LIMBO
by Sean Keith Henry

Akashic Books
New York

This is a work of fiction. All names, characters, places, and incidents are the product of the author's imagination. Any resemblance to real events or persons, living or dead, is entirely coincidental.

Published by Akashic Books
©2004 Sean Keith Henry

ISBN: 1-888451-55-6
Author photo by Christa Havenhill
Library of Congress Control Number: 2003116548
First printing
Printed in Canada

Akashic Books
PO Box 1456
New York, NY 10009
Akashic7@aol.com
www.akashicbooks.com

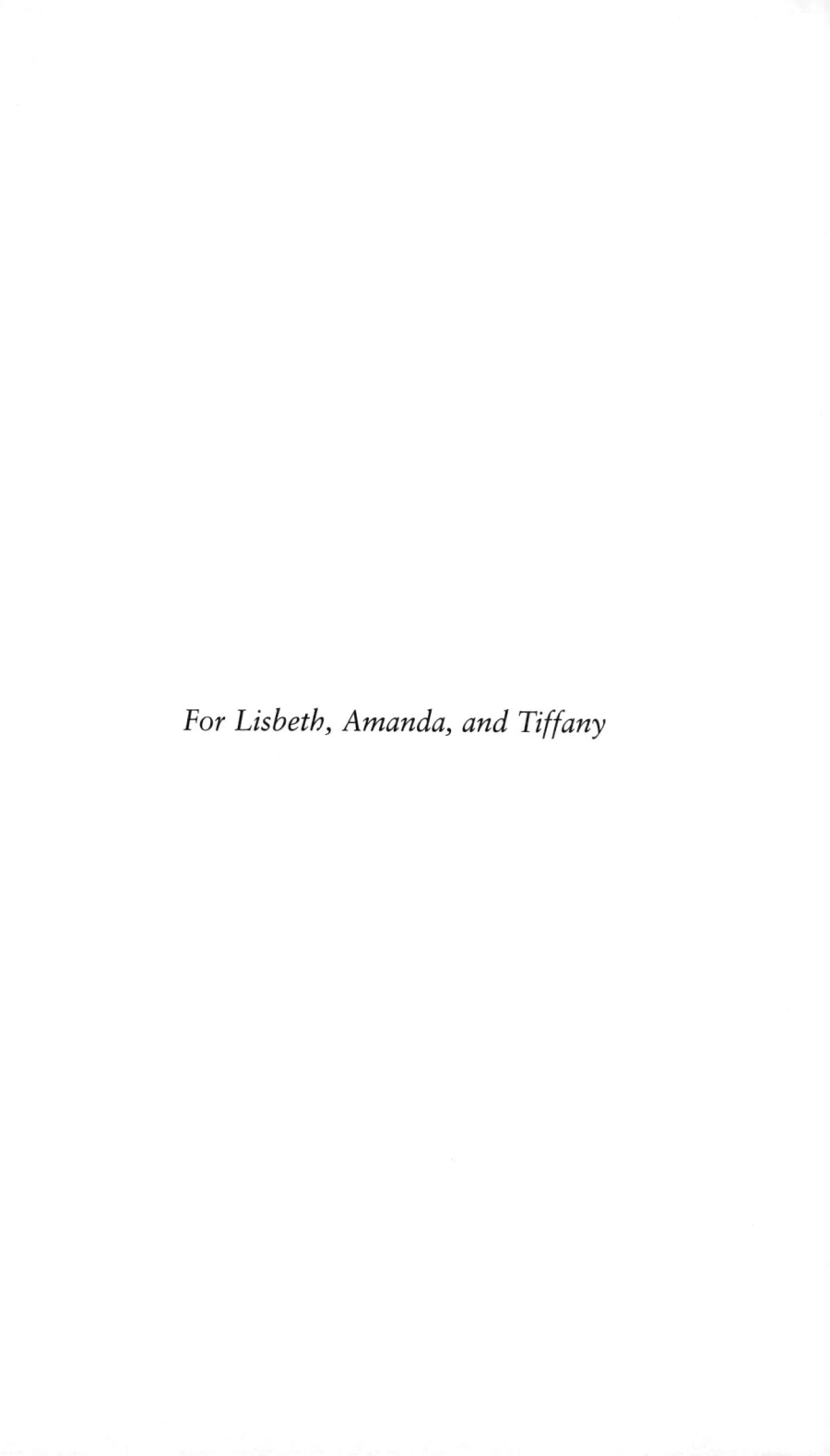

For Lisbeth, Amanda, and Tiffany

ACKNOWLEDGMENTS

Deep appreciation and gratitude to Valerie Sayers, William O'Rourke, and Sonia Gernes, who provided the environment for me to flourish at my craft. And a million thanks to Johnny Temple, Johanna Ingalls, and David Shirley of Akashic Books, three bright beacons in the publishing business.

PART I

Chapter 1

L ANDING IN THE MIDST of the descendants of vikings, the transatlantic flight with a one-year-old daughter and a wife teetering with apprehension has all but wiped out Pharaoh's capacity to *Chill out!* The phrase was embraced by his wife, Hannah, during her twelve-year sojourn in California, and she continues to use it officiously. *Let it go, hon* is another recent favorite. She says it to maintain her own sense of serenity, something, she admits, that has not been easy aboard their flight.

"Are you sure we want to go through with this?"

"I don't know. It's a bit risky, but it might calm you down."

"I'm calm," she insists, placing her cold hands in his and resting them on her lap. Perhaps she should be wearing mittens.

"You don't feel calm," Pharaoh says reassuringly. He covers her hands with his and tries to squeeze his warmth through her. "Come on. This might be our only chance to do this."

"What if we get caught?"

"We won't. And besides, we're married. We'll tell them we're on our honeymoon. What can they do to us?"

"You're probably right," she admits, looking with concern at Amaryllis.

"I wouldn't worry about our baby girl. She's out. She won't be waking up anytime soon."

"Okay." She nuzzles closer to him. He feels her warmth return while she allows him to continue covering her clasped hands in his as she murmurs, *"Jeg elsker deg."*

"I love you, too," he says, kissing her lips. They are still soft and warm, and they bring back memories of when he first kissed them, when she was barely out of her teens, when it felt like she was trying him out. She bows her forehead to his lips; he kisses her once above each eyebrow and they relax, leaning on each other like newlyweds.

"I'm ready, then."

"All right," Pharaoh says, relieved. "Let's go."

"Wait a minute," Hannah whispers. "How should we do this?"

"You go in first, then flush once and unlock the door. Then I'll come in." He squeezes her hands and tries to rub in more warmth.

"Have you done this before?"

"Of course not! This is my first time. Have you?"

"Don't be ridiculous. With whom?"

"I don't know. You're Norwegian. You're the one who has traveled a lot."

"Well, I've never done this sort of thing before, and I'm not sure I should, married or not. We're not teenagers, you know."

He feels as if he is about to deflower a virgin, and it arouses him to think that Hannah continues to have that effect on him.

"Speak for yourself. You keep this up and we might be doing this in baggage claim," he says.

Hannah places another blanket over Amaryllis and peeps above the heads of the passengers around her, hoisting herself upright from the armrests. A plump breast brushes the side of his face and remains protruding firmly at eye level. Pharaoh barely resists the urge to cover it with his mouth.

"Which one?"

"All the way back," he says, unbuckling his seat belt and pulling up an armrest to allow her to pass. "No need to take those shoes. You won't be needing them."

"Yes, I will. It's filthy in there," Hannah says, standing in the aisle and slipping into cabin shoes. She is an attractive woman, and has learned to intimidate people with her beauty by staring at them until they become uncomfortable. This works especially well with American women, who she claims are too jealous. Pharaoh watches as she limps down the aisle, still fitting her feet into her shoes. Her wiggle reminds him of an unsteady larva moving through a canal. She blames Amaryllis for her broad hips, but it is really her flat feet and wide, inchoate toes that are responsible. Flight attendants hustle back and forth with duty-free items and towelettes. When Hannah finally disappears behind the curtain, Pharaoh quickly follows, searching, trying to steal a desultory glimpse of his favorite flight attendant before Hannah changes her mind.

Inside, Pharaoh wastes little time. Ignoring Hannah's fuss and her torsional movements to find a clean and comfortable spot, he enters her vagina while she balances her buttocks on the edge of the basin.

"Hush! What's that noise?"

Pharaoh listens, still entering her slowly. "It's the goddamn engine. We're in the back of the plane, Hannah." Despite his excitement, their sex is not as erotic as he had expected. He does what he can to salvage things, fixing his imagination on a member of the cabin crew.

"Take it easy," Hannah says. "No need to get testy."

"Sorry, hon. Why don't you turn around?"

"No. The doctor said this way is best if I'm ovulating."

"Fine." Pharaoh closes his eyes and visualizes the flight attendant with graying hair and pimples, in her mid-forties. She probably has kids and a husband waiting for her in some remote part of the country. No reason to worry about ovulating. It isn't long before her image is complete. She slides on the basin as he holds her ankles tight and apart at the hips so that her legs form the letter M, pinned to his sides. She quickly unbuttons her blouse and lifts up her bra to release placid breasts. The skin on her abdomen does not match the tanned skin on her face. Her nipples are small and erect, almost the same color as her pimples. Pharaoh releases an ankle, sending her leg askew as he palms and squeezes the soft folds of her abdomen. He continues to thrust at her flesh. Her hands are curled in a tight grip on both sides of the basin; he tries, unsuccessfully, to pry them loose so that he can control her balance. He returns to her ankles, straightens them out so that her legs now form the letter V, and then places them along his chest. His hands are free to grab the bulkhead or whatever else he can reach, and then to hug her knees to him in his final thrust. When he opens his eyes, Hannah is looking at him as if he has just awoken from a coma.

"Was she in the Navy?"

"What?" He doesn't understand what she means at first. It was her idea that they try this up here.

"I think you've done this before," she says, while they fix their clothes.

"No, I haven't."

"Then how did you know where to put your hands in here with your eyes closed?"

"Come on, Hannah. It's not the first time I've been in the lavatory on a plane, you know."

"That's not what I said. You seemed to know what you're doing in here; that's what I'm saying."

"I was just excited. This is exciting for me, you know." He can tell she doesn't believe him.

"You go out first and check on Amaryllis. I have to sit here for a few minutes and keep this stuff in me so it'll take. I'll be out in a minute."

"You still love me?" Pharaoh asks, feeling the words stumble on his tongue.

"Of course I do. Now out!" Pharaoh does what he is told.

* * *

"I'm tired of being in here," Pharaoh says. The pilot's voice on overhead speakers welcomes passengers to the airport.

"Well, I have to admit I'm feeling a little better. You were right." Hannah's serenity arrives with momentous relief as the Boeing 747 docks at a gate at Gardemoen Airport, in Oslo. Superficial *goodbyes* and *good lucks* fill the aisle around them as Pharaoh nudges and drags their carry-on luggage forward.

"Thank you for choosing SAS and enjoy your stay in Norway," a flight attendant recites to him in English with a British accent. To Hannah, his flight attendant offers, *"Ha det bra. Lykke til,"* with the same British accent.

Baggage claim provides the most aplomb passenger with a moment for conscientious reflection. Amaryllis's stroller is waiting at the gate just as an SAS representative at LAX had promised. Restless passengers watch impatiently as Amaryllis awakes to her surroundings with belligerent screams that echo quietly in Pharaoh's ears. His grip tightens around the handle of the stroller.

"Relax, Amaryllis. You're in Norway," he says, as he inserts a pacifier in her mouth.

Sensing his anxiousness, Hannah sidles up to him and rubs the small of his back. "We'll be outside soon."

"I'm tired. I need a shave and shower," he says, sniffing at the remaining odor from a powder fresh stick of Secret he had applied to his underarms before leaving the pressurized cabin.

"We'll be home by midnight and you can take a nice long shower." She smiles and assures him that he smells fine. She nuzzles his cheek in a soft kiss, then beams at him mischievously. "Welcome home," she says with an appreciative embrace.

Pharaoh contemplates his fate. He wonders whether her mischievous and ginger steps are because she's trying to get his sperm to take or simply a sign of her belated enjoyment of their sex in the skies over Norway.

"You miss LA?" she asks.

Pharaoh has relinquished his residence in LA to take up residence in Trondheim, a city hidden behind mountains and fjords in the middle of Norway, steeped in its own dialectal, religious, and nationalistic history.

"Hell no!" Yesterday's *USA Today* is current news as far as he is concerned. He read it from front to back during the flight, more focused on what he is surrendering across the Atlantic than anything in the news itself.

The conveyor belt stops. A male employee in a bright red, one-piece uniform creeps out from a hole behind the stripped flap and slides pretentiously down the ramp to separate the luggage.

After fifteen minutes, their bags still haven't arrived.

"Where's the luggage? In Sweden?"

"I'm sure it'll be here soon." Hannah is calm, optimistic.

A passenger releases her dachshund out of its traveling cage, then has a difficult time coaxing it back in. The panting dog resembles a muscular rat. A thin woman with leathery skin drags a suitcase on wheels behind her, like a self-absorbed flight attendant, then stops to talk to the dog and its owner in Norwegian. The woman is wearing a white T-shirt. On its front is a daguerreotype of a man with a wide mustache curled up at the ends. Unfurled, Pharaoh speculates, it would probably measure about eight inches across his top lip. Together, the women manage to get the dog back in its cage but remain ensconced in conversation, their guttural phonetics blurring into a monotonous tone.

Pharaoh spots their first piece of luggage. He has forgotten to stop at the automated cart vendor on the way to the baggage claim. Hannah, however, has remembered, and she struggles with two oversized carts on her way from the rest room.

"What's the matter?" Again, she sees his distress.

An impatient woman has bumped him, more than once, as she strains to locate her suitcase among the suitcases circling by. On the third bump, he glares at her reproachfully. She responds with a timid smile. Not an adequate substitute, he thinks, for proper manners.

"Maybe I ought to get the luggage," he says, sliding the stroller toward Hannah. As he departs, the sports section of the *USA Today* tucked under an arm and both carts in tow, he gives the woman a subtle yet firm bump. Her timid smile takes on an embarrassing twitch. *"Oh, Unskyld meg.* Excuse me," he says sarcastically.

"Oh, that's quite all right," she replies in English with a British accent.

It is difficult to maneuver two luggage carts filled to capacity among busy passengers, but he manages. Hannah approaches with still another suitcase, smiling at her triumph. They have almost reached customs when Hannah stops, panic-stricken, and runs back toward the baggage claim. Pharaoh follows, half-running, half-walking. She returns immediately, pushing Amaryllis's stroller, her face pale and embarrassed because she is aware that she may have lost his sperm as she ran.

Outside it is raining and unusually cold, even though it's the end of July in Oslo, considered the height of summer. Sidewalks are slick and slope down toward the street, causing a constant hush from the sound of water draining over the pavement's edge. Pharaoh is dressed in black Caterpillar boots with steel at the toe, jeans, and a white T-shirt embossed on the front with a Los Angeles Lakers emblem, and a monogram design of the letters *"SHAQ"* on the back. His Caterpillars were purchased in anticipation of the rough terrain he expects to traverse here. But from the looks he has received so far, Norwegians have misinterpreted his intent, taking him as the sole member of an elite infantry. Amaryllis is awake and resumes her brittle tantrums. She will not be ignored.

"What happened in there? What was that all about?" Hannah asks, stopping to sit on the wet sidewalk and elevate her feet to a bottom wrung of the luggage cart.

"That woman had no manners. She kept bumping me. What a goddamn bitch!"

"You need to take it easy. Let it go. We're not in LA." She shakes her head at how he is dressed. "Aren't you cold?"

They are sheltered under an awning as they await her parents' arrival. According to Hannah's calculations, her parents ought to have been here by now. They were eager to see Amaryllis and had left Trondheim—Norway's third largest city, located north of Oslo—two nights ago.

"There they are!" He points at two people dressed in summer attire. They are very small. Thor, Hannah's father, has aged much since Pharaoh saw him last, but his wife, Trine, looks the same. They are both very healthy people, in their early-sixties.

It is Pharaoh's third visit to this little land, and his expectations upon moving here are optimistically guarded. On his first visit, Thor and Trine had taken him on an impressive tour of mountains and fjords in the middle of Norway.

Thor pretends to be a simple man. He has a large forehead with strands of grayish brown hair, and his ears are red and thick, as if frost bitten. They give him a weighty look. The masseter muscles of Thor's jaw are large and make him appear almost hound-like. The fingers on his hands are short and thick and stubby. He is a compact man and much stronger than he appears.

"Velkommen til Norge!" Thor is thrilled to see his daughter and her family. The force from his vigorous handshake pulls Pharaoh awkwardly toward him.

"Good to be here. Thanks for meeting us at the airport. Hannah tells me it's a long way to drive."

It is not a problem. The weather has been great. It is summer here in Norway, Thor explains, and no one is on strike. He is referring to Pharaoh's first visit here, when the sanitation workers were on strike. Thor had held himself personally responsible for the country's union woes. At a popular lake near his home, garbage had lay piled under trees while children and adults frolicked in the cold water and picnicked nearby. "Norway isn't always this dirty," he had explained. He had talked about the fjords and snow-capped mountains and his government's responsibility toward Norway's fragile environment. Pharaoh had carried the image with him back to LA, but his environmental enthusiasm was no match for the rotting food and used diapers that washed back and forth along the city's rocky shore.

Trine, Hannah's mother, gives Pharaoh a felicitous but expeditious embrace. She has small features, which crinkle up into a warm smile. She wears expensive bifocals, with shades that she attaches to the frames periodically. There is no sun, and Pharaoh finds her reliance on the shades to be neurotic and exaggerated. She is dressed in a light blouse, khaki shorts with one-inch cuffs, and black leather shoes that would look better with a dress. Occasionally, she stops to tug on the short white socks that have slid to just above her ankles. Varicose veins are visible on both her legs but she makes no effort to hide them. They are a testament to her five decades of manual work, not her age. Her hair is thin and reddish brown.

Trine quickly embraces Hannah, then picks up Amaryllis and carries her off in her arms, smothering her with hugs and kisses. Thor tries to keep up with his short arms and legs, but he has to reach forward to rub Amaryllis's cheek with the back of his knuckles. In her happiness and excitement, Trine has to wipe away tears that well up in her eyes. Hannah, too, is euphoric, but short of tears. She has come home to her family and her country, with a new family of her own.

Reaching Thor's Mercedes, Trine stops to examine Amaryllis's features. She has Pharaoh's eyes, nose, and mouth, but her V-shaped chin and pronounced forehead belong to Hannah's side of the family. It is conclusive. They all agree. She also has Pharaoh's big feet. Everyone laughs. Amaryllis smiles, too, but there is no consensus on whose smile she has. Trine presents the child with a miniature

Norwegian flag. When Amaryllis smiles again, Trine says, *"Det er et Norsk smil,"* and everyone laughs. Pharaoh pretends not to hear the entire sentence; what he has heard, he pretends not to understand. His Norwegian is underdeveloped, but it is improving rapidly. Pharaoh does not think Amaryllis has a Norwegian smile.

They are on their way north, homeward bound. When Thor believes they are far enough away from Oslo, where it is safe, they will stop for cake and coffee. Before leaving the airport, they met Beth, one of Hannah's many Gymnasium friends. Beth grew up in Trondheim, but now lives in Oslo. Trondheim, she explains, is not big enough to fulfill her life aspirations, although she seems unclear as to what those aspirations entail. She is a large person with a definite attitude, the type of attitude you'd expect from a beautiful woman. Attractive, thinks Pharaoh, although in a homely sort of way. Pharaoh had met her for the first time when she visited Hannah during a summer in California. At the time, Beth's attire was often a bikini top, a pair of nylon soccer shorts with a tight plastic waistband and thin stripes along the sides, and pool slippers. She was very meaty as a twenty-two-year-old, and Hannah had dismissed his observation to that effect as callous.

Beth has long brown hair that falls from her scalp to just above her lower back. It gives her an Indian appearance, in spite of her pale complexion, especially when she wears a headband. Her hair is parted in the middle and shines under the light, but the strands that hang along the length of her face are dulled by her pale skin. Her hair is lifeless, inanimate, as if in the final stages of hypoxia. She has brought Pharaoh and Hannah flowers, and a little dress and bonnet for Amaryllis. During her short visit, she is interrupted three times by the musical tones of her cell phone, apologizing after each call but also explaining that many people in Norway have cell phones. An indirect boast, suspects Pharaoh, about the advancement of wireless technology in Norway since his first visit. Upon her arrival, Beth had first spoken Norwegian, because of the presence of Hannah's parents. Upon their departure to walk Amaryllis, however, Beth switches to English. "So, Pharaoh, how do you like Norway?"

"The country is clean and the landscape is beautiful," he says, remembering his earlier visits.

She apologizes for the weather and asks about new episodes of *Seinfeld, Friends, Ally McBeal,* and *NYPD Blue,* which are scheduled to begin in the fall. She especially likes Kramer and Phoebe, she admits. Pharaoh explains that he has very little time for television. He prefers to read.

"Oh, yeah? Like what do you read?" It had been years since her trip to California, but she still remembers some of the dialect.

"Comic books, mostly."

She mentions that she has recently read books by Stephen King and Robin Cook. He counters with Jamaica Kincaid, V.S. Naipaul, and Derek Walcott.

"They're Caribbean authors," he explains, to allay her embarrassment at not recognizing the names, "not comic books."

"That's right," she says, shaking her head. "You were born in Trinidad. I always forget that."

The route to Trondheim is a natural spectacle. Rocks are high and dense. Trees are remarkably green and wet. The family travels over truss bridges and along the edges of rippling lakes. Thor clearly enjoys his role as tour guide behind the steering wheel. Trine taps Pharaoh on the shoulder and points at people submerged in water in moss-green rubber outfits, fishing for salmon. Then she raises his chin with her palm to direct his gaze toward the top of steep, rocky inclines and small waterfalls created by the melting ice. Pharaoh asks if the water might be too cold for fishing. The consummate tour guide, Thor pulls his Mercedes off the road to allow them to check.

"See there?" Thor says, pointing and laughing. "They are stupid fish. The water is shallow. Some of them are caught out there. They have no place to go. They are easy for fisherman or birds with sharp claws."

"Someone should put them in deep water to give them a chance," Pharaoh says, surprised at his growing awareness of nature's cold, harsh conditions.

"It does not matter. They taste the same in shallow water or deep," Thor says.

Hannah and Trine are busy talking in the backseat. Pharaoh realizes how dependent he still is upon Hannah to translate difficult sentences when multiple topics are being discussed, though he knows her lengthy explanations are somewhat interpretive. He apologizes for interrupting so often with his need to have things explained in English. Hannah thinks he will be proficient in Norwegian in about a year or so, but he is not so confident. "It will come," she reassures him.

"Nei, det går bra," Trine interjects. Thor decides to keep silent; he is not as optimistic. Pharaoh assures them that he will give it his best effort. Though he may never be fluent enough to conduct proleptic debates, he will at least be able to talk to Amaryllis.

Thor points to a distant rainbow, half of its arc a penumbra behind hilly, uneven mountains.

"It is pretty. Very pretty." Pharaoh chooses his words carefully, simple words, words he can remember to repeat. "Are you driving toward it?"

Thor is not a skilled driver, and the E6, an old major transportation route that extends across the length of this country, is not an easy road to navigate. On the map, according to Pharaoh's sister, Gwen, it looks like a long, serrated, uncircumcised penis with Sweden and Finland serving as scrotal sacs. For long stretches, the E6 consists of only two lanes. When signs permit him to pass other vehicles, Thor hesitates, lingering in the oncoming traffic lanes longer than is necessary, then races ahead. Once safely back in his lane, Thor's entire body relaxes and the engine resumes its steady, reassuring hum.

Hannah repeats Pharaoh's question in Norwegian.

"There'll be another one. We have many rainbows here."

Pharaoh and Thor fall silent again in the front seat as Hannah and Trine continue catching up. Neither of them knows if Beth has a boyfriend or lives alone, or where she works.

Pharaoh had noticed Trine's sericeous upper lip upon their arrival. There was no fuzziness over her lip during his last visit. Perhaps she had shaved regularly. He wonders if she is on medication, but dares not ask. She's too old for it to be a result of menopause, but too young for him to suspect old age. He is certain that Hannah has already contemplated her own genetic predisposition for a hairy top lip and varicose veins.

Trine has always seemed suspicious of Pharaoh's interaction with women, and his interaction with Beth is no exception. He hears Trine whisper, then giggle.

"My mom wants to know what you think of Beth."

"Beth is okay." He turns and smiles at Trine. Hannah is tired from the long flight, and he knows her new role as translator must be burdensome. He wishes they were alone and he could tell her how much he loves her and her family for embracing him and Amaryllis. Hannah closes her eyes for a moment, which he interprets as a momentary plea for relief from her duties. Everyone is quiet, waiting for her to resurface.

Amaryllis is wide awake as they approach Lillehammer, home of the 1994 Winter Olympics and a source of nationalistic pride for Hannah and her parents. They remind him of all the other cities that were passed over by the Olympic Committee in favor of Lillehammer. Spores and pollen whisk about the air as Pharaoh and Thor admire the modernistic buildings and residences, which still stand as a testament to Norway's past cultural glory. Thor suggests that Pharaoh might like to take some pictures.

"I've *been* here before." No one seems to remember. Thor looks puzzled. The wind has blown the strands of hair back over his forehead, giving him an ichthyic appearance. He squints, trying to recall when Pharaoh was here last. Trine also has her doubts.

"It wasn't quite completed yet, but I took pictures of the ski jump area and the hockey rink. Don't you remember?"

"Oh, yes. Yes," Thor finally says, turning to Trine. "But it was not as famous yet, and it was only half-built. Now it is finished. It is ready. And," he continues, smiling and grooming his long strands of hair with his thick fingers, "it is famous. So go ahead. Take some pictures."

"Let's get a picture of the Keillands with Amaryllis, then."

"What about you?" Hannah says.

"I'll take this one and you can take the next one." Amaryllis is wearing the present she received from Beth. It is easy enough to see now what all the fuss was about. She is a beautiful baby when she's happy and content. Her smile is infectious. Everyone smiles under the Olympic rings in Lillehammer. All Pharaoh can see is Amaryllis's four teeth.

CHAPTER 2

LOOKING AT AMARYLLIS reminds Pharaoh of why he has followed his family across the Atlantic to a remote area just below the Arctic Circle. Amaryllis is his first and only child. Her birth a year ago was not an easy or an appealing process. The romanticism of childbirth, much like the attraction between two people of the opposite sex, is often grossly exaggerated. For Pharaoh, it was like watching dogs regurgitate their food on the sidewalk or try to free themselves from being stuck together after fornication.

Hannah's obstetrician did precious little to prevent postpartum psychological trauma. He cursed, wrenched, cut, squeezed, pulled. And Amaryllis was born, silent, purple, with an elongated head. The event left Pharaoh mortified. He had often heard that the experience brings couples closer together and creates a more profound respect for humanity. In his case, it had done neither.

After coaching Hannah through the breathing stages, he was left with nothing to do but hold her hands and watch, spellbound, as her attractive features waned. The color faded around her face as a brackish, purple hue encircled her vagina. He could no longer recognize either part of her body. It was as if Amaryllis was being born of a stranger. He had been so distracted that he forgot to request to cut the umbilical cord, and the obstetrician had neglected to ask. The doctor reassured him that the strategic cut he had placed on Hannah's vagina was "minor, very minor surgery." While he sutured the seam, the doctor explained that everything would be as good as new, maybe even better, after the puerperium period. Pharaoh watched it all in horror and disbelief.

In spite of Pharaoh's repulsion toward the birthing process a strong bond had already been established between father and daughter. He had advanced on the delivery nurses as they transported Amaryllis to the nursery as if he was her bodyguard, pestering them with questions. "When will she be returned to her mother?" "Why aren't fathers issued medical identification bands?" "Are the forceps responsible for her cone-shaped head?" The staff seemed prepared for many more questions than they had answered. They had smiled courteously, pointed to where he could view and monitor the nursery, and then forgotten his existence.

Trine and Thor were also present for Amaryllis's birth, but their reasons for making the trip were not completely evident. Curiosity, a warmer climate in LA than in Norway during early April, and the birth of their first American grandchild all contributed to their arrival at LAX three days before Hannah had gone into labor. It was understood that Pharaoh and Hannah would, at some juncture, move to Hannah's native land. But until Amaryllis's birth, there were no concrete plans. In the past, he and Hannah had occasionally speculated about contrasting lifestyles, culture, environments, and people, but it was all very theoretical and superficial.

At Christmas, especially, Hannah's Nordic yearning grew more intense.

"I miss the snow, Pharaoh."

"Let's go skiing, then."

Hannah had been on a junior ski team in Trondheim, a good one by her account. Pharaoh had worn her ski cap on chilly nights in LA.

"Where? There's no snow here."

"How about Big Bear?"

"That is so California. It's too touristy."

"Oh. Call someone in Norway, then."

"We need to move." A telephone call to Norway would ultimately console her and persuade her to stay put. Their small apartment served as an outpost for Hannah's friends and family. To dismantle it would mean relinquishing her role as her family's conduit to a sunnier climate.

Serious consideration to move began when Trine had said to Pharaoh jokingly, *"Nå må du flytte til Norge."* They had made it all seem so simple. Each emphasized a particular area of interest. Trine stressed how important it was that Pharaoh and Amaryllis learn Norwegian. Here was an ideal opportunity. Pharaoh could learn easily from Hannah. Thor focused on nationality and, to a lesser degree, financial resources. It was important that Amaryllis obtain official citizenship status in Norway, even if the US does not recognize dual citizenship involving its own citizens. He promised to make the necessary inquiries and mail all the required forms. *"Det er veldig viktig,"* he said before they left—"very important." And so began a flurry of official forms from the Norwegian embassy that would eventually grant Amaryllis the most important legal document of any Norwegian citizen: the little red passport.

"It is very expensive to live in Norway," Thor had admitted sullenly. "All is expensive, especially gas. High taxes. You must bring your car."

Hannah had listened to his warning with a grain of salt. After all, her skill as a translator should be an extremely marketable skill. "Don't listen to him," she had said to Pharaoh when he expressed his concern. "He exaggerates everything. It's not as expensive as he says it is. He's cheap, anyway."

For Pharaoh, however, Thor's frugality with money was all the more reason to take his advice seriously. During his visit to LA,

Thor had never left the apartment without his tiny tablet and calculator, and he saved all receipts to make comparisons of prices on
items in LA and Norway. It drove poor Hannah crazy.

"It's probably not worth it. We ought to just sell the fucking car
and buy one when we get there," Hannah said, once she had learned
what shipping a car to her country from LA might cost. She had
become disenchanted with the whole process.

"I'm not leaving without my fucking car! I'm not moving all the
way to your country so my family can take the fucking bus!"

But first he had to get the vehicle there safely. It was the last item
they had surrendered before boarding the SAS flight to Oslo.
Throughout the flight, Pharaoh wondered if he and Hannah would
ever see the car again.

When the family finally leaves Lillehammer, the noise from the
heavy rain competes with rhythmic thuds from the single wiper
sweeping the windshield on Thor's German car. Pharaoh, now in the
backseat with Hannah and Amaryllis, was anxious to leave after
being held in Olympic thralldom for over two hours. The television
coverage of the Games had been more than enough, the city's streets
filled with drunken Norwegians. And now he was being bombarded
by Thor's tales of Olympic history and his tedious description of the
Olympic stadium, architecturally designed to suggest the keel on a
viking ship. Kristin and Håkon, the Olympic mascots, were everywhere, and their endless facts and figures regarding the winter events
and attendance left him exhausted from metric recalculations.

Back in the car, things have grown uncomfortable between
Hannah and her mother. Pharaoh has moved to the backseat in an
attempt to buffer the growing tension between the two. Though she
had actively solicited them, Hannah's descriptions of and confes-
sions about her past had left Trine feeling sad and anxious. And then
Trine's observation that her daughter "had kept on a few kilos" following her pregnancy had left Hannah seething, although it was not

meant in a malicious manner. Thor and Pharaoh decided to break things up as best they could. "Best for you to sit with Hannah. There is room enough in the Mercedes." Thor had calculated Pharaoh's height at 1.75 meters on his last visit to LA. "You look the same now," he said. *"You* are not fat." They both laughed.

Hannah is certainly not fat, though it is true that she has toes that resemble stunted sausages. A delivery nurse had made the reference while Hannah lay in stirrups on the delivery table. Her toenails are short, with barely a cuticle on each little toe. She can apply nail polish to only eight toes to achieve any aesthetic effect. She is short like her father, but solid if she maintains an exercise routine at a health spa. If she misses her routine for more than six weeks, a slant roll of flesh develops under the straps of her brassiere, and a keen ear can hear the rubbing of her thighs when she wears her tight Levi's.

"I wonder what we've gotten ourselves into," Hannah whispers.

"I am sure we'll be fine. You're just tired. Try to take another nap and keep your knees up or I'll have to ask Thor to let us out in the bushes."

She smiles and reaches for his hand. The need to supplant any further confrontations requires a surrender of sorts, even if it is only temporary.

"I'm beginning to think this wasn't such a good move," she says.

"Of course it was. They need to get to know Amaryllis, *us,* as a family."

"We should have just stayed in California and sent them pictures."

"Well, it's a bit too late for second guessing ourselves now," he says, aware that she is still tired.

Trine clips on her sunshades to protect her eyes from the glare of the rain. She looks ridiculous. Thor speaks to her in Norwegian. Although Pharaoh cannot follow their entire conversation, it is apparent that Thor is failing to lift Trine out of her stupor, in spite of his insistent good will.

"You should say something to your mom."

"Like what?"

"I don't know. Something."

It is a very inauspicious beginning to the next few years of their lives.

The salutary atmosphere has returned to Thor's German automobile. Hannah and Trine discuss significant changes in their family since Amaryllis's birth, and Pharaoh simply absorbs it all. Hannah's younger brother, Knut, and his girlfriend, Inger Lise, have purchased an expensive old house in the city. Hannah and Trine cannot see how they can afford it on his single income and with a newborn son. Hannah's older brother, Dagfinn, recently purchased another German car and sold a plumbing service that he began on his own. Hannah's elder sister, Kjersti, still drinks too much but at least she has a new boyfriend.

Trine also updates Hannah on the recent increase in violent crimes in Norway. Two taxi drivers in Oslo were robbed and shot, one fatally. "It is becoming like LA," she says. She hopes that Beth, whom she does not remember, moves back to Trondheim where it is safe.

"Do you have gangs?" Pharaoh asks.

"Of course we don't have gangs." Hannah is quick to come to her country's defense. Pharaoh sits silently as she explains that there are gangs across the border in Sweden. If gangs are here, they have been imported from Sweden; the problem is greatest in cities like Oslo and Bergen. While Hannah speaks, Thor continues to point to chapels, power stations, waterfalls, camping sites, mountain hotels, mines, and sea-level markers along the way. The rain has ceased, and Pharaoh is transfixed by the clearing sky. It is almost eight o'clock in the evening and the bright sun has finally appeared from behind the clouds.

Trine asks Hannah if Pharaoh has ever been in a gang. It is a question that is worth contemplating, if it is sincere.

"Yes. Tell her all my life."

"You're so full of shit!"

"All my life, I tell you."

"Well, you won't join one here." Trine and Thor await her translation. They seem satisfied with her edited version.

They are only minutes from Oppdal, a small winter resort where Hannah attended Gymnasium. Thor intends to stop there so that they can all use the rest rooms. Thor has sunken lower in his seat since their departure from the Olympic city. Hannah comments that he appears to be getting shorter in height than her mom with age. He turns to give her an admonishing stare and almost veers into oncoming traffic. She also mentions that Pharaoh can drive, if Thor needs to rest. He has driven across the US twice, after all. Thor agrees with everyone that it is a long way to have driven, but insists that he is not tired and can easily drive the rest of the way. He tells Pharaoh to sit back and enjoy the magnificent Norwegian sun.

Arriving at Oppdal, Trine and Hannah have bundled Amaryllis in a knitted sweater and watch as she stumbles along on her own, taking primitive gressorial steps outside of a local store. It is strange to watch them compete over Amaryllis's attention and welfare. Thor checks the hangar attached to his Mercedes to make sure it is still secure, while Pharaoh sits at an open table outside drinking coffee, trying to make sense of his new role, both as a son-in-law and with his own family here in Norway. Amaryllis, who has been asleep throughout most of their journey here, is clearly at the center of things. As Trine and Thor establish their new bond with Amaryllis and reconnect with Hannah, Pharaoh feels something eroding within himself. Watching Amaryllis grope at Trine's hands for balance while Thor busies himself with wiping rain marks from his Mercedes, Pharaoh wonders if there is any real role left for him here.

The local store closes in an hour according to a lighted sign above its doors. People on their way to the store slow down to stare at him briefly before entering. An old woman bundled in a feathered scarf in a nearby telephone booth speaks loudly into the receiver. She looks up to see Pharaoh smile at her and slides the door shut. Customers seem perplexed. They take furtive glances on the way out to their cars. The whole thing makes Pharaoh feel uncomfortable.

There is enough light for him to peruse his *USA Today* again. He notices a palinode referring to an erroneous statement about a Top 25 basketball program that he has missed. He is about to read further when a shadow descends on the page.

"You from the States?" The voice belongs to a customer dressed in a red and blue nylon sweater. The plastic bag hanging from his hand contains a carton of milk and other items. Pharaoh nods.

"What part?"

"California. LA."

"Nei," he says, sounding surprised. "And you're all the way out here?"

It must seem utterly ridiculous to him, thinks Pharaoh. The man's eyes search Pharaoh's attire as if he is looking for a tag that will tell him to whom Pharaoh should be returned, if found.

"I am afraid so."

"I could tell you're from the States."

"How so?" The man points to Pharaoh's now ragged copy of the *USA Today.*

"What will you do in Norway?" His questions are blunt. Because the man is the first person here to ask him these things, Pharaoh feels compelled to answer.

"I'm here to study."

That should suffice, but the customer wants to know what Pharaoh intends to study. Civil engineering? Geography? The fish industry?

"Norwegians."

The man fidgets with his bag as if it has suddenly become too heavy before he wishes Pharaoh good luck and departs. The old woman saunters by, staring at Pharaoh. He is tempted to chase her away, but instead he tramples her footprints playfully in the snow on his way to the vacant booth.

"Hi, Gwen."

"Who is this? How'd you get this number? You got the wrong number."

"Oh, Gwen. Come on."

"Oh, it's you. You sound like one of them already. You on the ground?"

"Yep, finally. Thirteen hours up in the air. Now eight hours left to go in a car and we'll be there. I feel like I'm still in LA."

"Child, don't lie to me like that. You meet any black people there since you touched down?"

"Well, not really."

"All right then. You're somewhere else besides LA."

"I'll be on the lookout, Gwen, and the first black person I see, I'll take a picture and send it to you."

"The first black American, child. There's a difference. I don't know any black American in his right mind, except my brother, who would pack up and go where he's not wanted, all because of a white woman."

"How do you know I'm not wanted here?"

"'Cause you're black and you're not an athlete; that's how," Gwen says.

"They don't know that," he replies. "I'll just pretend." He laughs at her simplistic reasoning.

"Nice to hear you laugh way over there in the cold."

"I can tell you miss me."

"How's my baby?"

"She's fine. They're spoiling her already."

"Yeah, well, I guess I had my little turn. It's theirs now."

"Come on, Gwen. Don't be difficult. This had to be done."

"No, child. It didn't. I hope you and that woman made the right choice. You're in someone else's land. All the rules have changed now. Remember that."

"They're nice people. You'll see when you come to visit."

"Child, you're crazy! You're not getting this chocolate woman over there. My people are right here in LA. I can't leave them."

He does not want to turn their first long-distance telephone call into an argument. "Have you heard from Timmy and Clint? Or Billy?"

"They're probably already in a heap of trouble. You know you were the only one keeping them on the straight and narrow."

"They're big boys. They'll be fine, but you should keep an eye on them for me."

"Well, they're in LA, child. They're part of my jurisdiction."

There is an awkward silence as he stares at the snowy landscape. People whisk past on skis and snowboards instead of skateboards and cars. He pictures Amaryllis on a snowboard and knows that Gwen is waiting for him to ask about their father.

"She'll be fine here," he says, finally. "Too many people love her here."

"Yeah? We got love over here too, honey. Well, she better be fine or you'll be hearing from me, child. I'll tell *him* you said hi, by the way. And pinch my baby for me."

They both hang up, and he has a strange feeling that not everything has been said that needed to be.

It has been twelve years since Hannah has been in Oppdal. Not much has changed, she thinks. A small room she rented is still here but now seems vacant. It is perched above a store and was without heat the entire time she lived there. Blankets and alcohol consumption provided warmth. Her graffiti drawings are still in place on the foundation of a local bridge. Trine and Thor seem surprised as she talks openly of parties and scrawled graffiti. They laugh as she continues to describe her youthful adventures, though a bit uneasily.

Hannah's parents were never as naïve as she believed. They had given their permission for her to attend school two hours away grudgingly and only when they were sure that they could monitor her. They knew when she left town and when she arrived. They even knew of her marks in school, despite her attempts to hide them.

At times, Hannah tells them, she had feared that she would freeze to death, if not in her room then certainly on the streets where she and her friends hitchhiked. She explains to Pharaoh that it is safe to hitchhike in Norway. Unlike LA, thinks Pharaoh. She doesn't actually make the comparison, however. She doesn't need to. Sometimes, she and her friends would stand on a street for hours and not a single car would venture by. "Of course it's safe to hitch-hike here—if no one ever gets a ride." For once, Pharaoh has the last word.

CHAPTER 3

L A IS LA. It is one thing to visit LA and quite another to live there.

Pharaoh's father has not spoken to him since he and Hannah announced their decision to move to Norway.

"We'll visit often," Pharaoh had said.

"Why can't *they* visit often? I don't understand it."

"Well, you made a similar decision a long time ago. It's the same thing," he had said. "You moved from your beloved country to the United States while we were still very young." His father had often explained that it was in *their* best interest at the time. He had grown tired of living in a country whose throwback to the British civil service bureacracy and parliamentary system made him wonder if Trinidad had really gained its independence.

"And it was a good decision," his father had said, proudly. "Your little sister is a pharmacist and you're a college teacher. If I'd stayed in Trinidad, I'd probably still be paying off a government official so that you two could get an education. So don't be too ungrateful."

Pharaoh had let him leave it at that. Both men knew, however, that Pharaoh's father's reasons for leaving were not entirely based upon concerns for his children. He had divorced their mother and had refused to pay court-ordered alimony or child support. And the civil service system he so vociferously complained about—along with its arm of retribution, the government police—had kept him in their sights. He had skipped to Bermuda, then to St. Croix, and finally to LA. Through letters and promises, he had somehow managed to persuade their mother that it was in their best interest and hers to surrender their custody to him. His mother, who had struggled with them at the time, had sent them to LA with a mutual friend, along with a stern reproof that their father would no longer have the luxury of watching lightning through her eyes. And so they had arrived in a great multicultural calabash, a six-year-old and a four-year-old thrust into a father's twisted notion of the American dream. Their mother had not even accompanied them to the airport. There had been opportunities for her to visit them in LA but she never came. She had suddenly become very religious. LA, she explained in her letters, was no place to practice her faith. Instead, out of pride and allegiance, she had decided to remain in her country of birth. Two years after the rest of the family's move to LA, she had died, unceremoniously, without her children at her side. She was only thirty-six years old.

The hospital had determined that she died of natural causes. Pharaoh's father had lambasted the nation's hospital officials, and ultimately its health department, as grossly backward and incompetent. This simply would not have occurred in LA. How can someone die of natural causes at thirty-six years of age in the twentieth century? Pharaoh and his sister attended the funeral in Trinidad, but they had been too young to grieve. To Pharaoh, Trinidad had seemed small and insignificant after his two-year absence. Natives still walked through coconut trees balancing themselves nimbly along wiry vines, as enthralled tourists looked on. Dirt roads with deep potholes, juxtaposed against oil refineries and sugarcane fields, had been a constant reminder of the government's priorities. The family had returned to LA with Pharaoh's father promising to write letters to the "Red House," the seat of the Trinidad government, until they responded. He had vowed that he would get to the bottom of their mother's death, but his enthusiasm waned after only two letters and no reply from the Trinidad government. That seemed to have been enough to absolve him of any personal or psychological responsibility for their mother's death.

Pharaoh's father had a strong penchant for older women. He quickly landed a job as an appraiser of houses for the city in an office managed by a woman in her mid-fifties. Their relationship lasted one year, long enough for him to move her into their home and then out again after he had secured a position as an assistant manager. Now he lives in a four-bedroom house in Inglewood that he has under-appraised. He would like to build a big house in Trinidad where he can retire peacefully, where people will give him the respect that is due a rich retiree from the States. He thinks that Amaryllis should be introduced to her roots and rich Caribbean culture in Trinidad. She is his only grandchild. It is one of the reasons he is so adamantly against her living in Norway, along with the antiquated antipathy he feels toward Hannah.

They pass a sign that indicates they are 111 kilometers from Trondheim and 565 kilometers from Narvik, a city farther north. It is not, however, the city farthest north, Thor explains. Tromsø is Norway's most northern urban center. He begins to expound on the northern lights phenomenon, but it is a hard concept to grasp when one lacks sleep and patience. Thor opens a floor console and hands Hannah a tablet with a picture of the Norwegian flag on the cover. Inside, he has written a list of important "to do" items. Hannah frowns. She doesn't like it when he takes being her father to such extremes. The inordinately long list includes visits to various public and private institutions in the city to ensure that Hannah and her family receive basic services in the basement apartment that they have agreed to rent in his home. They must register Amaryllis a.s.a.p. so that they can receive the equivalent of $600 each month until her third birthday. Thor also recommends that they should each obtain a Norwegian driver's license and discard their California licenses. And Pharaoh must contact the company that shipped their car to Norway to make certain that it does not end up in Sweden. They should also buy winter clothes at summer bargain prices, and Pharaoh should register for Norwegian classes early. The list goes on and on. Hannah interprets Thor's efficiency as anal-retentiveness. Whatever the explanation, he clearly is no procrastinator.

Hannah closes the tablet and passes it forward to Pharaoh. "Hang on to it," she says. On the surface, her request seems innocent, but it is also a way of trivializing Thor's list and the energy he spent compiling it. Pharaoh can tell that mother and daughter are still close. They work in teams. Trine asks for the tablet but cannot remember the name of the place she wishes to add. It will come to her eventually, Hannah tells him, like it always does.

They approach Trondheim in silence, like a visiting team in the final moments of a long bus ride to an opponent's arena. Little red buildings, set in landscaped plots some distance behind green and brown fields, rush by on either side of the E6. The patterns repeat themselves in different sizes for as far as he can see before they are interrupted by blue mountains. It resembles an enormous jigsaw puzzle. Cows and sheep graze in fields surrounded by electric fences. In some of the fields, white bales of hay that resemble giant rolls of toilet paper covered in plastic stand in rows of nine or ten alongside wood fences. There are no untidy fields. It is a serene atmosphere— not picturesque, but breathtakingly desolate when observed from a moving vehicle.

"What the fuck is going on over there?" Pharaoh breaks the silence, leaning his whole body toward the window to observe.

"Watch your language!" Hannah says. "Don't teach my parents those words." Everyone looks toward a field filled with cows grazing in muddy grass. Children in rain-slick clothes move stealthily around the animals.

"We must pull over and take a look. You may never see this again unless you and Hannah live in the country." Thor maneuvers his car off the road and turns off the engine. They remain silent as Pharaoh watches the scene unfold.

"Do you have such games in the US?"

"I certainly hope not," he says.

There are six kids crawling around in the mud. Some are on their hands and knees, and the others crawl flat using their arms and legs. In groups of twos, they rush a cow from its blind side and push it over, then return to safety to watch it wriggle in the mud like a newborn calf, the heavy bell around its neck clanging noisily but alerting no one as it tries to stand. After some time, the cow regains its footing and the herd resumes grazing. Immediately, the children attack again.

"They are only the children of farmers. We are not proud of how some behave; that is why we keep them in the country, away from regular Norwegians." Thor and Trine laugh.

"Let's leave! Haven't you seen enough?" Hannah snaps.

"Wait a minute. What's your hurry? Your dad said I may never see this again. I should take a few pictures."

"Like hell! Come on. I don't want to waste film on this stuff."

"Don't worry, it's my film." Pharaoh starts shooting photos.

"That's enough," Hannah says. "They'll see us."

"Damn! How big are those kids?"

Trine laughs.

"You don't understand," Thor says. "They are big. Farmers here eat what they produce. But it does not take strength to push cows over, only surprise."

"Well, it looks stupid and dangerous to me," Pharaoh says. "Some of those cows can get injured, and the children, too. Can't they?"

"Don't ask me," says Hannah impatiently. "I don't know."

"Those that cannot stand back up get slaughtered and are sold as beef. What the fuck! See that axe over there by the tractor?" Thor points a thick index toward a dirty tractor.

"Pappa!" Hannah snaps. "Don't use that word! See what you did, Pharaoh? Pappa, that is not a nice word!"

"What D fuck," Trine repeats like a parrot, laughing.

"Mamma, you, too! Don't use that word!" Hannah stares at her playfully, as if she, at least, should know better.

"Have the animal-rights activists heard about this?"

"Drive, Pappa!"

"Farm children must also have something to do," Thor says. He turns on the ignition and jerks his car quickly into traffic, accelerating too fast.

Everyone is silent again as they listen to the radio. They soon approach a two-lane toll station that bottlenecks traffic to a crawl. He apologizes for the traffic and interrupts the silence by switching the radio to a Norwegian music station. Trine hums along to a Gregorian chant.

The midnight sun is just that. It sits still high above the horizon, but there is a dullness to its luster that suggests something unnatural is occurring. Given the right occasion, though, the twilight can have a rejuvenating and enchanting effect. Perhaps, muses Pharaoh, he will celebrate his arrival in this country by attending a bar or a nightclub. He dozes off as they enter the city.

Pharaoh stirs as the Mercedes rolls noisily onto a gravel street that is narrower than he had remembered. The houses arc of different designs, constructed on similarly sized plots and out of the same wood material. Most are painted red, yellow, or blue, and many have dollhouses and kennels painted in similar colors. Large windows and balconies face the sun. Every homeowner knows when the sun rises and sets at his home. At ten o'clock at night, the neighborhood is silent. Television channels blink like neon signs through large living room windows; the same announcer appears on every screen. Amaryllis is wide awake, probably intending to play through the night. Hannah grows increasingly anxious as they approach the little white house where she grew up. It is a forty-year-old dwelling that Thor proudly admits he built from its foundation. As he maneuvers his car in front of the garage, he mutters, *"Velkommen til oss I* Byåsen. *Du er hjem."*

Pharaoh thanks him. But despite the warm welcome, he does not feel at home.

Pharaoh's friends in LA are probably gathered around a table at Baxter's beach house, their usual hangout, belching out bellicose laughter at the mention of his name and Norway. They are all previously enlisted Navy men. Timmy, an Ohio native living in LA, will attempt at first to rationalize the decision, but by the end of the night, after several shots of vodka chased by Coronas with limes, he will be calling Pharaoh a fucking idiot. There will be accusations about loyalty to longtime friends over family. Pharaoh's predicament is one of the reasons Timmy will never get married.

Billy, a Massachusetts native and the youngest of the group, will try to look on the bright side, even if his motives in doing so are self-serving. He and his girlfriend, Tia, have promised to visit Pharaoh only if they can buy hash in Norway. Billy's easy access to illegal drugs in LA is his only reservation about a visit. Hannah has always felt uncomfortable around Billy because of his affection for guns. She never knows what he's on or what he might suddenly produce from his pockets. And Billy is always eager to share.

Clint, an aspiring attorney and Pharaoh's best friend, will say nothing at first, collecting facts and opinions, taking a general pulse on what others say before dropping anchor on the subject. His theory is to never take sides unless it positively cannot be avoided. He is a coveted friend to any married couple, since he can always see the other side of an issue. During the LA riots, Clint claimed to understand both sides of the conflict.

The OJ Simpson trial is Clint's specialty. He can see the rationale behind the belief of most blacks that OJ was not guilty, or that he shouldn't be found guilty even if he was. From a white perspective, in the face of fundamental evidence compiled against OJ, Clint can also understand the belief that he should have been convicted.

Clint's sense of diplomacy abandoned him, however, when it came to Pharaoh's impending move to Norway. For Clint, Pharaoh's situation was "cut-and-dry" because of its uniqueness. "Only Norwegian I know is Hannah. If you want Amaryllis to learn Norwegian so that she can communicate with half of her relatives, you guys should make the sacrifice. And if you really love them, you'll get them out of this corrupt city." Clint, on the other hand, will never flee the States.

In the midst of their planning, Pharaoh and Hannah had sat down one evening to discuss what the move would mean to them. "I know you'll miss Clint and Timmy and Billy. They can visit anytime, and if you need a dose of LA, we'll come back for a vacation." It all seemed so simple and rational to Hannah. She had invited her friends to visit them once they were settled. To her, his emigrating was little more than a change of address. She understood from experience the longing and anxiety one struggles with at the very beginning, but she implored him to imagine how tough it would be if he had made the move all by himself, the way she had. Their love should make it so much easier. It is, muses Pharaoh, one of her appealing qualities. The world has no borders, as far as she is concerned.

Hannah was never even marginally interested in politics or public affairs, so it was difficult for her to understand Pharaoh's obsession with events that were seemingly beyond his control. "You don't have to be in LA to know what's going on in the States. We have good newspapers. Once you learn the language, it will be as if you had never left. And you can call Clint anytime. You guys can continue talking about OJ or the President and Monica Lewinsky." She simply couldn't appreciate why it was a big deal. OJ had "done it," end of story. And why were Americans in such an uproar about the President and Monica Lewinsky? From what she could tell, he was doing a good job. Her refusal to delve below the surface of things was a subtle source of contention between them. For her, the entire matter was settled by the simple fact, which she had heard on television, that other presidents had "done it." For Pharaoh, however, things were never so simple or so clear. His now-sullied copy of *USA Today* bears witness that his attention will always belong in whatever debate lies within its pages, even if those pages are two days old.

Chapter 4

AFTER THREE WEEKS at their new home, Pharaoh is still adjusting to climatic conditions. Byåsen is located in a mountainous region of Trondheim, and the sun sheds its warmth only after it fully clears the ski slopes. On weekends, the people of this small town shed various articles of clothing and move about as if they are tethered to the sun. It is late August and he can feel a brisk cold. Everyone assures Pharaoh that snow is not imminent, ignoring the frost that has blanketed the ground each morning since his arrival. The midday sun, when it finally appears, brings with it gnats and flies from the nearby forest that land harmoniously on exposed arms and legs. Only Pharaoh seems annoyed at their bites. Dagfinn and his wife, Anna, who live thirty meters away on Thor's lot, reassure him that he will get used to the insects. "They only bother you if you are an American," Dagfinn explains, smiling with snuff-stained teeth. "Once you have been here for some time they will think that you are Norwegian." They have been married for fifteen years and have two children, who are nine years apart. According to Hannah, Lena, a bouncy teenager, and Sara, an eight-year-old tomboy, hate each other and require close supervision when they are in the same room. One can reach out of a window on one side of their house and practically touch the trolleys as they amble by, their passengers seated stoically inside. The trolleys are noisy but punctual, and everyone reassures Pharaoh that he will get used to them as well. When the snow arrives, the trolleys will sound as if they are on skis. "Very soft and quiet. Whoosh, whoosh," Dagfinn explains.

Fresh tracks on frozen grass lead to the trunk of an old Volvo parked close to the fence and partially covered under a tarpaulin. It belongs to Anna and has been there for as long as they have been married. It is the first car she has owned, and out of nostalgia, she has refused her husband's offer to get rid of it.

On Sundays people from the city come for long walks in the mountainous forest beyond Dagfinn's house. The forest is inhabited by elks and Trolls, and its giant green Christmas trees, planted in clusters, make a dense pattern pointed toward the horizon. Children who get lost in its rocky caves after dark will never be found, according to folks here who want to keep their kids from venturing beyond the tracks. Trine is especially proud of the forest's proximity to her home. The house has a backyard garden, where she plucks different kinds of berries, flowers, and herbs. It's not unusual for hikers toting backpacks to spend weeks roaming through paths in the hills like nomads. Pharaoh must go on a tour, Trine insists, to experience its natural coziness. The family has spent nights there in sleeping bags. The air is fresh and clean. Of course, it is nothing like the forests in Brazil or Africa. There are no dangerous animals. And he will never get lost because there are always so many folks with cell phones out walking and enjoying the fresh Norwegian air.

Amaryllis has already been on one nature tour without her father. He is not that enamored by bush, dense undergrowth, and berries in their natural form, or with the jams and preserves he can purchase at a local kiosk. Trine and Thor attribute his lack of enthusiasm to participate in tours on Sundays in the forest to his upbringing in Trinidad. They believe he has seen it all. It must be beautiful there, they imagine, very exotic with different kinds of trees and waterfalls. And the people must be very natural with no need for winter suits and skis. Everyone would like to go there, especially Hannah and her parents. The forests in Trinidad must put this one to shame. They must all go sometime. It will be good for Amaryllis. Pharaoh does not enjoy insects, however, and sees no pleasure in trampling leaves and shrubs, his nostrils flaring as he struggles for air. In the forests, there are no outhouses, and Pharaoh is too civilized to stand and release his bowels like a primate. And, besides, Pharaoh cannot watch CNN in the forest.

Pharaoh and Hannah have had many visitors since their arrival, although they are far from being "settled." The apartment has one bedroom with two small windows, a living room that allows private access through a dank storage room to Trine and Thor's apartment upstairs, and a kitchen that has a small shower room in a corner. It is a basement apartment in a house with a foundation sunk three meters into the ground. The windows are high and provide a good view of grass and gravel at eye level, along with a wall of Dagfinn's house. Pharaoh has learned to identify people by the sight of their shoes and bare feet on the grass. Trine and Hannah occasionally acknowledge that the apartment is only temporary, a financial springboard meant to allow them to use the money they save from paying a low rent to eventually afford a nicer place. It is nothing like the big apartments that Pharaoh is used to in LA. His new friends explain that homeownership in Norway is simple if one has a job, but houses are still very expensive. It is a phrase he has already heard repeatedly from Thor. It is very expensive to live in a social democracy. Norway has the second largest income per capita, behind Switzerland, a statistic that enables Norwegians to afford higher taxes.

Pharaoh is sitting in a local café in the city with Hannah and Eva, a fellow ex–graffiti artist friend of Hannah's. A waitress makes surreptitious glances at their table. Outside of the café, Hannah and Eva had kissed, then had held each other in a strong embrace, both crying. For the past several years, their conversations had been largely restricted to postcards and brief telephone calls. Pharaoh rolled his eyes. An outdoor seating area, where white plastic chairs and tables are stacked in two rows close to the sidewalk, remains damp from the morning's rain. Pedestrians and cyclists compete for narrow paths on sidewalks outside, while Pharaoh fiddles with his espresso cup and listens to Hannah and Eva catch up on their lives.

"Shall I speak English or *Norsk?*" Eva has red hair now and remarkably deep wrinkles at the corners of her eyes. They are not crows feet, but claws. She has had a difficult time adjusting to the big 3-0 and is glad to have Hannah back to relive old times. Her daughter, Marit, is apparently a lot of work. Marit is eight, Eva explains, but wants to be seventeen so that she can attend pop concerts and meet the Backstreet Boys and *NSYNC. "Wait until Amaryllis gets there. It is so much headache. Norway is becoming so American. Our kids want to do everything they see the American kids do on TV."

The waitress makes her way over to the table and asks Hannah if Pharaoh would like a refill. *"Jeg vet ikke! Må du spør han!"* Hannah does not like the interruption, and her curt response alarms the waitress, who is barely out of her teens. While filling Pharaoh's cup, she glances at the top of his head and hands. He has on Levi's, a white golf shirt, and black Caterpillars, unusual attire for a damp day.

Eva is Hannah's height in a skinnier frame. A contraption in her red hair is meant to be fashionable but instead gives her head a crescent shape at the top. She is pierced all over. It is no wonder Marit is in such a hurry to be a teenager. Body piercing, among women especially, is not only a form of rebelling against a social system that does not promote individuality, Eva explains, but also a way of displaying one's capacity to endure pain. Both her earlobes contain studs and loops that end at the top of each ear. There is a brass loop in the middle of her left eyebrow and a diamond stud in her left nostril. She has a pierced navel and says that she is seriously thinking about piercing her tongue. But that is as far as she is willing to go. Suprisingly, Eva has no tattoos. She has considered getting a tattoo of a black panther with red eyes on her back, but worries it would make her look like a whore. She suggests that Pharaoh "be brave" and get something pierced. It will make him look European, she insists. Hannah disagrees. The two women stare at each other for a moment.

Pharaoh, too, disagrees with Eva. He believes that it is unnecessary for women to worry about displaying their ability to endure pain. His mind flashes back to Amaryllis's birth.

"Hannah thinks men look too feminine when they pierce themselves," he says.

"Well, it depends on where they put it," Eva replies. She grabs her espresso cup and puckers up to it. Then she reaches in a backpack on the floor next to her chair and produces an opened pack of cigarettes. "You want one, Pharaoh?"

"No, thanks. I don't smoke."

"Everyone smokes in Norway. That is why cigarettes are so damn expensive. The government thinks that people won't buy cigarettes if they make it really expensive, but we can always go across the border and get it cheap. Everything is cheaper in Sweden." Eva turns away from them whenever she has to exhale. It is a useless act, more a courtesy than a protection from smoke. Her thin lips barely cover the filter's tip. She has a wide face and, thanks to her thin lips, the look of a mouth with too many teeth. Pharaoh finds her attractive, though, in an odd way. Probably because she seems so courageous.

"How do you like Norway so far?"

"It is nice, a wonderful country right now. Ya da, ya da, ya da. But my opinion of your country could change with the first advent of snow."

"Then you must try skiing. It is so much fun. Hannah was a champion when we were at the Gymnasium. Maybe she can teach you how to ski, no?"

Despite her body ornaments and red hair, Eva has nothing on her hands. There are no rings on her fingers, and her unpolished fingernails are trimmed so short that they appear to be brittle. Like her piercings, they evoke feelings of pain and discomfort in the observer. Her hands are small, thin, and, unlike her face, wrinkle free. The tips of the fingers on both her hands have a yellowish tint.

Seconds after one cigarette is snuffed out, Eva reaches for another and apologizes. She smokes even more when she drinks espresso or alcohol. She says that she knows she must exercise more to keep up with her daughter and complains that she can barely make it to work on her bicycle without feeling as if she is about to collapse.

"My lungs are ruined. I am glad I live in Norway where the air is fresh and clean. I have seen the bad air in California. You have too many cars, Pharaoh."

Pharaoh notices that everyone has an opinion of California, even those who have never been there. He finds it oddly refreshing. At least people have an opinion, even if it's negative. Opinions about Norway in LA are hard to come by. Many people confuse it with Sweden, or compare its topography to the Dakotas, Wisconsin, or Idaho.

Eva's lungs may be ruined, but her full breasts keep them insulated and well protected. She is wearing a dark blue T-shirt, under a gray knitted longsleeved sweater, and baggy khaki pants. When they had arrived, Eva embraced him with exactly the same enthusiasm with which she greeted Hannah. During her embrace, he had noticed a slight sweaty odor emanating from her clothes, but it disappeared as soon as she began to smoke. Her elbows on the table, her sweatered but braless breasts sag slightly below the level of the table. She looks tired and haggard, and Pharaoh wonders how she could ever have been Hannah's best friend. As they recall past events, it is clear that parties and alcohol played a significant role in their early friendship.

Eva offers Hannah and Pharaoh an open invitation to dinner once they are settled. She is certain that she and Marit will enjoy meeting Amaryllis for the first time. "Marit loves babies and will want to babysit when we go to the bars," Eva says, smiling to Hannah. She assumes that Hannah will naturally want to resume old behaviors.

"It may not be anytime soon that we can go to the bars. Pharaoh and I are trying to have another baby," Hannah explains.

This comes as no surprise to Eva. She understands that this is why they are here and reassures them that Norway is a great place to have a kid.

Getting Hannah pregnant a second time is a scheduled event involving thermometers, calendars, pillows, and pregnancy kits. For some mysterious reason, dismissed by her LA gynecologist as "not abnormal for some women after their first pregnancy," it is difficult for Hannah to determine when she is ovulating without the help of external aids. But Pharaoh is in no hurry. Because of their clinical approach, the incentive to procreate seems lost. And besides, his cultural adjustment is the most important thing for him at the moment. School begins in two weeks, and he is in a country about whose culture, history, and people he knows almost nothing.

Hannah is well informed about her country, but her knowledge is limited to very general facts. In LA she often had to set the record straight, a task which sent her scrambling through geography books and old newspapers her parents had sent her. The same responsibility has suddenly been thrust upon him now after barely three weeks in Trondheim. Hannah's reluctance to fulfill her role back in LA stemmed from a lack of confidence in her capacity to be patriotic in a land where patriotism relies less on birthright than on creed. She was stunned and overwhelmed by the many ethnic groups that constantly professed love for God and the United States of America.

Pharaoh is willing to fulfill his assignment in Norway, even at the risk of alienating his family and friends back in the States.

He has expressed concern about the prudence of their decision to have another child. First he needs time to adjust, to feel secure in his new environment. Hannah brushes aside his concerns, insuring him that he, like millions of other men, will not regret his decision to have another child. Inevitably, they argue. She criticizes him for always expecting the worst, while he accuses her of trying to predict the future.

"Have you ever played poker with a fortune-teller?" he asks.

"That's a stupid question," she replies, wondering what he means. There is no immediate reprieve. Hannah is not ovulating anyway, so they have decided to try again in a few days.

Hannah has been called in for a second interview at a nursing home. She has left Pharaoh with emergency numbers and written instructions about Amaryllis's care. Anna, Dagfinn's wife, is at home alone and has stomped past the living room window on several occasions in green sweatpants and blue Adidas slippers. Although her movements suggest that she has a purpose, her steps slow each time she approaches the window.

According to Hannah, Anna has no formal education beyond Gymnasium and has failed English twice. As a result, she is reluctant to speak English to anyone, especially Americans. Pharaoh believes her timid manner involves more than language or shyness. On occasion, he has caught her staring at him, only to avert her eyes as soon as he returns her gaze. Hannah dismisses Pharaoh's claims as paranoia. And even if she has stared at him, Hannah explains, it might be a compliment, since Anna loves to draw.

"Anna is at home if Amaryllis gets too difficult," Hannah had said before leaving for her interview. "I am sure she wouldn't mind it if you took Amaryllis over to their place. She knows that you two are home alone, and she knows what to do if something comes up."

At Anna's lawn table, with his back toward the sun, Pharaoh watches as his daughter frolics in the grass around them. Her little legs stop and go as if they are controlled by the grade of a hill. Anna has provided coffee and waffles and, as if on cue, a neighbor, dressed in a light blouse, jeans, and dirty white socks with slippers, comes out and joins them. Anna and her neighbor's conversation has a laconic tone, their coded expressions suggesting a much longer acquaintance. Anna talks about the weather in Trondheim, comparing it to southern cities. Her neighbor, whose name Pharaoh cannot pronounce, produces a packet of tobacco and a filter. She has traveled to parts of Canada and the eastern US, and she speaks English better than Anna. The nameless woman explains that Anna is concerned about Pharaoh's move to Norway. She does not believe there is enough sun to sustain someone of his complexion. Her city, she says, enjoys playing hide-and-seek with the sun, but often neither can find the other. Anna also wonders about Amaryllis. How dark *can* she get? Her naïvete is embarrassing. To redirect the conversation, Pharaoh inquires about Lena and Sara, who are both at school.

Anna seems content with her role as a homemaker. She is a bit overweight and has an uneven, artificial sort of tan. Her brown hair is pulled back in a long braided ponytail. Occasionally, she tosses it forward, where it rests just above the tip of a small breast. While sitting here, she has unraveled the end of her ponytail three times and braided it again in the same twisting manner, proving, Pharaoh supposes, that it is easy to manage. It is nine a.m. and Anna already sports a full course of makeup that has left a dusty salmon-colored residue on her face. Her very blue eyes are surrounded by deep black eyeliner; the contrast with her unevenly tanned skin results in a very exotic look. She disappears inside for a moment and returns with a small pair of sunglasses, an unopened pack of chewing gum, a baseball cap, and a portable radio under an armpit.

"The sun is very hot for Amaryllis," she says in staccato English as she catches up with the child, who despite her coaxing refuses to wear the sunglasses.

Pharaoh's attempt is also of no use. "Oh well," he says, "at least she will wear the cap."

The trolley's approach drowns out his last words as it rumbles toward the city. They watch it disappear behind other houses and trees, its departure momentarily interrupting Anna's attempt to find her favorite station on the radio. Finally, she nods her head up and down to a beat Pharaoh recognizes as techno music.

"Perhaps Amaryllis will like a ride on the *trykk* soon," the name-less neighbor says with a British accent. "It is very fun for kids and leaves often, every seven minutes until eight at night. I remember riding on trains in Boston and New York. It was very exciting when they went into tunnels, but it is not a ride for kids. No one helps people with babies or strollers on the trains there, and passengers feel you in places where they shouldn't."

She is in her late-forties and she likes to talk. She rolls a cigarette methodically before stuffing it into her tobacco filler. Pharaoh learns that she is a single mom who ran away with her three-year-old daughter to protect her from a lying and abusive husband. Now her daughter is somewhere in Mexico, opening her legs everywhere. She is just like her father. During her remarks, the woman removes her light blouse and socks and places them in a ball behind her back. She, too, is tanned and leathery, but thinner than Anna. Her bra, a Maidenform, is extremely white, as if brand new, and droops a lit-tle along with the loose flesh above her abdomen. Her skin is wrin-kled, even the skin on her toes, and small knurled moles dot her chest and shoulders as she arcs herself toward the sun.

"We must enjoy the sun *uten snø* while we can. Soon it will be winter and there will be less sun," the neighbor says. "You are very lucky, Pharaoh, because you and Amaryllis do not have to worry about your tan."

Everyone looks at Amaryllis. The brim of the hat has slid over her eyes, slanting toward one ear. Bits of waffle litter the grass around her. Pharaoh suddenly experiences an intense need to protect her, as if the waffles pose some type of ill-defined danger. Even before he realizes it, he is in motion, walking across the lawn toward her. Once she sees him, her little arms and legs propel her spastically across the grass, then she drops on her hands and knees to gather speed. He chases her playfully, hustling around to block her path to the gravel. Amaryllis giggles, pivots, and is off again toward Anna and the nameless neighbor. Anna helps Pharaoh block Amaryllis's retreats, clearly amusing the other woman.

"You have a very beautiful daughter, Pharaoh. You must be very proud." She is in the midst of rolling yet another cigarette.

"She looks exactly like her mother," he says and thanks her, but it is not an entirely honest response. Hannah has already had to field questions about Amaryllis's ethnicity when he is not with them, especially from older women who seem only too eager to conclude that Amaryllis is adopted.

CHAPTER 5

THERE IS A NINE-HOUR interval between LA and Norway. While Pharaoh and his family are eating lunch in Trondheim, bartenders near Baxter's beach house in LA are signaling to their customers with the final call for alcohol. Pharaoh is desperate for information about his friends in LA, but no one has called. CNN keeps him up-to-date on things in the States, but not nearly enough. And he is not yet sufficiently at ease with his new language to follow Norwegian news broadcasts on television. Instead he lets his eyes follow the absorbing images, often covered by subtitles that take up a quarter of his television screen.

Just as he has begun to question the loyalty of his friends' promises to keep in touch, Billy calls. The overseas connection is hollow, filled with static and delayed pauses followed by echoes that make Pharaoh worry that the call is being monitored. Billy never says hello or goodbye. His friendship often seems like one long, uninterrupted conversation.

"What time is it there?"

"It's a little after one in the afternoon," Pharaoh says. His happiness at hearing Billy's voice prevents him from calculating the time difference immediately.

"I called at a good time, then. I was worried that I might wake up Amaryllis. How's she doing over there?" His questions sound rehearsed, exhibiting a maturity that Pharaoh is unfamiliar with but welcomes.

"Amaryllis is great. It's hard to keep up with her. She and Hannah are out on a stroll somewhere." Pharaoh purposely withholds the fact that it is raining. "You shoot anyone yet over there?"

"Not yet. But I just bought another one to add to my collection. A chrome-plated Magnum with a holster. I got it on right now, practicing my draw. You done any skiing yet?"

Pharaoh can hear Billy's delayed snicker on the line. It's four o'clock in the morning there, and he has a pretty good idea what Billy is up to. "Where's Tia?"

"Oh, she's right here. You wanna say hello?"

"Tell her I said hi," he answers, preferring not to hear her high-pitched voice. Clint has said that she belongs at Seaworld. "She's probably busy, anyway. So, Billy, tell me something new. What's happening over there?"

"The Lakers might not make the playoffs," he says. It is not the kind of information Pharaoh intends to elicit from him during their first long distance conversation. Nevertheless, they continue along the same vein. Billy supplies Pharaoh with trivial information partly because it is less complicated for him to store and manage in his state. He has no idea what Ken Starr is up to or whether Linda Tripp, whom he calls "a bitch," will be subpoenaed to testify. Even Billy is fed up with the situation. He asks for their address in Norway. Pharaoh feels a sense of trepidation when Billy wonders about the length of time it will take a package to get here, but he gives him the address anyway.

"Keep it clean," he says.

"Don't worry. It's a little present from me and Tia for Amaryllis. By the way, me and Tia are thinking about having a kid. We want a girl." Pharaoh does not know how to respond to this new revelation. He certainly wouldn't recommend it. Billy would be the kind of father who would give his kid candy to keep her occupied while he smoked his bong.

"It's a lot of work."

"We can handle it. Right, babe? What's the women like over there, by the way? I'm thinking of getting rid of Tia." He hears her high-pitched laugh.

"They're like icebergs, big and cold," Pharaoh says.

"Guess I'll keep her then." And Billy hangs up.

Pharaoh's initial jubilation at hearing Billy's voice subsides quickly as he reflects on their conversation. Given Billy's subversive nature, Pharaoh worries that he will use Amaryllis's name to funnel unwanted samples of his "stashes" to Pharaoh through the mail.

"He cannot be that stupid," Hannah says, defending Billy for the first time, when Pharaoh tells her about their conversation.

"No, but if he's high, who knows what he might stick in an envelope and place in a mailbox."

"You had better call him back and let him know."

He shares Hannah's concerns, especially since they share her parent's mailbox. Discovering illegal drugs in a sealed envelope addressed to Amaryllis from Billy would confirm their long-held suspicions about their daughter and LA.

Hannah's parents would often call her in LA right after they had watched episodes of *Jerry Springer* or *Sally Jesse Raphael.* "I thought your mom understood very little English," Pharaoh wonders aloud when Hannah tells him this. He's uncertain exactly who's to blame—the US for producing the programs or Norway for airing them. At any rate, watching them has definitely fueled Hannah's parents' mistrust of life in LA.

"She can read the subtitles," Hannah shoots back.

Pharaoh dials Billy's number the following day, at a reasonable time there though an ungodly hour in Norway, but he is not at home. Instead Tia answers. He listens as she tells him in her high-pitched voice how much she and Billy and the whole gang misses him. He promises to say hi to Hannah before getting down to brass tacks. The package, however, is already in the mail. Tia claims, despite his pleadings, that she cannot tell him what is in it because it would ruin their surprise. There is a "little something" in there for all of them, she says with delight. He promises Tia dejectedly that he will be on the lookout for it, but he does not tell Hannah about their conversation.

On most evenings after her shift ends, Pharaoh's sister, Gwen, doffs her white laboratory coat for a worn oversized shirt, cutoff jeans, and a dirty pair of hightop Reeboks. She is an avid gardener who has turned a small plot of dirt in the back of her home in LA into arable land. Life as a pharmacist has left her unfulfilled. It is too monotonous, and her interaction with the public, based solely on her instructions to them through a tiny cubicle window no bigger than her mouth, is almost minimal. She has been robbed four times, once at gunpoint, but refuses to seek employment elsewhere. Instead the parent company has enticed her with hazardous-duty pay, as if she performs a military service, and has also hired armed security personnel, installed cameras, and erected bulletproof partitions between the staff and the waiting room. Her clients are just kids, she insists, crying out for attention. She will not be intimidated.

Gwen studied botany at USC, then switched to pharmacy because the financial rewards out of pharmacy school were more immediate. Coded entrances and identification badges with magnetic strips were not what she had in mind, however. She is not an egoist but believes in making practical decisions. "A botanist has to work her way up to a decent salary, while a pharmacist reaps the rewards now. I don't want to teach anyone anything. I simply want a nine-to-five, a proletariat job where I can make enough money so that I don't have to depend on anyone. I'm not out to save the world, either, like you people, or fight for a cause. But I'll tell it like it is, call it the way I see it, and that is why we three can't get along." She has said all these things at one time or another.

It is also why she is still single. All her leftover energy is directed toward her garden and for creating discord in her personal relationships. "I am not here to pamper any man. If they think I've worked all these years so that they can come and lay claim to me because I'm a black woman, they're mistaken. I don't care who marched where or who sat where on a bus or who had dreams. I don't owe black men anything!" A pharmacy license and a $70,000-a-year income have given Gwen the freedom to speak her mind.

Gwen loves Amaryllis, but she berates Pharaoh for the mess she thinks he has gotten himself in. She accuses him of suffering from an identity crisis because of his marriage to Hannah. "And don't tell me you couldn't have fallen in love with a black woman, or someone with some color. This is LA! You had to fall for some European woman in the middle of LA? Baby, please. Give it a rest. I wish we had medication to cure what the hell you've got." Her criticism, although scathing at times, often stops short of defaming Hannah. His contention that true love is blind only serves to further infuriate Gwen. His over-romanticized, color-blind theory on love she considers nothing more than "bullshit on the sly."

While they lived in LA, Hannah had blamed herself for the hostility she sensed emanating from Pharaoh's relatives. She bought plants as gifts for Gwen's garden and had flowers delivered to them on their birthdays, when Pharaoh had forgotten to send cards. She overwhelmed them with cheeses, chocolate, and flavored smoked salmon upon her return from visits to Norway. Once, she had given his father a Troll, and Gwen an expensive bronze viking, as Christmas presents. Her effort did not go unnoticed by Gwen, but she continued to call it as she saw it. "It's not that I don't like your wife, Pharaoh. She seems like a really nice person. We've been out a few times, and to tell you the truth, we've had fun out there. But I cannot ignore who she is, nor what I see. I'm no good at pretending. You know that. I don't like how comfortable she is criticizing our people. She needs to pay some dues first before she can even think about that. Child, ain't nothing like watching lightning through black people's eyes if you ain't one of us."

"I haven't heard her," he had said.

"Child, you will. Just because she is married to you does not give her carte blanche. There is no such thing as a license to be black. You tell her that if she gets out of line. What's her point? Why is she really here, anyway? Is she after a green card?"

After Gwen had been robbed for the first time, Hannah, in her naïvete, had suggested that his sister stay with them until the police had caught whoever was responsible. "You don't know my sister," he cautioned. "She is tough, tougher than the LAPD who will never catch the culprit anyway."

Gwen's bitterness could also be traced to her continuing resentment over the couple's impromptu wedding. She had never forgiven them for their decision to get married in Las Vegas. Once again, she called it as she saw it. "You never even told anyone that you were getting married. What kind of wedding was that? Las Vegas? Only people who have something to hide get married in Vegas and they're usually back within a year. Oh, you're a movie star now because you're mixed up with a European woman? Bullshit on the sly, that's all I see. Bullshit on the sly."

After she learned of their plans to move to Norway, Gwen's attitude toward Hannah had undergone a sudden shift. She volunteered often to babysit Amaryllis and returned her with new teddy bears and clothes from Disney stores or baby GAP. She became preoccupied with Amaryllis's development and videotaped her at every turn. "Gwen," Pharaoh had said, "you know that you can visit us at anytime, and we'll be coming back for visits, too. It's not as if we all won't see each other again." But Pharaoh's words did little to reassure her or to relieve her despondency over losing Amaryllis from her life. She refused to talk about their forthcoming departure.

One early morning, an earthquake centered in the Mojave Desert sent tremors throughout LA County and San Bernadino County. It reached as far as Las Vegas according to some reports. Gwen, who had interpreted it as a sign, opened a small savings account in Amaryllis's name. "Consider it her war chest while she's over there," she announced. "When it's time for you to come back, you'll have no excuses."

PART II

Chapter 6

"*JEG HETER,* Pharaoh Chisholm. *Hva heter du?*"

"*Jeg heter,* Gawne Mandrake. *Hvor kommer du fra?*"

"*Jeg kommer fra* California. *Hvor kommer du fra?*"

"*Jeg kommer fra* Ohio, home of the fucking Buckeyes, and I'm here for some Norwegian pussy."

Pharaoh laughs. He and Gawne are practicing the basics of the language while they once again await the instructor's arrival from his search for a vacant classroom. They are outside one of the many entrances to a glass and concrete structure, designed to maximize the entry of sunlight and the retention of heat. Most of the students are fidgeting as they lean into a strong, chilly October wind. The campus, located thirty minutes from the city by bus, is set in a rural community with enormous satellite dishes attached to most of the homes. There is a pungent odor of manure, and from the buses, one can see the prop roots of corn as they strain with the wind in fields that straddle the roadsides.

There are twelve students, one more than is legally allowed on a cricket team, according to the only British student. They have quickly merged into cliques, the members self-selected along lines of nationality, language, and tastes. Perry and Grace have already established themselves as two of the instructor's charmed students. They arrived early and spent the summer advancing ahead of the class in coursework and Norwegian culture. Perry Delgado is a twenty-six-year-old Hispanic from Boston University who is slightly rotund. He is interesting to the class primarily because he is an American and a vegetarian. He is pursuing an advanced degree in Computer Technology and has a penchant for quoting dialogue from movies. Grace, a thirty-year-old Colorado native with a bachelor's degree in psychology, is tall, thin, and a newlywed. She met her Norwegian husband on the Internet.

"That is so fucking cool," Gawne says after she tells everyone, "way fucking cool!"

Grace acknowledges his fascination with a certain amount of caution. "Really? You don't think it's strange? Most of the people I've told back home act as if we're perverts because we found each other on the 'Net."

"Ain't nothing wrong with being a pervert. Baby, you've got mail. Bet you're not sleepless in Colorado no more." It is easy to picture Grace dilly-dallying her way around the web like a smolt in fresh water before getting snagged.

Hans Christian, the instructor, returns with positive news. He has found an empty classroom, but it is locked. "Someone will unlock the door in ten minutes, so I shall smoke with my students." His English is a bit rudimentary for someone who teaches a language at the university level. He joins a group of three African students who are in a heated discussion in English about the political situation in Nigeria. They are not smokers, but Hans does not seem to care.

"We are so big that we have two capitals."

"Or you are indecisive. You cannot choose," the student from Ghana says.

"Nigeria is a rich country, man, a very, very rich country. That is why we have two currencies. We have oil and minerals in the earth. It is the government who is responsible for all the violence. People cannot find jobs because the government supplies their own children with jobs first. It is what Chinua Achebe said. Have you heard of Achebe? A great man. *Things fall apart,* my friend. Things have fallen apart. It is the truth." The Nigerian student looks around for anyone who may have heard his ardent words, grinning as if he has won his case.

"It is not the government," the Ugandan student replies. "The government cannot be blamed for all Nigeria's problems. It is your oil and natural resources. It is a curse! It brings in big oil companies and businessmen from the West who pay you nothing and take everything away." The Ugandan has to repeat his name often to students. "It is a difficult name for the Western tongue to master. Oobamcee Moubuti. Say it! It is easy. It means prince of fortune."

Pharaoh has been watching the African students closely since he first saw them. Out of the three, Oobamcee Moubuti has assumed the unofficial role of silent leader of his continent. His opinions are deferred to and respected. Even among the other students he is approached with caution, as if a deep discussion is always imminent, one in which one's own passion and conviction seem no match for his resonant, oratorical voice.

Oobamcee is a thin man of average height, with a pronounced head. At age forty, he is the oldest student among them. Every day since the class began, he has worn the same oversized black jacket with sleeves that hang past his knuckles and a brightly colored shirt buttoned up to his neck. The rest of his attire consists of black slacks that are wrinkled and covered in lint, white socks, and polished black shoes. Oobamcee Moubuti's stay in Norway is indefinite. He has been awarded refugee status and will return to Uganda once the tribal fighting is over. When asked what he thinks of Norway, his reply is militant and evasive. "I am a displaced warrior. For now the fighting must go on without me, but I will continue to fight the oppressors of my people in my own way. It does not matter whether they are black and across the border in my country or whether they are white and here in the West. I am a warrior." There is no mistaking his claim. His face is wide and flat like the head of a spear. A receding hairline atop an oily forehead gives his head its pronounced look. There are four rows of jagged lines on each temple that everyone notices but no one dares to ask about. The markings remind Gawne of an armadillo he once saw on a music video on MTV.

Peter Nyere, a Ghanan exchange student, seems content to let his African counterparts embroil themselves in political argument. His role so far has been to lend support by nodding his agreement or disagreement or by presenting his outstretched hand for a handshake after the elucidation of some contentious point. He believes that all African conflicts that involve the West should be taken up by the United Nations and his fellow countryman Kofi Annan in New York. Kofi Annan, he continually reminds the others, is a very intelligent man. Peter is twenty-five years old. He chose the university because of its Civil Engineering program. He is here to learn how to build dams and floating bridges; his more academic aspirations will have to wait. He is unusually enamored with two of the German students who are unusually attractive, both of whom have also caught Gawne's roving eye.

Peter has offered Pharaoh his outstretched hand on several occasions. "How are you, Mr. USA? *Du er flink,* Mr. USA. German women are very nice, eh, Mr. USA." Pharaoh is the only American student to whom he refers to as Mister USA. Peter is tall with an athletic physique. He periodically scratches the tight curls of closely cropped hair on his head and face. They unfurl quickly, then roll back again into tight balls that resemble dung beetles. His vigorous scratching can be heard throughout the classroom during lectures. His complexion is dark with a bluish hue, and his constant smile emphasizes pink and black gums and stunning white teeth. Three finely woven gold chains hang from his neck, and he wears two gold rings set with diamonds on the middle fingers of his right hand.

Pharaoh cannot recall ever seeing anyone like him in LA. Despite his African-ness, his facial features are also somewhat Egyptian.

"You are very interesting, Mr. USA. You are married to a white Norwegian woman, no? In my country, you would be a respected man. You would rise to the top."

"In my country, it is the exact opposite. In fact, it can offend some people, especially those at the bottom. But my daughter makes it all irrelevant."

"It is only a hazard of love, Mr. USA. I have read about it and seen your American movies. But you have no jungle in America and you call your movies *Jungle Fever.* That is very interesting, Mr. USA."

"Oh, we have jungles in LA, but there are no trees, only skyscrapers and concrete freeways. And someday, it may all come tumbling down with an earthquake."

"Oh, oh. *Nei. Nei.* You are joking, Mr. USA. You are excellent with jokes." Peter's "Mister USA" has the potential to become annoying, but Pharaoh remains diplomatic.

Hans Christian looks at his watch and beckons to them. Inside the building, they straggle through throngs of students, remaining faithful to their groups.

"Look at Moses, parting the Red Sea," Perry says, as they follow the sounds of Hans's clogs on the tiled floor.

A few birds trapped under the glass ceiling flitter noisily overhead, dropping tiny branches and shit on students. Bulletin boards on brick walls are plastered with student and concert information, as well as police tips.

"How you ladies doing? What's happening? How you ladies?" Gawne's clumsy attempts to appear friendly and charming are greeted with passing nods or stiff smiles.

"I think Gawne will like it here. He's funny," Grace says, observing his flamboyant pimp strut.

"Señor Gawne is like a kid in a candy store. A little fastidiousness goes a long way here, Gawne. You'll see that eventually," Perry says.

"Give me a couple of weeks, bossman, and these ladies will know the man is in town." Gawne's eyes are fixed on the behinds of the German students walking ahead of him, holding hands like sisters. Despite his general confidence with women, he seems at a loss as to how best to approach the German students. They do not speak English, and no one in his group, except Hans Christian, speaks German.

"Christopher Columbus was not the first man to discover America. It was the vikings." Hans grins knowingly, as if he has told a joke. He points to each word on the blackboard and underlines *vikings*. Everyone laughs deferentially, a courtesy that is afforded to someone who is new at his position. The British, Canadian, and Ukrainian students cannot control their laughter, which eventually subsides to bowed giggles and furtive glances at the American students.

"Are you certain about that, Mr. Christian?" asks Pharaoh.

"Please, speak to me as Hans. You are not pupils here. We are a group," he says. "And, yes, I am certain. It is a historical truth. Why? Have you learned a different history from California?"

Hans is a small man in his late-thirties with shoulder-length brown hair and an untidy beard. His black pants are tight, displaying a well-formed gluteus. His shirt is loose-fitting and unbuttoned at the chest; both sleeves are rolled up to just beneath his elbows. His open-heeled clogs remind Pharaoh of the fashions of the 1960s. His girlfriend is always after him to shave and to cut his hair. She was born in Portugal and Hans speaks Portuguese fluently.

"There were others before the vikings," Pharaoh says.

"Who?" Hans's tone is accusatory.

"I'm not sure, but I read it somewhere."

"Well, students should be careful thinkers. Some history books make mistakes, especially in California." He places the knuckles of both hands on his desk and with his arms straightened rocks back on the heels of his clogs. His lips form a wry smile.

"Not this one! It is the same book where I read that vikings landed in America before Columbus."

"Er det noen andre ting om USA *I boken din?"*

There are slight murmurs from students. The switch to Hans's native language sabotages the exchange, effectively relegating Pharaoh back to pupil. Hans stands and scribbles both the Norwegian and English versions of his question on the blackboard, restoring at least some of his credibility.

"We were the first to land on the moon," Pharaoh says, "and the first to discover the rainbow." Staccato laughter fills the classroom.

"You are truly excellent with jokes, Mr. USA," Peter says. "Rainbows are everywhere."

"It is not a joke. It is what I have read." The silence that follows is only interrupted by Peter's head-scratching.

"We shall move on," Hans says finally. "We have had too many jokes for one morning."

Gawne cannot wait until Pharaoh's car arrives so that they can go cruising for Norwegian ladies. He is young, just twenty-one years old, and has no concept of the intricacies of marriage. His closest experience was a bitter relationship with an ex-girlfriend.

"Bitch was a white whore! Fucking all my friends behind my back in empty classrooms, holmes. Then she marries a Mexican beaner who has no idea that his wife is a whore. Hell, I'm never getting married, holmes!"

Gawne hints that he'd like to borrow Pharaoh's car—to impress the ladies. "It is difficult to rap to the ladies sporting your dogs or peddling a bicycle. And the buses are too fucking expensive, man. It's like three motherfuckin' dollars to ride the bus. I'll walk, holmes, before I give up three bucks. I ain't blown up." The two of them have become close friends, closer than they would have been had they known each other in the States.

"These bitches are hard to get to know, Pharaoh. I'ma have to run up on 'em and let 'em know I'm here, especially them Germs with their serious bumper kits. I need me some pussy before my shit turns into a raisin. They treating me as if I gots the applause. Shit, I ain't down with that! Man, at least you have a wife you can get it from. Me? I gots to do some recruiting, but these bitches ain't cooperating. You seen *Pulp Fiction*, holmes? Shit, I'ma have to get medieval on their asses. Don't make me get medieval now!" Gawne's threats are simply rhetorical, not meant to instill dread. As Grace explains, he is too cute to be taken seriously.

"Señor Gawne, you have too many gigabytes in your system," Perry advises. "Perhaps we must really find you someone soon. Your approach is wrong. It is a bit immature and somewhat primitive. I can help. Women are peculiar. You cannot approach them in the same manner as you would a well-done steak. Women prefer to be approached gallantly, even women in Europe. Here is what I suggest, Señor Gawne. You must have a party at your place and invite as many people as you can. Make sure you have invested in lots of alcohol. Women here love alcohol. Then when everyone is drunk, ask the women if they would like to see your room. If no one is interested, go into your room and secure the door. Make as loud a commotion as you can while you're in there. Tear off your clothes, too. Trust me, it is good theatre. Continue your bedlam for a few seconds. Then open the door suddenly and spring out naked, as if you have escaped. They will want to know who is in there and what has happened. Tell them it is the gimp. Tell them he did not appreciate the way you woke him up."

The reference to the gimp is typical of the film references and dialogue that regularly pass back and forth between Perry and Gawne. They are particularly fond of *Pulp Fiction* and *Top Gun*, filling their quotes with double entendres if the German students are present.

"Okay, which one of 'em you wanna do first, man?"

"Neither, I got Bumper. I'm gonna hit the brakes, and she'll fly right by, Periwinkle."

"Okay, Little Dick, do some of that pilot shit."

"Periwinkle, I've had about enough of this shit."

"Man, Big Dick here. Little Dick just caught him a couple flies."

"Break right! Break right! Watch the mountains, Little Dick."

"Looks like I caught you boys in the middle of breakfast. Sorry about that."

"Little Dick, that was some real nice flying, right up until the part you got shot down. But you never leave your wingman."

"You my wigga?"

"Yeah, it's me. Little Dick just quit."

"Okay, let's get in character."

Pharaoh catches Sail Ruleltu, the Nigerian student, staring at him with a blank expression on his face. It is a very disconcerting stare and difficult for Pharaoh to interpret. He stares as if he has seen Pharaoh somewhere before but can't recall the time or place, no matter how hard he tries to remember. Perhaps, muses Pharaoh, there is someone who looks like him back in Nigeria. Pharaoh looks away for a moment but decides to return his stare. When Pharaoh raises his eyes, however, Sail is no longer there.

Chapter 7

"YOU MUST BE VERY CAREFUL in Norway when you drive your car. You must never ever drink and drive or throw trash out of windows. It is very common in the USA, but we don't do it here. Norway is a little land, our pearl, and we try to keep it clean. People are filthy in the USA. What do you say? What do you call them? You have a word for them."

"Slobs," Pharaoh says.

"Yes, yes. Slobs," Knut says.

It is a trip unworthy of the company. Hannah had made all the arrangements after receiving a telegram that the SHO had arrived in Drammen, a port just outside of Oslo. Her brother and his friends had volunteered to drive him to pick up the SHO. She had prepared coffee, sandwiches, and waffles for the trip and had cautioned Pharaoh not to disclose what he had heard from her parents about Knut's expensive old house. Also off-limits was the time that Knut had recently spent in jail. Pharaoh had promised to keep it all to himself, but it was a difficult promise to keep.

During the ride to Oslo, Pharaoh learns from his companions that immigrants are attempting to turn Oslo into an "asylum capital" like Stockholm. Apparently, Stockholm, once a beautiful city, is now deteriorating faster than Scandinavia can build McDonald's.

"Muslims and Pakistanis and Africans all come here to seek asylum, and they never return to their countries. And then they behave as if *I* should feel like the foreigner when I walk on my own streets in Oslo. With their different languages, they are ruining the capital, turning it into an underground haven for drugs and prostitution and black market things. It is truly disgusting." Knut speaks with stiff, robotic movements. It is a topic that Pharaoh is not prepared to discuss, so soon out of the classroom and still getting used to this frigid new culture. Especially not with a twenty-six-year-old who cares more about Oslo's inhabitants than his snuff-stained teeth. Hannah had warned him that her little brother had been through some rough times and could be very opinionated. Pharaoh saw no reason why they wouldn't get along, however.

"Why are they seeking asylum here and not in Stockholm?"

"Stockholm isn't what it used to be. People cannot find jobs there anymore. Many Swedish people are coming to Norway to find jobs now. Ever since we found oil, they have been coming. We have become the Saudi Arabia of Scandinavia, but Saudi Arabia does not have these problems."

His two friends, both about Knut's age, nod their heads in agreement.

"We don't mean Americans. We all like Americans here in Norway. But *you* must understand. You have the same problems with the Mexicans in California. Is it not so?"

Nils is clean-shaven, overweight, and barreled shape, with tattoos on both arms. He has drunk most of the coffee and eaten most of the waffles. The four are crammed in a minivan, and Nils, who speaks no English, rests his folded arms on the back of Pharaoh's seat while chewing and talking on his mobile phone.

Robert is also overweight but has no visible tattoos. He is very blond and is wearing dark sunglasses. Throughout the trip, he flips through a case of CDs, most of them by rap artists, often leaning over from his seat to insert a CD himself. He does speak some

English, and occasionally challenges Pharaoh's statements as a show of support for Knut.

"I think some of your asylum seekers would like to return home. It must be very difficult for them here, especially if they feel as if they're not wanted."

Knut raises an eyebrow, as brown liquid oozes from the front of his gums onto his front teeth. In a single swallow, it disappears.

"We are getting too many. We are a little land. I understand that we must do our part in the world to help poor countries, but we are not as big and rich as the USA. And, as I have said before, they do much of the crimes here in Norway. There were never gangs here before we started letting so many people in. Now there are stabbings and rapes and shootings. Oslo is becoming like LA. Soon Norway will be like the United States." It is a comparison that Pharaoh has been waiting for. He is not surprised that mother and son share the same opinions.

"But I have seen on television that you have lots of pedophiles here. Seems like lots of your adult men like little girls and little boys. Maybe you are already like the States. Perhaps I should be worried about my daughter," Pharaoh stabs back.

"It is an Internet problem here," Knut admits, "but we have more to fear from gangs than from sick men on the Internet. We do not want to be afraid of each other like they are in the US. We do not want to become like the US."

"That will never happen," Pharaoh assures him. But Pharaoh worries to himself that it might already be too late. Knut's fear of immigrants suggests that perhaps he and his countrymen are halfway there. "And the United States does not have a king."

"You have the Kennedys. They are like kings in your country," Robert interrupts. "I am named after one."

"They are political celebrities and maintain their celebrity status because of the tragic events which involved members of their family that took place in America's history. They are not supported by taxpayers' money. Their pictures are not displayed at the entrance of every public building in the country, and they have no official role with respect to greeting foreign dignitaries. They require no bows or curtsies. They're just regular people to whom we give a little respect; that is all."

"But they are above the law. No one is above the law here in Norway. Look at Chappaquiddick. Nothing happened to the Kennedys."

"And OJ," Robert pipes in.

"The OJ trial was unfortunate, but it taught us some lessons," Pharaoh says, eager to espouse Clint's arguments. Knut, however, will not relinquish his point on the law.

"A civilized society, especially a democratic society, is supposed to treat all people the same. It should not matter how rich you are so that you can buy the best dream team of lawyers."

In spite of the arguing, Pharaoh suddenly realizes that he and Knut are actually getting along pretty well as the trip progresses. Like the rest of the family, Knut has embraced him because he is in love with Hannah.

"Some lawyers are better than others, Knut, and in a capitalist society, the great attorneys who know their craft and their own value can charge whatever customers are willing to pay. I am sure that if your Monarchy's diplomatic privileges were somehow revoked and they needed legal representation in the US, they would look for the best attorneys—unless of course they couldn't afford an attorney. Then one would be provided for them by the courts, free of charge."

Knut and the others have missed his humor, or perhaps they just choose to ignore it. He worries that he may have overstepped his bounds in the midst of their generosity. Knut quickly sets him at ease, however.

"You are very interested in Norway. That is nice to see. You are a good brother-in-law. I can see that my sister knew what she was doing. It is good that you learn much about Norway. Others do not respect our culture. They bring their culture and religion here and expect us to change our laws to respect their religion and culture. But you are tired of hearing this. It is not your problem. You have had enough in LA."

"No problem. I am here to learn."

They settle the conversation there, but it is an uncomfortable pause. Robert, after inserting a CD by Dr. Dre and Snoop Dogg, begins to sing along. His vapid tones provide empirical evidence of the power of the American music and entertainment industry, and of rap music in particular. Robert's rendition of "1-8-7 on an Undercover Cop" brings laughter from Nils and Knut.

"American rap music is full of life. We like it here in Norway, as you can hear."

"But you would not like the people who invented it if you had to live among them," Pharaoh replies. Knut's comment has made him uneasy. As they listen to the lyrics, his desire to defend rap music becomes more immediate. He wishes Gawne were here.

"Man, Robert, you sound like you from around the way here. You ain't no banger, are you? 'Cause I know you guys have some bangers in Trondheim. Brang the noise, man! It's coal nice to know that I'm hanging with some def fellas."

Knut and Nils both glance at Robert for some type of translation of what he has said.

"You know Dr. Dre and Snoopy?" Robert asks calmly, slumping slightly behind his seat belt.

"Word. I know them homeys. Man, we all from the USG. I used to hang with them brothas before everyone started bugging out. Seemed like they started icing brothas just so they can cut a CD. I got tired of that 3-6-9, man. I didn't want Amaryllis and Hannah to wake up one morning as roughnecks laid in the cut, hoping to put a cap in my ass. I even bought Hannah a deuce-five because some of the New Jills weren't giving her her props. But then we lucked out. A few of them got sent up, and we hatted out." Pharaoh reaches over and turns up the volume as the third track begins, bopping his head up and down softly. He can feel Robert's eyes peering through his dark glasses at the back of his head.

Knut's voice breaks their silence. *"Herregud!"* he says. A barrage of dialogue is exchanged in Norwegian before Knut finally translates on behalf of them. "We must listen to the news." Pharaoh does not mind. It gives him an opportunity to improve his Norwegian vocabulary.

After listening to the news, everyone sits quietly. Knut looks withdrawn, and his ride-a-longs, taking his cue, keep their thoughts to themselves. With less than two hours left on the trip, they listen to a talk radio program about immigrant taxi drivers in Oslo who are operating as pirates, outside of the city-sanctioned taxi drivers association. No one has asked if Pharaoh understands the host, who has a strange dialect, and no one has really bothered to translate. He sinks back in his seat and cannot wait for the long ride back in the SHO by himself.

Driving his black SHO at excessive speeds on roads built for European automobiles is tantamount to a narcotic rush. He is not on the autobahn. When motorists slow down to stare, he allows them to pass, then proceeds to race past them at almost double their speeds. It is a game in which he is the only player, the only one who knows the rules.

"You are new to our country?" the policewoman asks. She is in her mid-forties and, with her oily, beet-red countenance, does not appear to be in the best of health. Her hips are wide, suggesting either multiple childbirths or prolonged inactivity behind the steering wheel. She coughs and blows her nose in a handkerchief that she crinkles and stuffs in her front shirt pocket. There are two of them. Her partner is in his mid-twenties, probably a rookie, and seems more fascinated with the black SHO. He has circled it twice, lingering in the front and back on both occasions. It wouldn't surprise

Pharaoh if they were mother and son. Their uniforms are not familiar to him. They are dressed in light blue shirts, dark blue pants, black combat boots, green reflector vests, and hats reminiscent of those worn by small regiments in Eastern European countries. They are not armed and could easily be mistaken by tourists for private security personnel in charge of answering house alarms.

"You are a tourist?"

"Yes," he says.

"What part of Africa are you from?" she asks.

"I am an American," Pharaoh says, somewhat perturbed, as he sits with both hands on the steering wheel.

"I can hear that," she replies, sniffling. " I mean where in Africa are your African ancestors from?"

"The whole continent!" he says with emphasis.

"You have a nice auto," the other policeman announces. "There are tips from drivers about this auto. You drive fast, so we must stop you to investigate and to slow you down. Do not worry; we will not beat you up or rape you like they do in the States." They stand shoulder to shoulder peeping into his car.

"May we see your papers?"

"You mean my license?"

"No, your papers to have this car in Norway."

"My papers are in order," he says, smiling to himself as he hands them to her. His papers permit him to drive with a temporary registration certificate from Drammen to Trondheim only, and no farther.

"Who is Hannah?"

"She is my wife. She also owns the car."

"I see it," the policewoman says. She does not turn away her head to sneeze, instead uses Pharaoh's papers as a shield. After checking the papers, she returns them with a soft warning to "obey the speeds."

"More tips and you will have no license," the young policeman warns.

"I have been to Africa," the policewoman says. "You have a beautiful country. It is very natural, very big safari. It is easy to fall in love there." Pharaoh nods, though he isn't sure exactly what she means. He has never been on a safari anywhere.

"How do you like it here in Norway?" The policeman smiles. It is a smile that he expects will influence Pharaoh's response.

I am a quadroon house nigger despite my dark skin, so I am used to being indoors. The snow will not bother me, he thinks, before replying politely to the policeman's question: "It is a wonderful country. But I am worried about the snow and it is beginning to get dark too early."

"Oh yes," the policeman admits. "The snow is horrible! Horrible! Many people visit the South Islands in Europe during the winter. It is much warmer there. Or we stay at home and drink cognac. But we do not drink behind the wheel here. We are not like California." He is friendly but firm, much like a therapist. It's not the first time that Pharaoh has been spoken to this way here in Norway. It feels more and more as if he's become the center of an allopathic experience. Perhaps he is the entire nation's therapy.

They wish him *"lykke til"* and depart.

"Ha det bra," Pharaoh responds, waving to the policewoman. His words produce a big smile. She is still smiling as he drives away, the sheen from the over-productive oil glands on her red face gradually fading into the window of the idling police Volvo.

Chapter 8

COGNAC IS TOO STRONG. It is not a woman's drink, or at least not something she can drink without looking like a man, Hannah admits. They are at a disco in the city. It is their first night out. The vivacious laughter of Hannah and her friends is taking its toll on him. Three dance floors segregate revelers according to their rhythmic abilities. Six of them are sitting at a booth, across from a dance floor where young people jump in a pulsating manner to piercing computer-enhanced rhythms. Eva and her friend are on the middle of the dance floor, bouncing to the rhythms. Pharaoh enjoys watching them. Eva's friend is dressed in black leather, with silver chains hanging from his back pockets. His movements appear difficult and exciting. He jumps so high that the dance floor seems like a trampoline. The chains he's wearing appear to lash him into frenzy.

"You like this music, Pharaoh? Maybe they have this in America, too."

"It is not what I would listen to on a regular basis, but it's all right."

Dagfinn sips his cognac, then drags on his cigarette. He exhales toward the ceiling, above two large photographs of the King and Queen, who seem to be stoically monitoring the events. The King stands upright in one of the photographs in full decorative attire.

The Queen is seated in front of him, her gloved hands stacked in her lap. The image of the two is already familiar to Pharaoh.

Anna and Hannah discuss *Twin Peaks,* an outdated television show. They are trying to determine who killed Laura Palmer and occasionally interrupt Pharaoh to ask the name of a particular movie, actor, or actress.

"That is our King and Queen," Dagfinn says, as Pharaoh's eyes follow the cloud of smoke toward the ceiling.

"Have they been here?"

"No, no," he explains, taking slight offense at Pharaoh's irreverence. "This is normal for their photos to be up there. They are our tradition, but the younger generation believes they should go, that they are too expensive."

"It is important for every generation to recognize its tradition for what it is. They will probably change their minds as they get older and have kids of their own."

"I hope so," Dagfinn says. "I can see it in the Crown Prince and Princess. They refuse to follow their parents' way unless we criticize them in the press. The Prince wants only to go to parties at nightclubs or concerts and festivals in the city where there are disgusting people. And the Princess wants to ride horses and lay on the beach. They both want to be regular people, but they are not, of course."

"It is cool to be at nightclubs with people you like. We are at a nightclub. And some people really enjoy riding horses and lying on the beach. I have heard that for some women, riding horses can bring them to orgasm. Perhaps your Princess is one of them. Does she ride motorcycles?"

"Of course not! They are our future Statesman and Stateswoman."

"Maybe Mom and Dad should intervene, treat them like regular people, tell them to look for jobs. You might be surprised at how quickly they may turn around or resume their duties to the Monarchy."

Dagfinn frowns at Pharaoh's attempt to secularize the Monarchy.

"The women are wimps," Dagfinn says, as he checks their drinks and orders another round of cognacs. "My little sister says you have been to schools in LA. So you are a clever man, then?"

Pharaoh does not know what he means by "clever."

"I am kind of clever, but certainly not as clever as your King," Pharaoh says.

"Our King is mighty clever. But maybe he is not clever enough to deal with the children of his throne. Perhaps he shall be our last king. No more king, and we will be a republic." Dagfinn shakes his head sadly. Pharaoh can tell that he has given more than a casual thought to the prospect of a republic.

"Times change," Pharaoh says. "Sometimes it takes centuries and one only becomes aware of it gradually. But at other times, it hits like an earthquake."

"You are a clever brother-in-law," Dagfinn says, holding up his cognac. "We must dance now. But first, always before the King and Queen arrive somewhere, there are bells. Let us pretend they are arriving to join us for cognacs. Ding dong! Great bells! Skoal!"

"Skoal!" Pharaoh says, as they clink glasses.

"To Norway!" Dagfinn continues, as they clink again.

"To Norway," Pharaoh mutters.

"To our King and Queen! Great bells!"

"To your King and Queen. Skoal and great bells!" There is more clinking as Anna and Hannah use the opportunity to sip their wine and request refills.

"Are you getting drunk?" Hannah asks.

"We must dance, brother-in-law," Dagfinn says with a sense of urgency.

Pharaoh looks to Hannah and Anna for deliverance, even if it is only temporary, but they offer him no opportunity to sidestep the offer.

Single groups of females and males jump and prance to the DJ's synthetic sounds on the dance floor. The dancers began as couples, but everyone seems to have lost their partners to the larger group. To Pharaoh's dismay, Eva has left the dance floor. She wore a brassiere tonight, but it is no match for the voluptuousness produced by the pulsating techno music and a spirited partner. From the dance floor, he sees her collapse in his seat next to Hannah and push his cognac away. Next to him, Dagfinn's movements resemble a ceremonial Native American tribal dance. He hops from one foot to the next and bows, then applauds himself. Eva's friend, who Anna and Hannah have concluded is a punk rocker, has edged his way over to Pharaoh and Dagfinn. He is streaming with perspiration but will not remove his leather jacket. He is too cool, preferring to swim in his sweat.

"You must be very hot," Pharaoh says.

"Thank you," he answers, and continues his trampoline dance. The women look at them and raise their glasses.

No one gestures from their group, so Pharaoh flashes an impromptu peace sign. Eva's friend whispers in Dagfinn's ear, then opens his mouth and sticks out his tongue, revealing a silver stud pierced through the middle. They both look at Pharaoh wonderingly.

"I knew you could dance," Dagfinn says. It is not really dancing. Pharaoh is simply jumping in the manner that everyone else is jumping—everyone except Dagfinn and Eva's friend.

"I should probably get my drink," Pharaoh says, preparing to escape.

"I shall," Dagfinn replies, and bores his way through the jumpers and toward their table.

Dagfinn does not return with Pharaoh's drink. Instead, Anna places a drink in his hand and begins to dance. She does not jump, but only bounces her head up and down and side to side in a pretense of sophistication. Her arms sway at about waist level, as if she is attempting to untangle bracelets. She has a single, thick ponytail tonight with a curve at the end that seems capable of prehensile activity on its own.

"Rotten music!" she yells in his ear, tugging him by the arm toward the thumping loudspeakers before he can bottom up his drink. She is overdressed. Most of the revelers are in casual attire. Anna has on a black rayon dress that falls just over her knees, and black gloves that lace all the way to the knots of her elbows. It is an outfit designed for a younger, more curvaceous figure. Her black boots stretch atop her plump calves, and the six-inch soles suggest this exotic housewife is living proof of the Spice Girls' "Girl Power Revolution." She is thirty-five years old, but tonight she is in her teens.

Anna leads Pharaoh along ragged walls illuminated by black lights to look like moonscapes. It is obvious that she has been here before. Now and again, she stops abruptly to gain her balance or avoid losing his hand, his momentum sending him headlong into her back and soft rear end. They descend slippery, tiled stairs littered with empty beer bottles and plastic coke bottles, and end up at a long line filled with women waiting to use a rest room.

"I must pee," Anna announces. The words rush out as if she had been silently rehearsing them on her way here. A speaker above the wall ledge where patrons who are concerned about hygiene leave their drinks and empty glasses blares a P. Diddy tune. Suddenly Anna tugs, then pushes him through the men's room door and follows him in, pushing him toward a vacant stall. She enters and slams the door shut behind her while Pharaoh stands outside and shrugs his shoulders in disbelief, feeling every bit like a thrall.

Anna and Pharaoh are on the move again. He ignores her offers to lead him anywhere except back to their table. She points him in the general direction of their table and tells him that she must find her music.

"Come back to dance," she yells, and melts into the revelers, swinging her head and ponytail to and fro.

"Brother-in-law, what have you done with my wife, the mother of my two children?"

Pharaoh ignores Dagfinn's mock attempt to show vigilant concern about his wife. Dagfinn drains his empty glass, his eyes searching expectantly for the waitress and more cognacs. His search is interrupted by loud giggles between Hannah and Eva, though their joke excludes Eva's friend. Two revolving lights from the techno dance floor bounce off Eva's red hair and earrings, landing on the waitress.

"My little sister and her girlfriend are happy you are here, brother-in-law."

"Happy to hear it," Pharaoh says, as he ponders telling Dagfinn about the rest room incident. He decides that Anna will recite it better in her native language. "Anna went to look for her music. Perhaps you should join her."

"My wife does not dance well," Dagfinn says offhandedly, then bows his head and applauds, to remind them of his own dance prowess. "We don't like similar music. I am a jazzman. It is a more grown-up music. I am sure you know jazz." Dagfinn, with an outstretched hand, prevents him from paying the waitress. He is an American, Dagfinn's brother-in-law from California, with American dollars only, he explains, but the waitress does not care. She is on her way to another table as Dagfinn pockets his change.

"You boys having fun there?" Hannah asks as she frowns at the cognacs.

"We are not boys. Boys do not get drunk," Pharaoh replies.

"Remember, hon, tomorrow is Sunday, and only one of us can sleep in." Hannah and Eva look at each other and smile.

"Do not listen to the women. They are always a problem. We are men. We listen to no women, brother-in-law, except our Queen. To our King! Great bells!"

"To your King," Pharaoh says, as they clink glasses.

"And our Queen. Great bells!"

"And your Queen."

Eva's friend is in the middle of his second cell phone call, and his animated conversation causes Eva to sit up straight. The phone slips from his hand and falls to the floor. When he disappears under the table to retrieve it, Eva and Hannah give each other a conniving high-five.

"Where is Anna?" Hannah says, as if startled by her absence.

"I left her on her way to find music. She probably got lost. Let's dance," Pharaoh suggests. He thinks that she has finally had enough drinks to get up and dance with him—and to tell him what is going on.

"Let's wait for a good song," she says.

"What is going on?" he asks Hannah.

"It's none of our business."

"I'll go see if I can find Anna." He leaves Hannah and Eva spellbound over a conversation he cannot understand.

Pharaoh does not find Anna. She finds him. He feels a flat palm roughly knead his behind at the bar. When he turns around, Anna is smiling. Her eyes are bloodshot, making her smile sinister and mischievous. She hands him a half-empty Carlsberg, squeezes her way to the front of the bar, and then returns with a cognac and another Carlsberg. He explains, as best he can, the mood at the table. Hannah and Eva are probably on their third bottle of wine; Anna should hurry before they empty it. She is not ready to return and just sit, however. And Eva's friend is speaking to his wife. There's no need to hurry back.

"Two kids I am trying to lose," Anna says, and pinches her fleshy belly. Pharaoh has heard this one before. He does not believe her weight can be attributed to past childbirth.

"You can help if we dance," she shouts. So they dance.

The dance floor is crowded. People just arriving are stupid drunk. Anna occasionally loses her balance and leans on Pharaoh for support. He is tempted to let her lean on the floor instead, and smiles to himself at the thought. The DJ has played *her* song twice in a row—the Village People's "YMCA." Each time she has lost her balance making the "C." She likes many American songs but can only remember Green Day's "Time of Your Life" and Foreigner's "I Want to Know What Love Is." Green Day, she says, is her absolute favorite, as they dance awkwardly to "Time of Your Life." It is not a slow song to grind to, but Anna's movements suggest that it should be. The smell of sweat and perfume around them sickens him.

"*Gå det bra,* Anna?" Her embrace becomes heavy and snug as couples dancing around them grope at each other.

"*Nå, gå det bra,*" she says, smiling up at him as she presses her soft belly and hips into his thigh. She speaks in a rush of Norwegian and English. His skin is too smooth. She looks at him often through her window when he is at home. He is nice to look at. He explains that he can only see her legs from his window when she is outside. She does not believe her legs are nice to look at because they have balanced two kids and are always bruised because she is clumsy. He is welcome for coffee and waffles whenever he sees her at home.

The alcohol and dancing are taking their toll on Pharaoh. Should he return her invitation to coffee and waffles? Anna begins to sing the lyrics along with the music, oblivious to how close they are. Her shoulders barely move as they dance. He thinks she is falling asleep. The ponytail now hangs slack and lifeless from its knot at the back of her head.

He does not tell her that he has seen Lena, her eldest daughter, point him out to her friends, pat her hair, and press her nose flat against her face whenever he passes them on the street. Or that Sara asks on occasion why the palms of his hands are white and the backs of his hands are black. Or that she also folds her lips back to mock the thickness of his lips, and then laughs.

He is strong and good-looking with smooth skin, Anna repeats, as if she has finally arrived at the word.

"*It's something unpredictable, and in the end it's right. I hope you had the time of your life."* The lyrics repeat; Anna relaxes her hold on him and rubs both sides of his face with her gloved hand. He notices the outline of her erect nipples on her dress. She sees this and smiles. "You also?" she asks, and continues to sing the lyrics into his chest.

There are no thermometers or calendars, and the pillow is under Hannah's head. They are both drunk, but Hannah wants him to make love to her before she goes night-night. "Come here." He follows her voice, creeping cautiously toward it in the dark as he tries to avoid disturbing the soft snores from Amaryllis's crib in the corner of their bedroom. Their sex begins routinely with measured caresses, then escalates eagerly into a slight grapple as they both attempt to prolong, in their state, what is by nature a short, though ecstatic event.

While Hannah and Amaryllis sleep along with the rest of this quiet neighborhood, Pharaoh slips outside in an overcoat, sweats, and sneakers to find a place to smoke Billy's surprise. The need for secrecy is his only reason for wandering deeply into the forest. The sky is dark and clear over Trondheim. The moon hovers just above the heavy tree line. There are no trolleys operating at four a.m. Pharaoh, of course, welcomed Billy's surprise to Amaryllis, once it had arrived safely. Billy purchased two yo-yos, inserted three joints into each, and used Disneyland's address in nearby Orange County as a return address.

The joint takes effect almost immediately and has almost burned to a stub before Pharaoh is aware that he is squinting up at the moon. It's beautiful here at night, even as the moon dips behind the trees. It is also cold, a frost-like cold. He can feel blades of grass crunch beneath his feet as he steps. Anna's image fades in and out of his high. She had returned to the table staggering more than she did when she had left. Nothing was mentioned about their dance, only that he had found her and had brought her back. Later, while they were preparing to leave, she had asked him in a staccato tone if they had "jammed" on the dance floor. It was a new word for her, he guessed, although he could not be completely certain. She must have sought someone out, perhaps the DJ, to feel brave enough to use it. He had nodded in recognition that she had used the word correctly. "I must learn more English words so we can speak," she had said. He is flattered by her attention but also worried. What if her private declaration becomes an unspoken covenant to pursue and enjoy risks? Any further improvement in their vocabularies might prove unhealthy. Hannah and Amaryllis are tied to his navel, and he supposes it is the same with Anna and her family. Besides, her fascination with the smoothness and color of his skin will pass. It is the twenty-first century, and she remains unenlightened, pre-colonial. He has no obligation to teach enlightenment in Norway. It is not his responsibility, not why he is here. Yet he has to admit that he is attracted to her as well. He had repressed this attraction while they shared coffee and waffles with her nameless neighbor, and again when they danced. It is a strange feeling, and a strong one. And it is filled with a grave desire to hurt.

CHAPTER 9

WINTER OFFICIALLY ARRIVES and with it a barrage of snow. It is imperative that Amaryllis learns how to ski early, according to Trine and Thor. They have promised to buy skis for her first Christmas in Norway, and this leads to the first sign of contention between Hannah and Pharaoh over her parents' role in Amaryllis's life.

"Don't make a big deal out of this," Hannah says. "They are her grandparents. That's what grandparents do."

"Maybe they can buy her another present, one that I wasn't also thinking of buying."

"We never discussed buying her skis."

"It was going to be a surprise. I have already checked into it at ski shops in the city."

"Ski shops!" she says, incredulously. "Amaryllis is almost two. My parents were planning on buying her skis from Playworld, something she can play around in outside. She's not ready for cross-country yet, if that's what you had in mind."

"It's really not what I had in mind, Hannah," he says. "Amaryllis's first pair of skis should come from us, and her first bicycle, as a matter of fact. This is what dads do. It is what moms expect dads to do with pride. It may seem trivial or superficial, but it is important to me."

Hannah either does not see or refuses to see the point to his appeal. This isn't the first challenge to his parenting responsibilities by Trine and Thor. Trine already takes Amaryllis for afternoon walks around the neighborhood, turning it into a social event as she stops and chats with her neighbors. When Trine and Thor have visitors upstairs, they often ask Hannah if Amaryllis can come up for a short visit, which frequently turns into a lengthy one.

Pharaoh's household responsibilities are also dwindling. Whenever changes need to be made in the apartment involving carpentry, Hannah feels compelled to consult Thor, who takes it upon himself to make whatever changes he thinks are necessary. He has built a small dollhouse and a ladder for Amaryllis and has also built shelves in the bathroom, tasks which Pharaoh, too, could have easily performed.

"I don't see why you're getting so upset over this. Even if you buy her skis, someone still has to teach her how to ski. Did you grow up in the snow? You don't even know how to ski," she says.

"Well," he responds, "we can both learn. Amaryllis won't care if I am a beginner."

"Okay," Hannah concedes, "I'll let my mom know."

Hearing her tone, he feels he has no choice but to let it drop and succumb to her parents' wishes. Ultimately, Amaryllis will learn to ski one way or another. And Hannah is probably right—it is of little consequence who really purchases her first pair of skis. She is fortunate enough to have grandparents who are eager to shower her with gifts.

Hannah makes a reproachful inquiry about Pharaoh's father back in the States. They ought not to forget to send him and Pharaoh's sister a Christmas card with Amaryllis's picture in it.

She's clearly made her point, Pharaoh thinks.

Hans Christian is unhappy with their group's performance. They are not doing well. He accuses them of not being serious about learning his language. Their complaints about the difficulty of the language are summarily dismissed. They are at the absolute bottom thus far, compared to previous groups who have thrived under his instruction. The women are doing much better than the men, he points out, recommending that the men study more. Because there are no female Africans among them, the news does not bode well for the African students. They must be prepared to have more written and oral exams before July, he warns. His comments cast a somber mood over everyone. Even so, it is the final week of class before the Christmas holidays, and there is talk of the class going to dinner and a bar for drinks.

"What's there to think about, motherfucker? We could eat with them, then go hang with the homeys," Gawne says. They are in a large cafeteria where most of the students either have their heads bowed in one of two national tabloids or are preoccupied with sending messages from their cell phones.

The German women cannot attend the class dinner. They are flying home to visit their families and their boyfriends. It is a terrible blow to Gawne, but he claims it is only a minor setback. He expects that kind of shit from them, he admits, but he will never give up his pursuit of the ladies.

"We should invite everyone to go out afterwards," Grace says, pinching Gawne. "It shouldn't be only us four. That isn't very nice."

"What about Hans?" Perry asks. They remain silent.

"I agree with Grace," Pharaoh says. "And we should definitely invite Hans." So it is settled. Gawne volunteers to prepare a phone list and send emails to everyone.

The African students are at a table, huddled together as if they are conducting a private conference. Oobamcee is silent but contemplatively alert. Peter and Sail are deep in discussion, Sail in a more animated manner. Pharaoh has begun to spend more time listening to their discussions. It is like watching ordinary, afflicted men, unaware that they are becoming revolutionaries as they fight their afflictions. Oobamcee insists that Pharaoh actually join the discussion. Surely their comments must make him at least a little angry toward the West.

"Those homeys are always arguing," Gawne says, pointing his chin toward the Africans. "What's up with that?"

"Their countries are in turmoil. They're always fighting like they do in the Middle East," Perry says, barely glancing at their table. "It's hard to support them if you don't know who is right."

"Is it true Oobamcee has four wives? I've heard that he has three somewhere in Africa that he sends money to and one here in Trondheim. Have you guys heard that?" Grace has her back to their table but whispers anyway.

"Now *that* I can dig! Shit! Send my ass to Africa," Gawne announces.

"Señor Gawne," Perry says, as if he's about to begin a lecture, "why go to Africa when you can simply become a Mormon and live in Utah?"

"They don't have what I want in Utah, motherfucker."

"And what's that?" Pharaoh asks, joining the fray.

"Some sugar, homey. Lots of motherfuckin' sugar."

"I wonder how many kids he has? It's not unusual for families in Third World countries to have twenty or thirty kids each, you know. I've heard that the men are still fathering babies while they're in their sixties." Grace winces and looks at Pharaoh.

"I think," Pharaoh says in an attempt to rescue her comments from a primitive perspective to a cultural one, "their societies are different from ours. They rely on family and communities and tribes more than we do. And it is also a more patriarchal society. They're probably at the stage we were in, in America, when economic survival meant producing lots of kids to keep farms going or to make sure families survived diseases and epidemics. Didn't you guys take history? Their culture is different—that's all—just like this one. Look at where we were then, and look at where we are now. When they catch up, this world is going to be in for a fucking rumble."

"Don't we have a potty mouth," Perry says.

"But they won't ever catch up." Grace pouts and looks straight ahead. Perry and Gawne are up to something. Their eyes are locked on each other's faces.

"Well, check out the big brains on Pharaoh. You're a smart motherfucker, Pharaoh!" Their attempt to mock Pharaoh's statements annoys Grace further. She excuses herself to call her husband on her mobile phone. Perry and Gawne continue their word play, but Pharaoh is not in the mood. He'll see them in class. His departure does not even interrupt their banter.

"You guys mind if I join you?"

"Mr. USA, of course you can sit with us." Pharaoh shakes Peter's outstretched hand. Sail looks over his shoulder to see who is left at the table and nods, happy to interpret Pharaoh's move as an obvious choice between two cultures.

"Your friends can sit with us, too, if they wish," Oobamcee says. Today he is out of his usual attire. Under his oversized black jacket is a white shirt with no collar. An overhead lamp illuminates a slight perspiration on his forehead that he occasionally brushes back into his hair with his palms.

"They are not one of us," Sail says. His comment registers a short, disturbed frown on Oobamcee's face.

"Have you seen many rainbows today, Mr. USA?"

"It is too late for rainbows and too cold," he says, and smiles at them. Pharaoh tells them about the ensuing plans after the class dinner and extends them a cordial invitation. Peter and Sail respond that they were not strong drinkers in Ghana or Nigeria and that they do not intend to become drinkers here.

"Norwegians are to alcohol what our people are to dance," Peter says. "Students get drunk and pee outside the windows of our rooms all the time during early morning hours on weekends, both the men and the women. It is very funny."

"It is not only Norwegian students who behave this way," Pharaoh replies, laughing, "I have also gotten too drunk and peed where I should not have."

"This is not a laughing matter," Oobamcee says.

"They do not disturb me. It is okay," Sail admits, assuredly. "In my country, I have slept through gunshots."

"And you are proud?" Oobamcee's question dangles as an accusation. Sail must be weak if the gunshots he speaks of are part of a tribal conflict or war. It is Sail's mistake to disclose passivity to a declared warrior.

"Yes, I am proud. I am a Nigerian. I am an African. A fox that sleeps today will be awake to eat yet another day. I do not think, comrade, that we are all that different. We all see a United Africa, a kind of US of A. You have chosen your method of combat, and I have chosen mine."

Peter scratches his head.

Pharaoh is no longer certain of his decision to leave Perry and Gawne at their table in favor of the Africans. The political climate here is tense. Oobamcee has pulled out an envelope with the Norwegian Monarchy insignia stamped on the flap. Above the insignia, written in italics are, *The African Knights Economic Advisory: Peace and Understanding Serving Earth."*

"Perhaps I have interrupted your meeting," Pharaoh says, suddenly aware of how trivial a night of drinking may seem to them.

"Do not be alarmed at our talks," Oobamcee says. "It is common among Africans. We believe discussion will lead to a better understanding of the many conflicts taking place inside and outside of our countries. I have heard many Americans say talk is healthy, and you have many television programs in our countries to heal many people."

Pharaoh refuses to be dragged into their discussion despite Oobamcee's oblique criticism of Americans. Oobamcee is a clever man, and it is only a matter of time before they will argue openly. But that time is not now. They both seem to realize this, even before Pharaoh once again extends the invitation to go bar hopping after the class dinner.

"Perhaps warriors also do not drink," Pharaoh says.

"Quite the contrary," Oobamcee counters. "Warriors drink, but they do not get drunk and pee in places where they should not."

"Then I will never be a warrior."

"That is not what I see," Oobamcee says.

"Your wife is also invited. I have heard that your wife is also here."

"Ah, yes!" Oobamcee exclaims, as if he has discovered Pharaoh's point of attack, his strategy. "This is the truth. My wife has the responsibilities of a mother. She cannot drink alcohol. She has a baby to concern her. It is a responsibility she does not take lightly and one that I am sure you know well. I, too, have heard that you have a child at home. Your wife, is she coming also?"

"Perhaps," he says. "However, if she cannot come or chooses not to, I hope it is not because she is a mother."

"Ah, yes. Of course. She is a Western woman." Oobamcee's clothes continue to hang slack on his small frame. A large sweat stain, visible through his opened jacket, has moistened the front of an armpit. Despite the weather outside, the sleeves on his white shirt are short.

"I would like to meet your wife, Mr. USA," Peter says.

"Only if you promise to behave like a gentleman."

Sail does not appreciate Pharaoh's remark, even in jest, and looks to Oobamcee for a rebuke that does not come.

"Oh, *nei!* You are kidding again, Mr. USA. You are still flink with the jokes." Peter's bright smile broadens into an avid laugh. He is too easily amused, a quality that affords him an immediate cloak of deception.

"Tell me, Pharaoh, have you thought of visiting Africa?" Sail asks.

"I have been to Africa," he says.

There is a look of consternation on their faces. Oobamcee clasps his hands and interlocks his fingers to assure Pharaoh of his full attention.

"You are not serious," Peter says. "You are still with the jokes."

"Really. I am serious. I have been to Africa."

"Africa is a very big place. Where in Africa have you been?" Sail asks accusingly.

"I have been to Kenya. Mombasa, actually," Pharaoh continues nonchalantly. "But it was more in an official capacity. It is a very beautiful city."

"It is not so beautiful," Sail admits. "It is overcrowded and polluted with skyscrapers like your cities."

"Perhaps that is why it is so beautiful. One can see from its architecture that it is a very advanced city, a modern city." Oobamcee's silence is conspicuously pronounced. The black hairs on his clasped knuckles are coarse and curled. "Do you not agree that Mombasa is a beautiful city, Oobamcee? While we were in Mombasa, some of my friends wanted to go to Uganda across the border, but they were advised against it."

"My country can be a dangerous place for tourists if they are not careful," Oobamcee replies. "We are a country at war." They exchange glances, and he slips the envelope resting on the table under his arm as if preparing to leave.

Sail is the first to rise from his chair. "You spoke of an official capacity. What kind of official capacity do you speak of?" he asks.

"I was in the Navy."

"So you were a military man? You were on an American warship then when you visited Mombasa?"

"Not exactly," he answers. "I was there in a different capacity."

"Ah, yes. I see. You are covered in mystery," Oobamcee says, smiling. "It is very well, Pharaoh."

* * *

Hans Christian enters the cafeteria, slapping his clogs against the tiled floor as he approaches their table. He calls out to them from a farther distance than is normally expected in Norwegian culture. He has informed their class that Norwegians are timid and shy, and that they never shout to each other from across the street, in the way many other cultures do, to greet people. Norwegians will first cross the street and then wait until they are within arm's reach to say, *"Hei eller god dag."*

"Har deres glemte klassrommet deres?" asks Hans.

"We did not forget the classroom," Pharaoh replies ostentatiously. "We were just on our way there."

"Snakk Norsk!" Hans Christian reminds them, his knuckles pressed onto the edge of their table. There is a sudden sense of trepidation among the three African students, though Pharaoh is not sure of the reason.

"Unskyld," Pharaoh says. *"Vi har bare glemt å passe tiden. Vi skal gå tilbake nå."*

Hans smiles approvingly and hands Pharaoh a folded note before departing toward Perry and Gawne.

CHAPTER 10

PHARAOH MANEUVERS Amaryllis's stroller around patches of snow and ice and headstones. They follow a small procession of mourners at a careful pace to an open grave. Amaryllis is awake and occasionally stretches a gloved arm out of the stroller to touch the shiny black stones. Kjersti's pallbearers are all the men she has left behind: a boyfriend, two teenage sons, Knut, Dagfinn, and Thor. There is an extreme haste to get her into the ground. It has been three days since Kjersti's death, and only Hannah appears to be experiencing any deep grief.

Pharaoh arrived at the hospital soon after Kjersti's death to discover that funeral preparations had already begun. "Kjersti is no more," Thor had said to him. *"Hun er død."* It was an easy word to understand in this context.

A small Lutheran church in the middle of the cemetery is covered in snow. Three-fourths of the building's height is in its steeple. It is a historical monument built by the Germans to bury their soldiers during the war. It sits in the midst of a few acres of land filled with headstones adorned with spry bundles of flowers that have been recently set into the snow. Kjersti was no soldier. Hannah and Trine walk arm in arm behind the men. They both hold each other upright as mourners approach the grave. It begins to snow at an angle to the ground and across the gravestones. There is no priest, pastor, or bishop for last rites. It is a bare ceremony, but an efficient one, fit for an adult woman who everyone but Hannah knew would someday take her own life. She has left behind two thin teenage sons and a perplexed boyfriend. According to those who knew her best, she was evil and ill-tempered toward everyone except Stig, a small affenpinscher whose constant *"woof woof"* sounds like an irritating cough. She had taken time to prepare obscene notes on pink Post-it stickers and place them throughout her house before shooting herself in the head. It is an unfortunate event and an inconvenience for the survivors. Pharaoh worries that it will be especially traumatic for the youngest of her teenage boys, who had found the body and to whom everyone has expressed sympathy. The other boys have accepted it perfunctorily, with frail handshakes and as part of the ceremony.

As the coffin is lowered into the ground, Amaryllis begins to babble. "This is not a playground," Pharaoh whispers. "Cut it out!" But she ignores his order, expressing her own capricious mix of discomfort and boredom. No one seems amused.

Once Kjersti's body is in the ground, people at the graveside begin talking about her. According to Hans Christian, many Norwegians believe that Trolls eventually uproot the buried bodies of people who commit suicide in this little land and drag them deep into the forest. He has expressed sympathy and surprise because, according to statistics and history, it is not very normal for forty-eight-year-old women to commit suicide in his country.

"What were the notes all about?" Pharaoh asks Hannah.

"Her first husband and her boyfriend," she says defensively.

"I cannot believe she wrote notes. It's as if, on top of everything, she wanted to make sure she had proved her point. What kind of person writes notes everywhere? And where did she get a gun? I thought guns are hard to get in Norway."

"Can we talk about something else?"

"Fine," he says. "Of course. I understand that you are still griev-
ing."

"She hadn't even spent time with Amaryllis. I spent so much time
with her boys while they were growing up and she was a single
mom. She was really selfish when you think about it," Hannah
complains, as if Kjersti's suicide would have been absolved had she
first fulfilled her obligation to spend time with Amaryllis.

"She was never too fond of me."

Hannah sticks to her request to change the subject. While
Pharaoh watches Ally McBeal be neurotic, Hannah cocks her ear to
the footsteps upstairs and decides that her mom must still be awake.
She begins the climb upstairs again, for the third time in the past
two hours, and he is left alone, while Amaryllis sleeps, to sort out
what Hannah must be feeling.

All the pictures of Kjersti in their apartment have disappeared.
Even those in Hannah's old photo albums have been removed.
Hannah's attempt to erase Kjersti's memory is not simply retaliatory.
For Hannah, Kjersti's memory since her death evokes depression,
confusion, and pain. Her teenage sons have gone to live with their
dad, whom Kjersti had accused of raping her during their first sep-
aration. The rape had resulted in the birth of her second child and
an attempt at reconciliation. It is an accusation that she maintained
throughout her life and alluded to again in the notes she left behind.
Trine and Thor have not escaped her bitter accusations. There are
insinuations of abuse and molestation by Thor. Kjersti's suicide has
sent tremors across this family, and everyone is trying their best to
pretend that things are back to normal. Trine and Thor prefer to let
the accusations pass, but it clearly exacts a toll. They are in dour
moods and seem older than they were only a few weeks ago. Thor,
especially, has shrunk in stature. His proud lectures to Pharaoh
about Norway have recently been suspended and his German automobile remains parked outside of his garage under a blanket of

snow to accommodate the affenpinscher's temporary stay.

Pharaoh has begun to feel alienated from the rest of the family as they deal with this tragedy. He senses a certain vibration, an emission of dread, that they have somehow attached to him, perhaps as a way of coping. His presence among them has come into question, as well as his religion, as they struggle to deal with Kjersti's suicide. Pharaoh begins to feel a rising sense of paranoia as Trine suddenly expresses interest in the kind of religion blacks practice in America and the Caribbean. Her vague references to Jim Jones and voodoo are not completely innocent, he worries. Whom else could they blame for bringing this tragedy on the family?

"We never have those names here in Norway," Kjersti had explained when she first met him.

"Well, you don't have people like me in Norway," he had barked back.

"What kind of name is Pharaoh?"

"It is Caribbean."

"You are sure?" she asked.

"I am sure." They had been invited to Kjersti's home for coffee, and to his surprise, had sat across the table from each other, along with the coughing affenpinscher, while Kjersti served confectioneries, coffee, and cognac. She had consumed three glasses of cognac to his one cup of coffee while he watched the affenpinscher lick its testicles clean.

"When I heard that Hannah fell in love with a black man from LA, I was afraid for her," Kjersti said. "But now I have met you since you came here to Norway to visit. I am pleased. We are happy about it now." It was the first Pharaoh had heard of a "we." "We love our only sister, so it is well that you are in Norway. We were very worried about the LA people."

"I understand," he replied.

"You will have beautiful mulatto children," she said, refilling her glass for the fourth time. Their conversations were frequently interrupted while she consulted Hannah for the English translations of words she could only express in Norwegian.

"You have never been to the States?"

"No. It is too far, and I do not like to be in planes," Kjersti explained, as the affenpinscher stood on its hind legs and wagged its tail. "It is unnatural."

"I understand. It is a long flight." The ambiguity of her words made him uneasy. What was "unnatural"—the flight or his relationship with her sister?

"You and my little sister are brave." She lit a cigarette and congratulated Hannah on quitting, reluctantly acknowledging Pharaoh's influence in her decision. Family portraits, as well as pictures of female artists, politicians, and athletes, hung throughout the room. Kjersti had described many of those pictured as "simply Norwegians," whom he would not have heard anything about in the States. After her fifth glass of cognac, Kjersti had begun to cry. Her life, she confessed, had been very difficult while she and Hannah were growing up. They had not been true sisters. She blamed Thor. At the mention of his name, she squeezed her eyes shut and sobbed between sips of cognac. Her behavior had come as a surprise to Pharaoh. Hannah, too, had begun to look teary-eyed. As her face grew flush, her resemblance to her sister seemed to steadily increase.

Kjersti was five centimeters taller than Hannah, but outweighed her by about ten kilos. In her casket, her dimpled chin, which jutted out to meet the relaxed, turned-down collar of her turtleneck, had lost its prominence. Her thin, brown hair, fastened near the end by a small butterfly clip, covered both ears like gills and hung loosely between her shoulders. On the day Pharaoh met her, she had worn black culottes with thick black wool socks and a black turtleneck sweater with a zippered front. Her sobs had continued sporadically, despite Hannah's efforts to console her. She promised to be a good sister again if Hannah and her "man" ever moved to Norway. It had been a manipulative plea, one Pharaoh dismissed at the time as ridiculous.

"You must visit our fjords."

"He is not much into nature," Hannah had replied and begun to cry herself. Her outburst sent the affenpinscher scampering from the room. It had been a pathetic display, Pharaoh recalled.

"We are sorry. We have not seen each other for a long time, and I must give my sister's new man a hug also." Kjersti had stumbled into him with her hug. "It is true that you are strong," she said, as if she were making a startling discovery as she regained her balance. "Stig!" she had yelled, and the affenpinscher appeared, coughing and wagging its tail in a frenzy.

None of the surviving members of Kjersti's family are willing to assume care of Stig, whose temporary stay in Thor's garage has come to an end.

"We are very busy," Thor says. "It is a matter for her boyfriend."

Hannah agrees with Trine that it is not realistic to expect Kjersti's boyfriend to take care of Stig. Not after the notes.

"He must go to sleep, then," Thor concedes. Everyone agrees. It is a surprisingly simple decision for the family, yet no one is fully prepared to carry out the agreement. Instead they discuss the cost of putting Stig to sleep in an animal hospital, as opposed to the hazards of releasing him far into the forest. He will not survive on his own in the forest, Hannah says, and starvation is inhumane, a slow death. She will not sleep well knowing that the only thing her sister cared about is roaming the forest waiting to die. They finally agree to pay to have Stig put to sleep in a proper manner. Hannah's eyes appoint Pharaoh to volunteer to take the damned affenpinscher to the animal hospital.

Chapter 11

*E*R DET MANGE INDISKE *restauranter i* California?" Hans
Christian asks.

"Not many Indian restaurants, not in LA," Pharaoh replies, "but
there are quite a few Mexican restaurants."

"The meat is a bit tough," Grace says with her face close to her
plate, poking at pieces of meat, skeptically. "And this sauce is too
spicy." She is in her favorite alumni sweater from the University of
Colorado.

"It's supposed to be spicy, baby. That's what you ordered, spicy."
Gawne winks at Grace. Her husband, Gil, sits beside her, his entrée
buried behind a deep rice bowl that resembles a chamber pot. They
are an image of contrasts. He is shorter than Grace, with an
abdomen that protrudes clumsily over his belt and prevents him
from sitting upright and closer to the table. His eyes are small
behind wire-rimmed glasses and seem to rove suspiciously on people. He finds Hans Christian especially humorous because they
grew up in the same community. He laughs in a quiet cackle whenever they share a joke in their native dialect.

"Where is your wife?" It is the first time Meg, the Canadian student, has spoken to Pharaoh directly. She is seated next to him and
seems uncomfortable.

"My wife could not make the dinner, but she will join us at the bars later."

"Anyone else ordered the curry meat?" Grace is still bowed, manipulating pieces of food on her plate.

"Maybe you should send it back if it's too spicy," Perry says, frowning at her. "You can do that, you know."

"Well, here. You taste it, then."

"I don't eat meat, Grace. I am a vegetarian!" Perry snaps.

"I ain't," Gawne replies, and pushes his plate forward to accept the morsel. The restaurant is small and located on the water at the mouth of a pier in the city. There are small boats tied to the pier, and a hovercraft used for transporting passengers across fjords has just docked, causing the restaurant to sway slightly. On the cover of the menu are pictures of two Indian men, presumably the owners, and a short declaration in Norwegian signed by the King and Queen.

Ian and Greta sit at the far end of the table sharing a pitcher of beer. They have been thrust into a friendship because they are the only students who smoke. Ian does not like America. "We Brits drink and smoke. That's why we have so many pubs," he explains. "And you Yanks do drugs and fight. That is why you have so much crime."

Greta, who is only nineteen, but looks much older, does not seem to share his sentiment about America. She is happy to be away from her country and isn't ashamed to admit that she is in search of a Norwegian husband.

Gil gently taps his fork on a half-empty glass of beer to get everyone's attention. He has an important announcement to make, he says, then defers to Grace, who suddenly turns crimson. "I am pregnant," she announces. It is a while before she regains her color. Pharaoh is the first to reach across the table to congratulate Grace and shake Gil's hand. Gil's belly and unsteady gait make it seem like they're both on a gangplank. Peter begins to applaud from the other end of the table. Although everyone joins in, Pharaoh's applause is the loudest because Hannah is not there to hear the news.

"*Gratulere med et Norsk barn,*" Hans says, and raises his glass. "*Neste gang må du si at du er gravid.*"

"Perhaps in your condition you should drink water instead," Perry says. Grace acknowledges his paternal concern with a blush and a smile.

"It is only one beer, peewee," she says, but it is apparent that it has been one too many.

While Perry and Hans calculate everyone's portion of the bill, Gawne and Pharaoh surreptitiously make plans to smoke a joint as the night wears on. Gawne cannot contain his excitement, slapping Pharaoh five and calling him "a motherfuckin' brother," "a god-damn holmes," and his "best bitch." His comments do not go unnoticed by the African students.

At the Handball Club, sports events and rock-and-roll collide. The students are seated at four small tables that a senior waitress, in a full body apron fastened behind with bows at the waist and neck, has eagerly arranged as one long table at the edge of the dance floor. Nokia televisions in metal frames are suspended from various points along the ceiling, and a giant four-sided white screen descends to just about the level of a disco ball. The screen is illuminated with revolving black spotlights that make it appear like a giant twirling die.

Hans is explaining that this is his favorite place outside of the classroom. While the waitress takes Oobamcee's order, Hans waves to the DJ, a balding fat man with a long, curled mustache who, without his headphones, could easily be mistaken for a bouncer.

The slow mournful introduction to Lynrd Skynrd's "Freebird" startles Gawne. "Man, that motherfucker better start playing some G-funk up in this here establishment before I come back from the rest room or I'ma have to come unglued!" He is dressed in baggy

Tommy Hilfiger jeans and a long Nike T-shirt. His head gestures toward the exit, but Pharaoh isn't ready to smoke.

Hans expects a full house and a ripe environment for students to practice speaking to "real" Norwegians.

"I am here to get drunk," Perry says.

"Me, too. Where's the waitress?" Meg blurts out, and then withdraws, as if surprised by her initiative.

"Baby, what do you want to drink?" Gawne nuzzles up to Meg.

"I'll get it," she says, brushing him off. The waitress returns with a Planter's Punch for Oobamcee, a cognac and beer for Sail, and a Galliano shot for Peter. She deposits them all on printed napkins. Pharaoh realizes that he has been mistaken in his assumption that warriors do not drink alcohol. Oobamcee pays for their drinks. His tip evokes a deferential smirk from the waitress, who, exercising diplomacy, curtsies and sidesteps to their end of the table. As the last chords of "Freebird" begin to fade, the DJ offers a spirited welcome on behalf of the Handball Club to Hans's international students. His next track is dedicated to them.

Hannah is late. When Pharaoh calls home, she tells him that she is in pain. She has just gotten her period, and her cramps are intense. She will have to stay at home for the evening.

"Everyone wants to meet your wife," Meg says when she learns that Hannah will not be coming.

"I am not sure why. Perhaps they want to see who would marry someone like me," Pharaoh says.

"Right. Maybe we want to see if you really have a wife." Meg smiles.

"Sure. Lots of men say they're married when they're not, honey bunny," Perry adds.

"Well, I'm not one of those men. I have a wife and a kid."

"Oh, I believe you," she says. "Why else would you be here?"

It is a question that has kept him preoccupied of late. He is still in love with Hannah, but he has begun to feel alienated among her family. It's not just because of Kjersti's suicide or the cold temperatures. There are all sorts of little things that he can't put his finger on precisely. He can hear the wind and snow at night spinning outside his window, and each morning while he shovels a path around the house and garage, neighbors on their way to work try not to stare. He shovels the snow out of gratitude to Trine and Thor for allowing him to pay a low rent. At times, their smiles as they drive to work are friendly and respectful, but increasingly, he can sense something condescending behind their pleasantries.

Pharaoh can also feel Amaryllis slipping away from him, though he tries to keep his hold on her. It is a slow, subtle distancing, but he feels it nonetheless. "She is not even two yet," Hannah says defensively whenever he tries to talk about his concern. "How can you tell that your bond is breaking? Even if it is breaking, it's probably just a temporary thing. All kids go through that with their parents. Soon it'll be my turn."

"It is difficult to explain. I see it in her eyes, in the way she responds to my voice, especially when there are other voices in the room. It is something you would notice as a mom, too, Hannah, if it were happening to you."

"Fine! Maybe we should talk to someone about it, a professional."

Pharaoh is at first reluctant to consult a counselor about Amaryllis, though he eventually decides that it might help. But first he has to be certain that his fears are based on fact, and are not just imaginary. He will spend more time with Amaryllis, even if it means treading on the time allotted to Trine and Thor.

He decides to be the first one to tell Amaryllis everything he thinks she needs to know. He feels that whatever he says will stay with her throughout her life, or at least up until she begins to think and reason for herself. "You will grow up to be a tennis star like the Williams sisters and represent the United States at the Olympics," he tells her. "You will never represent this country in anything. And don't let old people disguise their ignorance as feeblemindedness when they assume that you are adopted." He makes little fists out of her hands, playfully covering them with his mouth or prying them loose with his lips. "This is how you use this finger to make a very important means of expression, when you're older." He helps her point her index finger toward the sky. "Not a private gesture, a public one." Amaryllis's giggles are hardly encouraging, but he vows to keep at it.

Back at their table, Perry and Gawne suddenly lift their bottles and offer a toast to "fine" women.

"So what now?" Perry asks.

"What now? I'll tell you what now. I'ma call a couple of hard-pipe-hitting niggers to go to work on the DJ here with a pair of pliers and a blowtorch if he don't get funky in a minute. You hear me talking, hillbilly boy? I'ma get American on your ass!"

"Naw, man," Perry replies on cue. "I mean, what now between me and you."

"Man, we got to make a request is all."

"Okay," Perry says laughing, having misplaced his dialogue.

On his way to the disc jockey's booth, Gawne points to Pharaoh with an index finger and a stiff arm. "When I get back, homey, me and you are gonna have words!" His statement is half-friendly and half-menacing. Without Grace, who is constantly reminding Pharaoh that Gawne's demeanor is cute and harmless, it begins to lose some of its charm.

"You need to talk to him," Meg says, removing her shoes and placing them next to her purse under her chair.

"Why?"

"Well, I don't think they appreciate some of his comments. It might be insulting to them," Meg says, leaning in to Pharaoh to encourage him to whisper his response. She frequently attends class in oversized dark sweaters and blue jeans, but tonight she is wearing an oversized sweater and an ankle-length, roomy skirt that clings to her stockings. She has relaxed enough to allow the materials to cling.

"I'm sure they realize that he is harmless."

"You think so? I don't know," she drawls. "They don't like him."

"Well, he's cool," Pharaoh says, feeling a sense of betrayal that they are even talking about Gawne.

"Do they like you?" he asks.

"No, they don't. But it's different with me. They want to fuck me," Meg says.

"All of them?" he asks smiling.

"Yep," she says, rolling up the sleeves on her sweater to expose arms that are as shiny as if a liniment had been recently applied to them. "Especially the tall one who keeps calling you Mr. USA and likes touching people when he talks to them. I hate that! And you don't have to hide your smile, Pharaoh. I didn't say they wanted to fuck me at the same time, although I wouldn't be surprised. Who can tell with them?"

"You are very observant."

She sheds the compliment by returning it and signaling the waitress. "You, too. But I already knew that. You wouldn't know that about me, though, because you never talk to me."

"I should probably be glad I haven't. You might think that I want to fuck you, too."

"You ever think of telling him to call you Captain USA instead?"

"Why?"

"I don't know. It beats 'Mister,' and it fits your ego." Meg drains her glass and reaches for her purse as the waitress makes her way toward their table. Gawne, too, is in tow, making unflattering movements with his eyes at the woman's bottom as she stops and delivers more drinks to the Africans. As she does, she bends slightly to exhibit her aging wares. Her earlier diplomacy has been reduced to simple flirting for tips.

More people have begun to stream in preparation and anticipation for a televised event. Waitresses suddenly step up their paces amid a flurry of orders, and customers look around for the nearest television screen.

"Where is Perry?" Gawne asks, as he swings his chair around so that the back is up against the table. He straddles the chair.

"I don't know. I didn't even see him leave," Pharaoh says. REM's "Losing My Religion" permeates the room. Pharaoh and Meg look accusingly at Gawne.

"Y'all best get the fuck outta here with that shit. That ain't my motherfuckin' request. This DJ don't make no fuckin' sense! He ain't got no Warren G, no Snoop, no Ice-T. Hell, he ain't got shit! Regulate that shit, motherfucker!" Gawne shouts.

"There's Perry," Meg says, and points to a crowded entrance. Perry looks older than before, mumbling to himself as he squeezes through people. Maybe he's practicing his movie dialogues, thinks Pharaoh. As he approaches, it is obvious that he is only singing along to REM's song. His shirt is neatly tucked into a pair of gray Dockers pants.

"Where've you been, wingman?" Gawne asks.

"Checking the place out," he replies, trying not to interfere with his rhythm.

"You find out anything?" Meg asks.

"I'm sorry. My name is Perry. You are?"

"Not drunk enough to find that real funny."

"That's the maple-leaf chick," Gawne interjects. "Looks like she's cool."

Meg responds to Gawne's off-handed approval by lifting the loose neck of her sweater closer to her chin, as if attempting to hide hickeys or scars from self-inflicted wounds. The image of the quiet person in class returns, but it is fleeting, a sober moment.

"Would you like to dance?"

"I don't dance," Meg says. Her response is almost automatic, out before she realizes that it is Peter who has made the request. Her demeanor shifts from one of embarrassment to annoyance because she was blindsided with his request.

Peter smiles dazzlingly and gently pats her on the shoulder. His smile belongs in a toothpaste commercial. "Thank you, madam. I'll call again," Peter says, bowing as he makes an about-face.

"That was cold, baby," Gawne says to Meg. "How you gonna dis a motherfucker like that? It ain't nothin' but a dance, baby. Come on! Can't you hear the party alarm?"

"You're not a dog, are you?" Meg brushes off the spot where Peter's hand touched her shoulder.

"No, baby."

"Then quit humping my leg."

"She doesn't have to dance if she doesn't want to. Not everyone likes to dance or can dance, man." Perry's defense of Meg sounds like a personal admission. The waitress places a drink on a napkin in her tray and lowers it down to Meg, then deposits two ashtrays on their table as an afterthought. Meg places a bill on the table, but the waitress quickly taps the bill and pushes it back. Her drink has been paid for by a gentleman, explains the waitress, who, responding to Meg's questioning look, points a thumb over her shoulder at the lone African student on the dance floor.

"Oh shit! Baby, you got to dance now. Homey bought you a drink and all. Ain't no charge! Shit. You got to dance. Give that man a dance, baby. He's out there all alone now. Come on!" Gawne's plea is tinged with derision, despite his coaxing.

"Hell, he's got some moves," Perry says, as they turn around to look. On the dance floor, Peter does not look like a man preoccupied with fucking Meg. His movements are wide and panoramic, as if he is dancing with several imaginary partners, all of whom are performing dance steps that variously incorporate line dancing, the twist, and the beat of a waltz. He has not scratched once.

"Maybe we should all join him. He looks like he's having fun," Pharaoh says.

"See. He didn't need me," Meg offers weakly. She blushes, but tries to hide it by again sinking most of her chin beneath the collar of her turtleneck sweater. She is overcome by all the attention she has been receiving. It feels as if she has passed an impromptu initiation into the group. Suddenly overwhelmed with emotion, Meg bows her head in both hands and begins to cry. Pharaoh starts to touch her but instead asks if she would like to smoke a joint outside. His gesture makes her even more emotional, however, and her sniffles erupt into a convulsive sobbing.

"*Går det bra med,* Meg?" It is Hans, rising from his chair.

"*Det går bra,*" Perry answers. Oobamcee and Sail look on in silence, confused but continuing to sip their drinks. Meg finally removes her hands. It is obvious that she has been laughing behind them.

"You serious?"

"As a heart attack," Pharaoh says. She collects her shoes and walks out to Peter, who is still twisting and twirling his arms around like they are luxurious silks on the dance floor. Meg stops him with a tug on his arm and stands on her tiptoes to yell something in his ear. He responds with a wide toothpaste smile.

"Let's go," she says to Pharaoh when she returns to their table, her shoes still dangling from her fingers. Pharaoh signals to Gawne, who follows right behind them. Perry also decides to follow, making Pharaoh feel like the Pied Piper as they make their way across the dance floor toward an exit. He isn't worried, however. There is plenty for everyone.

The Handball Club is packed. People at nearby tables bend forward and converse as if they are discussing secrets, while others remain lethargic, bluffing themselves through verbal onslaughts like geriatric patients. According to Hans, Rosenborg, the local soccer team, is the only Norwegian team talented enough to qualify to play in Europe's prestigious Champions League. It's a distinction that rallies Norwegians behind Rosenborg as the unofficial national team.

"It's a pussy sport," Gawne says in a dismissive tone. "Hell, any-one can play that game. I've seen elephants playing soccer in India. It's for pussies!"

"I'd hardly call elephants pussies," Pharaoh says.

"The way they chase that ball, they ought to be, holmes."

Hans seems eager to discuss differences in styles and techniques between countries in Europe and South America. *"Norge og Tyskland spille på samme måte.* Norway and Germany play the same kind of football," he replies, still teaching. Gawne's complete repu-diation of the sport, however, contains no ambiguity.

"Gawne, you've never even played the game," Pharaoh says, expressing his contrition for Gawne's remarks and trying to control whatever damage has been done.

"That's cause I ain't no elephant, and I ain't no pussy neither. Do I look like an elephant? Do I look like a pussy?" It is no use. Gawne's comments force Hans to the other end of the table where he watches tonight's match on the big screen and smokes a cigarette with Ian and Greta. Pharaoh agrees with Meg that even at a social event Hans needs to have the last word, or not talk at all.

It's halftime and Rosenborg is demolishing the German team. They have scored three unanswered goals in the first half, one a bullet from midfield by a flamboyant short player nicknamed Mini. Gawne is on the dance floor dancing to Sly Fox's, "Let's Go All the Way." He is surrounded by women waving black-and-white scarves, the official colors of Rosenborg. The DJ interrupts the music to inform customers who are unfamiliar with the fight song that the lyrics are printed on their napkins. Peter, too, has returned to the dance floor, accompanied by a woman with long black hair. She is an older woman, attractive under the flattering light, and dances with a purse strapped over her shoulder and through one arm. Most of the men are either at tables clustered around television screens or in line at the urinals.

"Fy faen," Meg mutters and begins to giggle. She has doffed her shoes again and sits yoga-style on her chair while she sips her drinks and stares at Sail and Oobamcee, who have begun to loosen up a bit. Meg, too, has become more vibrant.

"What the hell are they so happy about?"

"Peter has found a dance partner."

"Good. I'm real glad." Meg's tone is sarcastic.

"It means you no longer have to worry about his preoccupation with fucking you," Pharaoh says.

"You've brought that up a few times now. Maybe I shouldn't have said anything," Meg says, covering her mouth with both hands. It is difficult to see if she is embarrassed or ashamed. He thinks her behavior would be more appropriate at an encounter group, not a nightclub. "Or maybe you want to fuck me, too, Pharaoh. You can if you want . . . In your dreams!" She laughs.

"I don't dream," he says.

"Of course you dream. Everyone does."

"Not me."

"You just don't remember them; that's all. Everyone dreams."

"How can I remember something that never occurs?"

"Not even wet dreams?"

"What kind are those?"

"You know. The ones that I'm in," she says, still laughing.

"I'm sure I'd remember those."

"See. Aren't we having a good time together?" There is a glint in her eyes. They are the eyes of an owl, huge, so there is no mistaking the glint. Her head and neck rotate 180 degrees to either side as her eyes follow people across the room.

"Perry! Perry!" Meg yells. "Is he asleep?"

"He's probably just relaxing," Pharaoh says.

Perry stirs and resumes a conversation as if his nap was a momentary interruption. He has not reacted well to getting high. After two hits, he had begun to get drowsy, referring to Meg as Scully. He found the resemblance uncanny and was surprised he had not noticed it before tonight.

"You guys should come to Boston sometime. It's a cool place. Did you know that *Ally McBeal* and *The Practice,* and, oh yeah, *Dharma and Greg,* are filmed in Boston? Not to mention the gang on *Cheers.* Remember *Cheers?* And people forget about our beaches. We have nice beaches with lots of sand and horseshoe crabs and shit."

"*Fy faen!* Is that all you did back in the States, watch TV?"

Perry reaches across the table and points to an imaginary spot on Meg's sweater with his index. "What the hell is that? You need a bib?" When Meg bows her head to look, he flicks her chin playfully with his index and laughs. "Come on, Scully. You fell for that?" His antics garner smiles from Oobamcee and Sail, who are making a grand show of ignoring Peter and his female partner out on the dance floor.

Hans eases back into his seat alongside Perry and joins the conversation by cautioning Meg about her use of profanity in Norwegian. They are often the first words students learn. But while they may sound funny to people from other countries, to Norwegians or Scandinavians they can be insulting. He says this while leaning forward, his arms folded on the table. Meg agrees and thanks him, but she is not sincere.

"Shit! You're no fun!" Meg blurts out and giggles.

Hans glances at Pharaoh as if he is responsible for the obvious change in Meg's personality.

"Fire in the hole! Will you look at that loco?" They turn to see what has brought Perry out of his drowsy stupor. Gawne is sandwiched on the dance floor between two solidly built women whose moves resemble a porno flick. His dance is equally lewd, though the women are doing most of the gyrating in their thick-soled shoes. The women continue to dance with each other while Gawne does his rendition of a Beavis and Butthead shadow dance, where he pretends to be receiving fellatio while slapping his partner. To most of the crowd, his movements appear more comical than offensive. Meg sticks two fingers in her mouth and whistles, but it is barely audible through her giggles.

"You hear that? That was my party alarm!" Meg shouts over to Gawne.

"Go, wingman!" Perry says. "Looks like our toast worked. How'd you like to bring him home to dinner?"

"I wouldn't," Meg says.

"Me, neither," Pharaoh agrees, just to get on record.

"Are there many more like him in America?"

"There are many like him everywhere, even in my country. You have them here also," Sail says. His tone and quick reply reveal an undisguised contempt for Gawne.

"Wow! He speaks." Sail ignores Meg's comment and addresses his remarks to Pharaoh.

"Have you not seen them here also?"

"No one quite like Gawne, I'm afraid," Pharaoh says. "At least not yet."

"He is a different man," Hans says. "I do not think we have many like him. Very original, but very arrogant."

"Oh, but you have," Sail insists. "I see them on your buses, on your city streets, at your kiosks, and at your airports."

"What's your girlfriend's name?" Meg asks, almost shouting to Hans.

"Hun heter Felicia."

"Hvor gammel er hun?" she replies.

"Hun er kanskje så gammel som du er," Hans says with an encouraging look on his face.

The look on Sail's face, however, is one of irritation. His inability to use the language has reduced him to a spectator.

The disc jockey updates the scores of completed games that might affect Rosenborg's position in the league. The crowd roars after he announces the last score. Hans is ecstatic. He waves to the disc jockey, who acknowledges him and the rest of the crowd by mixing in a song by a Swedish group. The crowd applauds and sings along. *"Sommer tid, hei! Hei! Sommer tid!"* It is a song about summer and sunshine, and almost everyone in the club seems to know the lyrics.

Gawne arrives back at the table sweat-stained and dejected. "Let's roll, y'all. Time to take steps. This place ain't happening."

"Yeah, right. You looked like you were having a good time out there a minute ago," Perry says. "What happened?"

"Them bitches were lesbians, man."

"No way."

"Yes way," Gawne replies.

"And you couldn't tell they were lesbians?"

Gawne looks at him. "Shit no," he says. "Could you, mother-fucker?"

"I guess not," Perry says.

"That should have been a challenge for you then," Meg pipes in. There is a thin coat of perspiration on her forehead, and her cheeks look warm. Yet she is very at ease perched on her chair, fully aware that she has irritated Sail by relegating him to silence.

"Man, we got to find some real women is all." Gawne signals to the waitress to bring him a beer, while everyone listens to Perry try to market Boston to Hans. It is a great place for students and urban professionals, he insists, with Harvard, MIT, Quincy Marketplace, the Red Sox, the New England Patriots, and a great transit system. The "T" will get you anywhere. It moves about 1.2 million people a day, according to Perry, who shuts his heavy eyelids to contemplate the prospect of moving so many people at a time. Hans finds the number staggering. It is a quarter of the population of this land. He wonders where so many people go during the summer. To the beaches mostly, as well as to concerts and theme parks, Perry explains. He also talks proudly of the Boston Common and the

Back Bay area, where his family lives. Along the beaches, it is not uncommon to run into lobsters with giant pincers and horseshoe crabs. Boston, says Perry, is not only known for its political history but also its fine seafood restaurants. Hans counters that Norway, too, is known for its fish, especially laks, or what Americans call salmon. But Norwegians do not eat in restaurants as often as people in Boston, Hans concludes. It is too expensive.

"Let's eat after I'm done drinking my beer," Gawne proposes.

"You sure? You might have your hands full, buddy." Perry smiles. One of the women Gawne has called a lesbian is burrowing her way over to their table.

"Will you dance?" Her request surprises Gawne.

"I'ma raise the roof, y'all." He sets off toward the dance floor with his exaggerated pimp walk, his hands shadowing the curves of the lesbian's ass as she toggles in thick soles that resemble cloven hooves.

"Your second chance," Meg grumbles. Another uproar is taking place around the television screens. Hans dashes to a nearby television.

"Boys will always be boys," Meg continues in her cynical tone. "I take it you don't care for this sport, *ay*."

"Not really. I'm much more of a basketball boy. Too slow," Pharaoh says.

"Me, too. I'm into B-ball. See, again we have something in common. Who'd figure!"

"What else do we have in common, Meg?"

"You like bats? I like bats," Meg says. "They are beautiful creatures."

"Nothing's beautiful that has claws on its wings, Meg."

"They're so peaceful."

"Yeah, as long as they're hanging upside down in a cave sleeping. I wouldn't want one as a pet."

"I would," she says. "They're cute."

"And they get cuter the more alcohol you consume, I suppose."

Gawne's beer arrives and Perry volunteers to pay for it. There is another uproar, followed by distinct groans that send the waitress frantically on her way.

"That means the score is three to two," Perry says. "Two quick goals by the German team is not a good sign. Those Germans are good. Football to them is just another substitute for war."

Meg nudges his arm. "Did you know that we invented basketball?" She grins, as if she has won a round of Trivial Pursuit. Her face is small, with tight lips. Her nose is partially covered by the wineglass she is tilting to her mouth. Perry is right. At times, Meg definitely resembles Scully from *The X-Files,* but only at times.

"Where'd you get that piece of trivia?"

"The same place you got your rainbow trivia. I read it somewhere."

Pharaoh ignores Meg's smirk. The African students have stopped drinking. Oobamcee produces a pen and pad and begins to calculate numbers with the efficiency of a street vendor. His fingernails are a pale, fluorescent white, in stark contrast to the coarse black hairs clustered on the back of his fingers and hands. Sara, Dagfinn's inquisitive daughter, would be sure to notice.

"Are you sure about that?"

"Yup. It's actually a Canadian sport when you think about it."

"I believe you are wrong." Sail's lips are parched, but he has no time to lick them. He is determined to speak.

"No, I am not!" Meg makes a quarter turn in Sail's direction, then challenges Pharaoh. "Look it up!"

"He was born in Canada, but he moved to the US and worked there, I believe. He invented the game in the US, so it cannot be a Canadian sport. We have learned this in school. It has become a popular sport in Nigeria also."

"Whatever. We're probably both right." She addresses only Pharaoh as she concedes his point. Pharaoh understands neither their mutual hatred, nor their hopeless civility.

The crowd grows suddenly silent as the music fades. Everyone, even the people on the dance floor, stare at the big screen as if they are witnessing an historical event. The German team has been afforded a penalty kick. Despite the grand fanfare of Rosenborg's players who jockey for position away from the ball in the event of a miss, the ball slices past tangled defenders and goalkeeper and into an upper corner of the net. At the stadium, the German fans jump in their seats, but here the Norwegians stand in dumb silence. Finally, someone in the crowd screams out, *"Nei!"* One voice begins the fight song, and the others quickly join in.

"Not good," Perry says. He is halfway through Gawne's beer. "Even Steven."

Sail taps Oobamcee on the wrist. When he looks up, the markings on his temples are raised. Pharaoh turns to see Peter hurrying toward them with a bloody handkerchief over his left eye.

"See? See what I mean? And you guys jumped down my throat for not dancing with him. What's a matter, you ran into a wall?" Meg's humor falls flat immediately. The amount of blood oozing out from behind Peter's handkerchief means he will require stitches.

"It is nothing," Peter says, making a feeble attempt to laugh. "Only a battle scar."

"We should get Hans," Perry says.

"No!" Oobamcee raises a palm adamantly. "We do not need him. It is okay."

"I did not expect them," Peter mumbles. "It was an ambush."

"He should get that looked at by a doctor. That's too much blood."

Meg nods in agreement with Pharaoh's suggestion.

"He will live. We must first hear what happened."

"It is okay. I am okay. Madam, we must dance." Meg blushes, then turns pale at the sight of his bright smile and all the red blood.

"Enough! Tell me how this happened. Who has done this?" Oobamcee's stern rebuke gets Peter's attention.

"We were talking outside, the woman and I. It was a friendly conversation. Then I walked with her to a bus stop. On my way back, I was attacked by three men."

"Hell, this is freaky. Just like in the fucking movies," Perry admits.

"What did they want?" Oobamcee glances at Sail, who has donned his coat.

"What did they look like? Did they say anything?"

"They were white. One wore glasses, and another was bald. They said nothing, but there was a Norwegian flag on the sleeve of a jacket. It happened very fast. I thought they wanted to dance." It is not a time for levity, but Peter is doing his best to lighten the situation.

"That was foolish! You have put us at risk!" Oobamcee says.

"It isn't really his fault," Pharaoh says to Oobamcee.

"We should report this. Assholes!" Meg does a 180-degree turn to see if the three men Peter described are still in the club.

Pharaoh takes one look at Oobamcee and Sail and knows immediately that reporting the incident is not an option. "No. The bleeding has stopped," he says. "And we should get Peter home. But we must find these guys first."

"Don't be stupid," Meg says, stepping into her shoes. "We don't need any fucking heroes tonight! Let's just leave."

"I am all right," Peter says to Oobamcee, but he does not look all right. He is embarrassed and humiliated, and he collapses in his chair. Oobamcee and Sail share a short glance. Oobamcee will take Peter home to fix his wound. Sail has been instructed to go with Pharaoh. Perry and Meg have also decided to tag along, but neither volunteers to tell Gawne that they are leaving. He is having too much fun, sandwiched between his two lesbian friends.

"Man, hold on! Hold on, now! You mean three white boys threw down on one of our homeys and you guys are just now telling me?"

Gawne is clearly upset. Two unarmed bouncers are refusing to allow him to take his drink outside. "Son of a bitch! I paid for the mother-fucker!"

"It is the law here." The bouncer seems tired and distressed. Gawne finally relents, at least partly because of Sail's urgent stare.

It is cold and slippery outside. Black snow has hardened on side-walks and streets in the city from the constant wear of vehicles with studded tires and pedestrians trudging on sanded ice. There is no one on the street where Peter said the ambush occurred. Outside of apartment windows, Rosenborg's colors flap in the cold wind.

Meg's fear has transformed her into a Pollyanna. "If we find them, let's just get their names and addresses and report them to the police. Okay, guys?"

"Sure, you right," Gawne says. He ducks into an alley and kicks loose a frozen rock. He picks it up with his gloved hand and grins at Meg. "Something to write with."

They walk in a 3-1-1 formation. Perry lags behind them, com-plaining about the cold. He is not dressed for prolonged outdoor activity. Sail anchors the formation, but he seems to be concentrat-ing more on maintaining his footing on the ice than on looking for the three men. Meg's owl-like vision spots three men who fit Peter's description entering a kiosk at the far end of the street. Pharaoh's head is filled with warnings. He hears Hannah's voice telling him in Norwegian how much she loves him and reminding him in English that he is no longer in LA. Maybe it would be best to take Meg's advice: Get their names and addresses and file a formal complaint.

When the people exit the kiosk, laughing and smoking, it becomes obvious that they are not men, but teenagers. They invin-cibly swagger on the slippery sidewalk instead of taking the sanded path up the hill.

"Hey, motherfuckers!" Gawne shouts. No response.

"Easy, man. Maybe it's not these guys."

"Sure, you right. It's them!" Gawne rushes toward the three.

"Unskyld, motherfuckers! Yeah, I'm talking to you!" He slams one to the ground with a single blow. The teen topples softly onto his face. Bright red blood spots the ice as a pair of wire-framed glasses slide toward the kiosk. He gets up quickly and seeks shelter behind a parked car. Another teen, whose head is shaved, tosses his cigarette and tries to flee, but he slips and falls flat on his back. He rolls over, and Pharaoh buries the steel-toed tip of his Caterpillar into soft flesh.

"Smoke this!" Pharaoh grunts.

The third teen disappears down the road, with Perry and Sail in pursuit. Gawne catapults the rock from his hand toward his earlier opponent's face, but it misses its mark and burrows through the window of a parked Volvo. The teen is cornered, though, and a fierce blow from Gawne quickly reduces him to a feeble moan and then stillness on the ice.

"Oh my God! Oh my God! You guys happy? Look what you've done!" It isn't as bad as Meg makes it out to be. *"Nei! Nei!* Are you crazy?"

Pharaoh ignores her hysterical cries for him to stop. He feels surprisingly lucid, completely in control of his actions and his thoughts. He thinks of his love for Hannah, of Sara's questions, of Anna's irrational lusts, of his growing sense of displacement in this little land.

Gawne leaves one motionless body on the ice. "Listen to this asshole snivel like a bitch. You a bitch, motherfucker?" He spits on Pharaoh's victim, who is sobbing. The spit lands on the teen's bald head in a soft, viscous glob. It is not a spit for good luck. Gawne crushes a lighted cigarette nearby.

"Shit! Let's get out of here," Pharaoh whispers.

Perry appears at the top of the hill, shivering. "Damn! Things got a little messy, I see."

"Where the hell were you?"

"Me and Sail took off after the last one."

"You catch that motherfucker?"

Perry explains that he was not just twiddling his thumbs while Gawne and Pharaoh were in action. He and Sail chased the third guy over the hill, but conditions were treacherous for walking, let alone running. They both fell. Perry managed to grab onto a fence, but Sail kept going, sliding flat on his back all the way to the bottom. He does his best to laugh off the embarrassment.

Sail is limping when he returns. "We must go!" he shouts upon seeing bodies on the ice.

"Did you find him?" Perry asks.

"We must go quickly before we are caught."

"Where is the maple-leaf chick?"

"She must've left," Perry says, happy to talk about something else.

"We must leave this place now," Sail repeats imploringly.

"You catch that motherfucker, holmes?"

"I did not catch him," Sail says, as if disappointed with his effort. "He was too quick. He kept running. Perhaps one day he will stop."

They advance toward a busy intersection and hail a taxi. Sail decides to walk to Oobamcee's place. He is gone before Pharaoh can persuade him to stay.

They settle in a taxi, a late model Mercedes-Benz that smells of leather, tobacco, and snuff. "Our first rumble in Norway," Gawne mutters to Pharaoh.

"I hope it is our last rumble anywhere," Pharaoh replies. He realizes now that he is shaking. Perry is seated next to the talkative driver, who has visited the United States and thinks it is a big place with too much crime.

"Keep an eye on the goddamn meter up there, holmes!"

"Where to?" Perry turns around.

"McDonald's," Pharaoh says. There is a sudden increase of traffic and pedestrians on the streets. It is almost eleven o'clock, and crowds of people with dejected looks on their faces are exiting bars and clubs, many attempting to flag down their taxi by jumping in front of it.

"Out of the way! You are too drunk. I don't want you to throw up on my seats. It is fine leather. Use your bus card. You, beautiful lady, I shall come back for." The driver's comments are an entertaining diversion. "People here become hostile when Rosenborg do not win games they should win. I am sure it is the same with the Chicago Bulls."

"Man, what you talking 'bout? I know that motherfucker ain't comparing my man Jordan and the Bulls to this pussy team!"

"Be quiet back there, fool!" Perry says to Gawne, resuming his conversation with the driver, who admits that for many of the people on the street tonight football is simply an excuse to get drunk.

"On second thought, I should go home," Pharaoh says suddenly. Gawne and Perry immediately agree to call it a night. Pharaoh has come down off his high and is no longer in a festive mood. They each in turn ride silently to their respective homes. There is a shared sense among them that nothing good will come of this night.

CHAPTER 12

AMARYLLIS'S IMMUNITY from infections is over. It is two days before Christmas and another twelve before she completes her antibiotic therapy. Pharaoh administers rectal suppositories and suctions her nostrils around the clock. Every sneeze requires suction.

This is what Hannah enjoys the least about being a parent. "You're so much better at it than I am. She holds still for you. I have to fight with her too much." She cannot understand his enthusiasm to stay at home and nurse Amaryllis back to health. "You're sure you're okay with this? It means that you'll have to spend more time with Amaryllis after your classes, and you'll have to put her to bed."

But Pharaoh is taking it all in stride. *"Det er ingen* problem. She is my daughter, too," he assures her. Pharaoh's recent changes in attitude have injected new life into Hannah's efforts to conceive, which have somehow shifted from *her* elaborate preparations to *his*. All his underwear are summarily inspected and discarded, if they are found to be too tight. His sperm needs to breathe. Boxer shorts and lukewarm compresses encourage strong breathing and robust swimmers. Hannah has dismissed as rubbish his contention that underwear can have sentimental value. She balks at his desire to wear only American underwear, specially ordered from the States. He swallows large adult capsules as big as suppositories that contain fish oil. Hannah has determined, conducting research through magazines, the exact time of day that he has his optimum sperm count. In her zeal to conceive, she has also solicited advice from a few of her friends, as well as Trine, who has suddenly become quite interested in knitting wool socks and long johns for Pharaoh's use. She has allowed Pharaoh to open one of her Christmas presents early, and he has used the long box that contained a knitted pair of knee-length socks to enclose an abacus for Amaryllis. It is hidden behind the base of a broad Christmas tree that absorbs most of the space and light in their small apartment. To console Pharaoh over Amaryllis's skis, Hannah assures him that his gift will be the first one that their daughter will open tomorrow evening at the traditional family Christmas party.

Hannah and Trine have decorated the Christmas tree with most of the shiny, delicate ornaments at the top, safely out of Amaryllis's reach. It has given the tree a sparse, naked look, one that Trine jokes should remind them of Christmas in LA, *uten snø*. A thin string of miniature Norwegian flags encircle the tree from the star to the naked section, where even the twinkling lightbulbs stop. In an unexpected show of support for Pharaoh's country, Trine has knitted from leftover yarn a small rugged American pennant to hang on the Christmas tree. Five small, white buttons represent the fifty States. Amaryllis is waving the pennant in a closed fist under the tree as she watches Pippi Langstrompe skip and toss her orange ponytails from side to side on television. Pharaoh is grateful to Pippi, a skinny, pimply faced child with supernatural strength who frequently balances horses and overweight grown-ups on her head.

Pharaoh barricades himself in the kitchen to prepare dinner by placing the small kitchen table on its side at the entrance to the living room. A note on the refrigerator prioritizes his instructions for the evening. He is to cut Amaryllis's fingernails, but not down to the quick so that it hurts the following day. He must also remember to remove the covering from the suppository before inserting it, and he is to make certain Amaryllis eats a healthy dinner and brushes her teeth well before he puts her to bed. Any problems he encounters can be handled by Trine, who has raised four children in this house and is now making her way on soft snow toward their apartment.

Pharaoh's habit of locking the front door while he is at home has been met with ridicule. Everyone assures him that his actions are perfectly unnecessary, especially since spare keys to the entrance upstairs are kept in the garage.

Trine stamps her shoes on the mat outside and enters with a newspaper folded in two places. *"Hei, hei,"* she greets him, and immediately makes a beeline for Amaryllis, who welcomes her by sneezing. She wipes Amaryllis's nose with a corner of the knitted flag and hands it to him along with the newspaper. She has found work for him, she announces, as she leans into him balancing Amaryllis on a hip while tracing a nomadic finger along the classified section. The veins on the back of her hands are as blue and pronounced as the varicose veins on her legs. Her finger comes to a stop on a telephone number in a column enclosed by similar classified ads, all of them seeking instructors for language courses. "You must ring them up and tell them you will do it," she demands, banging her index finger on the paper in a percussive manner. She interprets his nod and his attempt to read the small print as interest both in seeking employment and in learning her language.

"They are grown-ups, so you will not have to speak to them in Norwegian, only English," Trine explains, leaning forward over the kitchen table to see what he is preparing for dinner. The aroma is spicy and pungent. Trine tells him to use the exotic seasonings manufactured by Norwegian-owned Black Boy products. She offers to loan him whatever bottles she has upstairs if the onions, tomatoes, and garlic he is using aren't enough. She doesn't understand his reluctance to use Black Boy products.

"I will call them tomorrow, bright and early," he promises. His assurance does little to satisfy her, however. She bombards him with a busy itinerary of left turns, bus routes, historical landmarks left over from World War II, and bridges. He is already lost. She leafs through the paper from back to front, commenting out loud on articles she has had all day to read, while she balances Amaryllis's twisting arms and legs on her hip with remarkable dexterity.

She has circled three death announcements in the obituary section, which she now points out to Pharaoh. *"Han er død. Hun er død og han er også død."* They were all people she knew, and she will attend their funerals. Amaryllis shall live a long life in Norway, Trine insists. *"Liker du sport? Futbol? Rosenborg?"*

Pharaoh pretends that he is too busy with the dinner preparations to respond seriously to her questions.

"Se her," she says, holding up a picture of students being escorted in groups away from a high school in Texas by policemen and ATF agents. More evidence, she thinks, of how fortunate Norwegians are to live in a safe country. Sensing his diapproval, she turns to the front page and a picture of a body covered in white plastic with the photo insert of a boy's smiling face in the upper right corner of the page. *"Han er død. Nei, Jeg tro at han var drept!* Murder!" she declares. She tries to imagine an explanation for the crime. He may have belonged to a gang because his body was found in a manhole on the other side of the city where Muslims live. His head and hands have disappeared from the rest of his body, she whispers to Pharaoh. It is too horrible of a crime to have happened here. The murderers may have been immigrants from Pakistan, she says, for this is not the crime of a Norwegian.

"Have you seen the paper?" Perry's voice is controlled, almost unnatural, when he isn't reciting movie dialogue.

"I am looking at it now." It has been hours since Trine's exhortation about the breech in her little land's serenity.

"Are you thinking what I am thinking?"

"It's probably not the same guy. Nothing has really been confirmed," Pharaoh says, fully aware of how ridiculous and feeble his spin is, if Perry is right.

"We need to find out. Can you get hold of Sail?"

"I'm not sure that is a good idea. Besides, he might be home for the holidays."

"So you *do* think it's him. Jesus Christ, Pharaoh! Can you fucking believe this? I knew those guys were trouble. It's in all the fucking papers and on TV, for crying out loud. You have to ask him."

"It is not our business, nor is it our fault that a Norwegian is missing."

"Missing?" Perry says, incredulously. "Try *dead*, burned beyond recognition and castrated, too. Shit, Pharaoh! Someone really didn't want this dude identified."

"What paper are you reading?"

"Oh, you didn't get that part, huh?"

"Hey, it was only a kickass. This has nothing to do with us."

"It does if Sail decides to implicate you or me or Gawne. No way! No fucking way!" Perry whispers. "We have to straighten this out!"

"I think you're taking this thing too far. Don't get carried away, Perry."

"He's lying!" Perry says.

"What do you suggest, man?" Should I interrogate him, then make a citizen's arrest if I think he's hiding something?"

"Can we do that, make a citizen's arrest?" The news has rattled Perry. His sense of humor and facetiousness have disappeared completely, leaving him nervous and naïve.

"Probably not. It was only a joke. Relax, man!"

"Relax? Relax! How can you be so calm, Pharaoh? Are you high? I don't get you sometimes. You certainly have the most to lose from all this. We can get into some serious trouble. I'm talking kicked out of the program—or the country, for that matter."

"You think? And that will be, what, a bad thing? Relax! We've done nothing wrong. Let's keep our mouths shut and see how this thing unravels."

"Okay," Perry agrees. "But you have to confront Sail on this. I think that son of a bitch lied about not catching the guy."

"You don't think the guy could have outrun him and gotten away?"

"No way," Perry says. "And this has nothing to do with where he's from; so don't go there with me! Shit! My roommates are back. I have to go. You need to straighten this out, Pharaoh. By the way, have you heard from Meg? I haven't seen or heard from her since that night. I hope she's all right."

Perry is not alone in his concern about Meg. Pharaoh's emails to her, acknowledging the veracity of her claim that a Canadian invented the game of basketball, have elicited no response. Perhaps a reply will confirm that Sail, too, was right, and Meg would prefer no such confirmation. They have nothing in common except their preoccupation with the African students, but she has had an immediate effect on him. Since the Handball Club, he's missed Meg's candor more than anything.

Chapter 13

HANNAH COMPLAINS ABOUT her hectic shift as she soothes a restless Amaryllis. She complains that she receives little help from her coworkers at the state nursing home. Everyone is preoccupied with discussing the charred body discovered in the city, especially when the news is televised. As a new employee, Hannah has to orient herself to the surroundings by trial and error, often interrupting people on cigarette breaks to ask questions. And they all have opinions about the US once they know that she has lived in California. She finds it unbelievable that she now has to defend the US. The fact that she has returned to Norway simply reinforces her coworkers' anti-US bias.

She likes her patients much more than most of her emloyees. "They have better characters, and they shouldn't. I mean, hon, they're sick. And some of them are really chronic, too, but they're so cute. I mean, you should hear them laugh and tell jokes. I hope we get like them when we are old and gray."

Amaryllis begins to wiggle and cry in her crib as Hannah attempts to insert an oral syringe filled with cherry-flavored medi-cine between her pursed lips. It is a task that requires two pairs of hands if Amaryllis is half-asleep. Something maternal prevents Hannah from performing these basic duties with Amaryllis at home, even though they would be routine at work, where her patients are more critical. She believes the problem will solve itself once they have a second child.

Hannah announces her desire to relax in a hot bubble bath with oils and natural emollients that she received from Eva as an early Christmas present. "I miss our bathtub in the States," she says. It is close to midnight. Hannah strips to her underwear, wraps herself in a towel, sticks her fleshy toes in a warm pair of moccasin-like slippers, and waltzes off to use her parents' bathtub.

It is a long time before she returns, pale, scented, and swaddled in her towel, eyeing him suspiciously. Soaking in a bathtub has revived with heightened urgency her desire to move. "We should start looking through the real estate section in the papers so that we can move as soon as you get a job."

Her sudden reference to his prospective employment makes him anxious. The city is still tense from recent events, and he worries that the risk of random questioning by the authorities may prove too big a sacrifice for seeking employment.

"I can call about the job tomorrow, if you want," Hannah says. He watches as she brushes her wet hair back, pulling the brush tightly along the nape of her neck.

"I'll call about it first thing tomorrow and send them my CV."

She responds with alarm and a vigorous shake of her head from side to side. "No, no. That's not how we do it here. You have to go down there and talk to them. In fact," she continues, "you don't even have to call. I would just go down there with my CV in hand, if I were you, and let them know that I am interested in the job. I can come with you, if you're not comfortable doing it alone."

Despite Hannah's counsel, he is reluctant to barge into an office unannounced and without an appointment. But he is not a child. He assures her that he will do as she says, but on his own.

She approaches him, still brushing her hair, and kisses him on the mouth. "That's for good luck," she says.

He thinks he will need it. He caresses her slick hair and parts the towel at her thighs.

"I think I need a little more luck than that," he says, smiling and unbuckling his belt. Hannah lets the brush hang in her hair and lowers herself to the floor, kissing him playfully.

"This is for good luck, too," Hannah says, and covers him with her mouth. As his erection stiffens, he wonders why their sex has become less frequent in her little land. He pushes her away from him before reaching his climax and then enters her quickly before she can remove the brush from her hair and rest her head comfortably on the floor.

"I really miss you, Hannah," he says between muffled grunts.

"I know it," she says. "I know you do, Pharaoh."

The office occupies an entire floor atop a flower boutique in an old granite building that also houses a music store, an optometry office, a mobile telephone office, and an Internet café. On one side of the office are large windows which look out onto snow-covered trailers and parked cars at a construction site. The windows are shielded by aluminum louvers that are drawn up, allowing a stream of sunlight to warm the room. Pharaoh's eyes scan a giant desk covered with papers, a computer terminal, a portable television set, and a coffee maker with the small red light on. Behind the desk are shelves filled with green folders with large single holes along the thick spines. The holes are bordered by silver rings around each rim and seem to have no particular purpose. A pair of skis lean upright on the wall facing the desk, and a huge duffel bag and snow boots prop up the bottom of the skis. A golden retriever sleeps quietly on the parquet floor next to an opened umbrella. A long winter coat hangs from a clothes hanger on the wall.

The introductions begin with a handshake at the reception area followed by an informal admission to Rigmor's.

"Forgive the mess in my office. You have come at a right time for

I am leaving for my winter vacation at the end of the day. My husband and I shall go skiing in Oppdal. Have you tried skiing yet?" Rigmor is a tall woman in her mid-fifties with graying hair. Her skin is tanned to a leathery texture. Pharaoh glimpses the outlines of soft muscles in her upper arms and back as she closes the door to her office and offers him one of the two empty chairs in front of her desk.

"We have new wooden floors. Aren't they very nice?" She seems genuinely excited. She removes her shoes and shrinks an inch or so onto the parquet floor before shrinking even further into the brown leather chair behind her desk. Pharaoh, practically tiptoeing in his shoes to avoid scratching the parquet, is offered a cup of coffee, which he politely refuses while explaining why he is so far north. Rigmor hands him her business card. She and her husband visited Seattle, Wisconsin, the Dakotas, and San Francisco during the late-seventies and had a great time, he learns. They have never been to Los Angeles. "I will read this now," Rigmor says of his CV, and turns her face toward the sun.

The interview is successful and proceeds with a casualness that is unexpected, but appreciated, by Pharaoh. He will begin teaching adult students to prepare for an English certificate exam in June. The course will be taught in three-hour evening sessions twice a week at a local high school, and he will be paid after he has signed a contract. He accepts copies of the text along with cassettes and a key to a storage locker that, according to Rigmor, contains six cassette players and other supplies. She is happy with his experience and pleased that he came in today. It means that she can prolong her forthcoming vacation, enjoying skiing, snow games, and hot chocolate with her husband and friends.

At the end of the interview, Rigmor accompanies him into the elevator and out to the street without her coat and umbrella. It is a professional, yet warm gesture, sullied only by the stares of pedestrians and motorists as Pharaoh and his new employer seal their agreement with a handshake. Despite the sun, a cold, slight wind curls snowflakes about them. Rigmor wishes him, *"God Jul og Godt Nyt År!"* She also warns him about aquavit, a distilled drink made from potatoes and flavored with caraway which Norwegians drink with meals during family Christmas dinners. There is nothing else quite like that taste in Norway except *"gammel ost,"* she says. She hates both of them.

Pharaoh's short walk to the trolley stop takes him past a construction site where men in bright orange uniforms are moving about wrought iron structures at a leisurely pace. The workers turn their heads as he walks past. A few turn their entire bodies. Happy from finding employment, he nods to acknowledge their inquisitiveness. Policemen stroll along the sidewalk in twos. Pharaoh's successful interview almost makes him wish they would stop him and ask him questions. This is one of the few times he has ventured into the city during daylight and on foot. He feels like a vampire. And that is probably exactly what Norwegians see when they look at him.

The restaurants, cafés, and stores on King Street occupy compact spaces along narrow sidewalks. Because of the ploughed snow, pedestrians walk next to large, decorative bay windows kept warm by spotlights and display signs. The streets have become crowded since his interview. Pedestrians hurry across an intersection in a diagonal stream at the sound of an alarm from the traffic signal. Almost everyone is dressed in black, as if they are in mourning over the still-unidentified body draped in white plastic that has become a common image on television newscasts and on the front page of the local newspapers. At a kiosk located near a busy traffic roundabout, pedestrians stop and stare at the laminated front pages of newspapers on display. The police have brought in special cadaversniffing dogs from Germany to track down the original place of death. There is a sense, according to public-opinion polls represented by a colorful step graph at the bottom of one front page, that the police are ill-equipped for what they are up against. Theories abound about who might be responsible, ranging from the Russian Mafia to Pakistani enclaves living in high-rises in an underdeveloped section of the city. The crime has sparked new debates about religious freedom, acculturation, and the integration of Muslim immigrants within the Norwegian community. Many people recall an earlier uproar at a local school over a Muslim parent's refusal to allow his daughter to participate in swim classes if boys were also allowed in the pool. *"They are too different to fit in,"* read the caption at that time under the picture of a Muslim woman whose identity was masked by her veil. There is a picture in the current paper of the Norwegian Crown Prince standing uncomfortably amongst black and Hispanic students at UC Berkeley, decrying racism in his homeland and promoting multiculturalism from abroad. It is clear from all of the articles and pictures in the newspapers that this local incident has gained national significance. Pharaoh cannot let himself believe that Sail is somehow responsible.

A black obelisk stands at the center of the city with a statue of a man steeped at its top. Falling snow has created a sheath of ice around the statue's surface. At the base, people have placed lighted candles, wreaths, and flowers to commemorate the dead body. Pharaoh barely notices, however, his mind focused on his excitement about the interview with Rigmor and his new job.

The news of his employment has Hannah and her family fishing for information about the Folk University. They bombard him with questions that he cannot answer and that leave him embarrassed and uncertain about the interview. Trine wants to know more about Rigmor, and his evasiveness results in more and more questions. Thor thinks it is a good, private, adult school, from which Pharaoh will receive a large salary. He is busy estimating taxes with his calculator, based on what he believes Pharaoh's services as an American are worth. Pharaoh has grown tired of Thor's calculations. It was

Thor's meddling, after all, that convinced Hannah that it would be more cost-efficient for him to ride the trolley to the city this morning than to drive the SHO. A satisfied smile spreads across Thor's heavy jaws as he transfers his calculations to yet another tablet with a Norwegian flag on the cover. After taxes, Thor announces, Pharaoh's salary will be nothing to make a fuss about. But it cannot be avoided. It is what all Norwegians must deal with.

Hannah is surprised but pleased that Pharaoh's very first job interview in her country has been a positive one. In spite of Thor's calculations, there is talk of them eventually buying a two-bedroom condo in the city, or investing in a month-long vacation in California.

"California, here I come," Pharaoh says.

"Oh, I almost forgot," Hannah says. "Did you tell your classmates you were going on a job interview?" They are upstairs drinking coffee with Trine and Thor in front of frosted windows. Pharaoh can see smoke emanating from rooftop chimneys. Sara, a nine-year-old tomboy in baggy jeans and a Mighty Ducks T-shirt, fondles Amaryllis's hair, infatuated it seems with its texture.

"Well, you were very popular this morning," Hannah says. "Perry called, and then a little while after, Gawne called, and then Perry called back again. And someone named Oobamcee called. That one had a nice accent. Where's he from? You should invite them all to Christmas dinner."

"We'll see." He makes no inquiries about their messages.

"Var det en damer som ringte deg fra skolen?" Trine asks. Thor laughs behind his cup of coffee. Hannah attempts to translate, but it is unnecessary. Hannah assures Pharaoh that her mother, who is still smiling to herself, is just kidding.

"Did Oobamcee leave his number?"

"On the table downstairs," Hannah answers, frowning at Pharaoh's departure.

* * *

"We must meet and talk." Oobamcee's voice is deep and resonant over the telephone. It is not an accent or a tone of voice that Hannah would consider nice.

"How is Peter?"

"Peter is fine. His injury from the fall was not serious."

"What fall?"

"He fell on the ice and cut himself; perhaps you did not notice," Oobamcee says.

Pharaoh awaits further explanation, but Oobamcee remains silent. "Where is Sail? Is he okay?" Pharaoh finally asks. He can imagine the lines above Oobamcee's temples fixed in contemplation. There are sudden noises from children in the background, as if a door has been opened, and then Oobamcee silencing them in his native language.

"I believe he is at home asleep, but I cannot be certain."

Pharaoh's incredulous laughter startles Oobamcee, who is not one to joke. There is, after all, no reason Sail should not be sleeping. Hannah enters the living room noisily, mumbling about Pharaoh's cold coffee, and then heads for the kitchen. She opens the refrigerator to get Amaryllis's antibiotic, then removes a syringe from a draw, eyeing Pharaoh suspiciously as she walks past.

"Where do you live?"

"Not far," Oobamcee says. It is all the information he is willing to impart over the telephone. In the background, Pharaoh hears the distinct voice of a woman admonishing the children. A series of vacant clicks indicate that Oobamcee has placed the receiver on a hard surface. While waiting for him to return, Pharaoh stares at Hannah's handwriting in Norwegian on a yellow Post-it note. She has begun to post written information everywhere to assist his learning of her native language. He hopes it is not an ominous sign. Her penmanship is neat with X's over I's and J's, and lines that curl slightly at the beginning and end of words. She has an appointment at a salon in the city tomorrow and will take Amaryllis.

Oobamcee finally returns, without any reference to his momentary absence. Pharaoh conveys Hannah's Christmas dinner invitation to him and his family, as well as to Peter and Sail. Despite his previous reluctance to commit to social invitations involving their class, Oobamcee accepts readily. The Christmas dinner is only two days away.

PART III

CHAPTER 14

THE SEARCH FOR CLUES to the identity of the severed body found in a manhole leads investigators to Drammen, the city outside of Oslo where Pharaoh picked up his car. The papers describe it as the cesspool of Norway, because of its diverse immigrant population and high crime rate. He is not surprised that an association, however weak, has been made to Drammen.

Despite constant images from old cases on the newscasts, there is no new information on the progress of the investigation. Pharaoh believes it's a sign that the authorities are close to making an arrest. The cadaver-sniffing dogs have left for Germany along with the sincere thanks of the police inspector and the mayor on behalf of their city. Residents are instructed to stay alert. Although thousands of tips have come in to police, no arrests have been made, according to a police spokesperson, who apparently forgot to remove his snuff before going on camera. The offer of a reward has generated renewed interest in the kind of weapon used. A polled majority of Norwegians believe it is the work of an exotic tool, like a machete, while a majority polled among heavily populated immigrant communities believe a more common tool, like an axe, is the likely murder weapon.

Gawne does not care what people here believe. He describes the local police as amateurs and dickheads. He has just returned from an impromptu trip to Stockholm, where the cops remind him of those in Ohio. "Man, I ain't letting this shit worry me. We don't have anything to worry about. You seen *First Blood* with Stallone? Well, them white boys struck first. Payback's a bitch, ain't it?" He does not believe that Sail is even remotely involved and dismisses Pharaoh's updates on the case to announce that he has finally gotten laid. He has had two whole days of fucking, and he would still be there had it not been for her parents. His dick is sore, bruised, and blistered. "Shit, man! Met her on the bus, holmes. All she had was a backpack and a bus card, oh yeah, and her pussy! Can't forget that. That pussy was tight, but I tore it up! Hell, I ain't like the chef. I like it when my balls stick! We gotta go to Stockholm, Jack. They got some serious pussy across the border, motherfucker."

Gawne's embellished tales of his sexual exploits is a welcome distraction from the heaviness of the holidays. He tells Pharaoh that he has purchased small souvenirs for him and for Perry, which he must remember to bring to the dinner. Perry has already telephoned three times since his return. "That boy needs to chill, holmes." He laughs at Pharaoh's suggestion that Perry, too, might benefit from a trip across the border. "Can't say that I know where homeboy can get his ass plugged, but if he's looking for pussy, pussy'll find him there. If he's looking for scrotal clamps, black mambas, and wire dildos, or if it's dick homeboy's after, well, he's in the right place." Pharaoh smiles. Even with his recent conquest in Sweden, Gawne is unable to hide his resentment over how difficult it has been for him to meet women in Norway. He decided to cross the border after looking up at the sky one afternoon and seeing clouds take on the form of vaginas.

"Hell, homeboy is as gay as they get." He returns to the topic of Perry's sexual orientation. "Don't tell me you haven't noticed. He's never ever worried about getting some pussy. Shit! How long has he been here? Hell, where you been?" he asks incredulousy.

"Those aren't reasons to assume he's gay. And not everyone talks about sex the way you do, man, or craves it on demand the way you do, for that matter. Perhaps his life doesn't revolve around getting laid. I'm sure he has a girlfriend, and if not, then that's his business." But Pharaoh isn't certain about a girlfriend. He defends Perry out of a sense of obligation as a friend and because he is not present to defend himself. It's clear that for Gawne the matter has less to do with determining Perry's sexuality than with proving that his street savvy is superior to Pharaoh's. The signs are everywhere, Gawne claims, but a discussion he had with Perry about *The Crying Game* was the real clincher. Pharaoh is surprised that Gawne acknowledges having seen *The Crying Game*. What will he be talking about next, the Maplethorpe exhibit? "Serious business, holmes," Gawne insists, trying to collect himself. "It was a dead giveaway."

With his street savvy in question, Pharaoh admits that he had his suspicions about Perry all along. "I just had a feeling," he says. "I just knew."

"Bullshit! Knew my ass," Gawne scoffs. Before their conversation degenerates any further, Gawne instructs Pharaoh to round up all the single ladies in his neighborhood in preparation for his visit. It is, after all, what Norwegians do when the Crown Prince is expected at a local event. But in Gawne's case, it's really worth the effort; his dick is hung lower than the Crown Prince's.

People arrive with bouquets of flowers and gift-wrapped presents that Sara collects promptly, with a hushed announcement of the recipients, and arranges strategically under the tree. There is a level of excitement throughout the house that has little to do with the spirit of Christmas or all the preparations that have gone into expanding the dinner to include five guests on short notice. The excitement has exhausted Amaryllis, who is fast asleep in her crib downstairs.

Trine and Thor have conducted research on Africa so that they won't appear as ignorant hosts to the African students. Thor's research involved looking up the respective countries in an old atlas to check for average mean temperatures during the Norwegian winter months, sizes of population, and per capita incomes. An old Norwegian travel guide confirmed for Trine that African meals are laden with spice, so she has purchased a small bottle of Tabasco sauce.

"I hope she's not expecting them to pay for the dinner," Pharaoh says jokingly to Hannah, but with immediate regret. Her parents are not that bad, she reminds him, and he should not judge them as harshly as he does.

It is seven minutes after seven as the trolley rumbles by. From a kitchen window, one can see Knut and his family approach on a worn snow path from the trolley stop. Knut balances presents on a stroller while his girlfriend, Inger Lise, walks a few paces behind, chewing energetically. She is large and dressed in a long, brown fur coat. Her jerky movements resemble a bear walking on its hind legs. Pharaoh volunteers to help Trine and Hannah carry food the short distance from the kitchen to the living room while Thor makes final seating arrangements. But Hannah insists that he will only be a nuisance; she doesn't have the time to translate Trine's instructions. Instead he should check on Amaryllis and, on his way back, fetch extra rolls of toilet paper from a downstairs storage room and place them in the hallway lavatory.

Up close, Inger Lise and Knut have almost identical features—round faces with red cheeks and expansive foreheads. After removing her hat and fur coat, revealing a snug fitting gray bodice and ankle-length black pants, she is congratulated by everyone except Thor and Pharaoh for her recent weight loss. "Baby fat," she grins, showing small, snuff-stained teeth. For the first time since her pregnancy she has had a few sips of Kahlúa, which Knut cheerfully admits has made her drunk and wobbly.

"Brother-in-law, congratulations on your new job in Norway," Knut says, removing his shoes before entering. He is smartly dressed in a blue shirt and a brown tie that is wide at the end and ironed stiff. It dangles between his abdomen and belt buckle and reminds Pharaoh of the beak of a duckbilled platypus.

"Tusen Takk," Pharaoh says.

With both hands stuffed in his pockets, Knut enters the living room and walks around the table for a perfunctory inspection, dragging his wool socks on the parquet floor. Most of the living room furniture has been shifted to accommodate a makeshift table covered with a hemmed red tablecloth. The table seats sixteen and is arranged diagonally across the room. Knut gingerly twists three bottles of aquavit around so that their labels are aligned in one direction. Thor, looking as if he belongs at a trendy nightclub in his black shirt, black tie, black pants, and white suspenders, places single bottles of beer on cork coasters. He is too busy to respond to Knut's compliment that he looks considerably younger than most men in their fifties.

The doorbell rings and Sara, in a longsleeved yellow dress and white tights, rushes to collect more presents but returns with a frightened look and a battle cry. *"Amerikaner! Amerikaner!"* She bumps into Hannah, who consoles her with an embrace and gently escorts her back to the front door to be properly introduced.

Perry and Gawne have also done their research and are an immediate hit, presenting flowers to Trine and a bottle of cognac to Thor.

"God Jul," Perry says. *"Takk for invitasjon."*

"Vær så god," Trine and Thor say in chorus. Perry's Norwegian is impressive, and they make inquiries about how long he has been in the country. He is fully prepared for questions about what he thinks of Norway and answers like a parrot on a wire, but there is a nervousness about him that Pharaoh hopes the dinner will quell.

"My parents think your Norwegian is good." Hannah is dressed in a pair of loose-fitting black slacks with an elastic waist and a white blouse. She has forgotten that her translation is unnecessary. She smiles offhandedly at Gawne and Perry after they compliment her outfit and hair, then smirks in Pharaoh's direction.

"The homeys here yet?"

"Not yet," he says. Anna and Dagfinn arrive and introduce themselves to Perry and Gawne with bows and handshakes. Trine and Thor immediately put them to work.

"We must have Christmas music. My father has forgotten the music," Dagfinn says. Sara giggles at his English.

"I think Alzheimer is to blame. It is what you have to look forward to on your next birthday," Knut says and laughs, pinching snuff from a tin.

"Hello, little brother." Dagfinn lowers his eyes to Knut's midsection, and laughs. He is dressed in an expensive black suit that he bought on a recent visit to Germany. He does not bother to remove his shiny shoes. Anna is dressed in a black ankle-length skirt, a white blouse, and a knitted blue sweater. Her perfume leaves a lingering scent after each trip to the dinner table. Her hair is combed neatly over her shoulders; two clips on each side of her head create a thick covert flap of hair down the middle of her scalp that straddles her collar. It is a conservative look, one which makes her seem closer to her own age. She catches Pharaoh observing her and smiles, drawing a candle from a pack in one hand and tilting its wick ritually to the flame on another.

"Man, she's checking you out, holmes." Gawne is at Pharaoh's shoulder in his traditional baggy khaki pants and oversized white shirt, buttoned to his throat. He has separated from Perry, who has joined Knut and is busy examining a family photo on a wall.

"That's my sister-in-law, man. How about some respect?"

"Easy, holmes. Where's your Christmas spirit? Sounds like you're stressed. You ain't beginning to trip about that shit in the papers, are you? You getting just like homeboy over there. Y'all need to relax. I told you. Chill. That ain't got nothing to do with us." Gawne stuffs both hands in his pockets and nods his head rhythmically as if he is listening to music on headphones. Far from reassuring, his comments suggest that he has been following events closer than he is willing to admit.

"Just don't scare anyone. Let them get used to you."

"Now, is that any way to talk to a homey? I'm cool, Jack. Chill!"

"That is what concerns me, man. You're just too cool."

"Yeah, sure, you right. I'll chill. They'll get used to me just like they got used to you, holmes." Trine walks by carrying a large Pyrex dish with flesh-colored hot sausages. She encourages them to speak Norwegian to each other; it is the only way they will learn the language.

"This is for you, before I forget. Compliments of Sweden." Gawne hands him a small package wrapped in wrinkled aluminum foil and says, "Merry Christmas, motherfucker!"

Pharaoh hurriedly stuffs the small pipe in his pocket.

"Any chance we can use that before dinner?" Gawne grins. Pharaoh initially entertains the thought, but decides the risk of discovery is too great. There are large windows on both outer walls in the living room, which give unimpeded views of the yard and street. Thor is outside shoveling snow and placing lighted candles along a path to the front door. He has manufactured them himself by placing wax and upright wicks in empty Turtlewax cans that he has saved over years of polishing his car. The cans are submerged in the snow to hide the manufacturer's labels. The flame lasts for about six hours before the wick extinguishes itself in a pool of clear, hot wax.

A loud crash in the kitchen is followed by Norwegian profanity. Inger Lise's fur coat is on fire. She and Anna stand nearby, transfixed by the creeping flames singeing the fur. Dagfinn hustles to the scene, steps on a lighted candle lying next to the coat, and then rushes upstairs to get a fire extinguisher. Pharaoh grabs the fur coat by its collar and tosses it outside in the snow. Anna begins to laugh, as Inger Lise continues to gaze with a sanguine look at the empty spot.

"It's okay. *Det går bra,*" Perry says, arriving with Knut, who does not look surprised. A smoke-detector alarm goes off. Knut reaches up, opens the front cover, and violently tugs the battery loose. Everyone is silent except Trine, who can still be heard swearing in the kitchen.

"How 'bout that joint, holmes?"

Hannah appears stealthily behind Gawne, holding Amaryllis, who is dressed in an elf outfit that once belonged to Sara. The child looks disoriented in Hannah's arms and squirms as Pharaoh prepares to accept her. Pharaoh attempts to ignore Gawne's blunder, but it's too late.

"I hope I didn't hear what I think I heard."

"Yeah, a loud noise. Your mom okay in the kitchen? I hope that wasn't the dinner." Pharaoh moves to a nearby window with Amaryllis and Gawne, and they watch Thor's frantic attempt to smother the fur coat's flames by beating it with a shovel. Dagfinn looks on, a fire extinguisher at the ready. Hannah follows Pharaoh with an admonishing stare, and he braces himself for the words he knows will follow.

"*You* know what I mean," Hannah says.

"Damn, holmes! You got a cute-ass kid. I know she didn't get all her looks from you." Gawne's effort at damage control fares even worse than Pharaoh's. Amaryllis responds to his voice with a sneeze that produces a green glob of snot that enlarges like an inflated balloon. He wipes away the bubble.

"At least you're good for something," she says to Gawne, couching her rebuke with a smile. Amaryllis has finally cleared her nostril, something Hannah claims she was having little success with before they heard the smoke alarm and came upstairs.

"Are you married, Gawne?"

"Nope. I'm single," he says proudly, offering his outstretched arms to Amaryllis. "But I got lots of cousins and nieces and nephews." Amaryllis climbs into his arms without hesitation.

Hannah looks from Gawne to Pharaoh as if she has made an important discovery.

"Well, we're hoping for another one soon. Amaryllis needs someone to play with," Hannah says.

Neighbors wander outside of their homes to get a closer look at Thor's antics and the simmering black patch in the snow. Most of the fur coat is now buried. He watches along with Dagfinn as steam and smoke seep through the condensed snow. Thor does not permit any further interruption of his routine. When Inger Lise finally stumbles outside to apologize, he sidesteps her approach and resumes his manner as if nothing has happened. He enters his garage, then returns with a lighted lantern and a wood carving of a small boy in a Bunad with painted, rosy cheeks. The carving is about two meters high and Thor plants it upright in the snow at the entrance facing the street and hangs the lighted lantern from its arm. Anna pokes her head out of the kitchen, conducts a place count, and then instructs Sara to get her sister, Lena.

"What the hell is keeping those guys?" Perry asks.

"What guys?"

"Oobamcee, Peter, and Sail. Are they coming?" Perry is agitated. The African students are late, and he is recommending that the hosts begin without them.

"They'll be here," Pharaoh says.

"Yeah, if they're not out chopping off someone's head. Maybe they've been arrested," Perry mutters.

Knut ambles over after Perry to continue their earlier conversation. Their discussion has left Knut with a fiendish demeanor.

"And what do you think about it, brother-in-law? Your American friend here does not believe our women should sunbathe without their bikini tops at our beaches. He believes it is uncivilized behavior because it is not done in America."

"Damn, holmes! You shitting me? Don't listen to him," Gawne

says to Knut, and then glares at Perry. "I can't wait until summer's here. You better believe I'm hitting the beaches, and it ain't gonna be to check out the surf."

"That figures," Perry admits. "We're not surprised. But it is another way of exploiting women, even though it may seem like an individual choice. It is unfair to both sexes, really, because men can't walk around without their swim trunks."

"Yeah. I bet you'd like to see some trunks, homey." Gawne guffaws as he tosses Amaryllis and her startled smile up in the air and then catches her.

"I have nothing against it," Pharaoh says, trying to avoid any angst among the guests before dinner.

"You got something on your mind, buddy?" Perry looks accusingly at Pharaoh as Amaryllis continues to giggle in Gawne's arms.

"We agree, brother-in-law," Knut says. "We are liberal here in Norway with the human body. It is not something to hide. But we are becoming more and more conservative like your Texans. Your Hollywood tells us that we in Europe are primitive because we are not ashamed of our bodies. I have heard the jokes."

"*Unnskyld meg,*" Perry says. "Allow me to respond. Hollywood cannot be blamed for everything. But if women decide to keep their tops on because they have been enlightened by a movie, then that is a good thing."

"Yeah," Gawne interrupts. "It's because of Hollywood that women in Europe shave their armpits and legs today."

"Shut up, man! You're not helping," Perry snaps.

Inger Lise's presence temporarily halts their conversation. She brandishes Baby Thor in her arms, gently swaying him from side to side before she offers him to Knut. Baby Thor begins to cry. His parents try to determine what's bothering him, as Gawne and Perry eye each other hostilely.

"You got something to tell me?" Perry says.

"Uh uh. I think you got something to tell us." Gawne includes

Amaryllis as his ally. He has hoisted her atop his shoulders where her little green legs straddle the white collar around his neck. She enjoys the height, and her bouncy laughter makes it difficult for Perry to remain annoyed.

"Finally, Señor Gawne has someone he can relate to on the same level." Amaryllis's bottom lip begins to tremble. Her laughter becomes a terrified whimper, as if she has been insulted. Hannah's maternal instinct draws her to the living room like an agitated magnet.

"I'll take her," Pharaoh says, but it is too late. Amaryllis is already being lowered into Hannah's arms.

"You snooze, you lose," Gawne says in an attempt at consolation.

"There is the source of her anxiety," Perry says, tilting his head furtively at Inger Lise breast-feeding a now content Baby Thor in her lap. She does not care that she has been drinking or that her exposed, bulbous breast is a sight of discomfort for others. There is a small, discolored tattoo of a snail above the areola, which is surrounded by bruises. Stretch marks run along the tip like collapsed veins on a drug user's arm, suggesting that her milk might not only be contaminated but poisonous. Everyone averts their eyes, but like a malignant growth, Inger Lise's bruised breast is difficult to ignore.

"Jesus Christ, holmes. You see that? Either your brother-in-law's been knocking some serious boots, or he's been using homegirl's breasts as a punching bag. Hell, that ain't even my thing," Gawne whispers.

"Don't go there!" Perry cautions. "It's not our concern. We don't know how she got them. Perhaps they're from breast-feeding an overanxious kid. There might be a simple explanation."

"Yeah, right. And I need an enema. Hell, maybe her old man's been breast-feeding, too," Gawne mutters.

"I agree with Perry. It's their problem, Gawne. Leave it alone," Pharaoh says. But when Hannah returns with a diaper and Amaryllis in tow, Pharaoh accepts both dutifully and tries to get her to acknowledge what he and his friends have seen.

"Make yourselves useful," she commands. "Don't just stand there and stare!"

"Has someone burnt an effigy of us outside?" Oobamcee asks Pharaoh. "We are sorry we are late. There were problems to solve and it was difficult to find your home." He has entered with only a knock, trailed by Lena, Peter, and Sail.

"You need one of these," Lena announces in a childlike voice, curling strands of wet hair behind an ear as she flashes her cell phone like a badge. She is in summer wear that exposes a paunchy midriff.

"Oh, yes, Western technology. It is too complicated for a simple man like me," Oobamcee remarks. Lena giggles and hurries to greet the relatives.

"I am sorry we are late," Oobamcee says again, with a volume and sincerity that bring everyone to the entrance, including Trine with her camera in tow.

"I am glad you are here. We were beginning to think you weren't going to make it," Pharaoh says.

"Yeah. Now we can eat," Gawne says, his eyes shadowing Lena's naked midriff. Each of the new guests hands a present to Sara to place under the tree. Peter seems genuinely happy to see Pharaoh, as the two pump hands. There is a small bandage above his left eye. From the jagged outline, it is apparent that the stitches beneath it are homemade.

"Mr. USA, I have not had an opportunity to thank you properly. In my country, such a gesture must be rewarded."

"I do not need a reward, and besides, you are not in your country," he says, returning Peter's smile. "We did what was right."

"We hope," Perry says aloud. Sail nods at Pharaoh and surveys the room. For a moment, he acts as host, performing introductions among stiff handshakes and cautious smiles. Knut advises Inger Lise to stop breast-feeding as the African students enter the living room.

His attitude toward the human body becomes decidedly less liberal in their presence.

"It is okay. We must not interrupt a mother in progress."

"She is finished," Knut replies.

"I see," Oobamcee says, turning to Pharaoh. "And where are you hiding your daughter?" Pharaoh points to Amaryllis, who is busy, to Sara's dismay, scattering presents under the Christmas tree. When she sees Oobamcee, she stops her mischief for a moment. She looks from Oobamcee to Peter, but they can't compete with decorative paper.

"A wonderful offspring," Peter announces, clasping his jeweled hands as if conducting christening rites.

Anna and Lena can be heard in a muffled argument together in a corner of the kitchen. Their argument does not bode well for Lena, who stomps out of the kitchen and out of the house swearing at her mother in a mix of English and Norwegian. It is his first glimpse of Anna as a parent. Hannah, who is also present, reaches over and rubs the small of Anna's back as a gesture of comfort and empathy. But it is clear from her body language that Anna does not appreciate the attention.

"We must talk later. It is very important." Oobamcee's whisper is deep and suggests a level of complicity with which Pharaoh, although he acknowledges it, is uncomfortable.

"I have been questioned by the police," Oobamcee says once they are alone. "And it seems that your friend, Meg, has been deported."

At the dinner table, there is a short silence for Kjersti and Stig, the affenpinscher, before everyone begins to eat. Anna is seated next to Pharaoh, and he can feel her leg press against his under the table. He breathes in her perfume and feels when her elbow brushes against his arm as she flattens a napkin in her lap. The disagreement between mother and daughter remains unresolved. Lena's hair is still wet, but she has opted to wear a short leather jacket buttoned over her blouse. In a continued show of defiance, she interrupts her meal to read and send messages from her cell phone.

"You know," Oobamcee says to Lena from across the table, "it is against the law in some countries for people to bite their fingernails." It is not the kind of attention she covets. Eyes zoom in on her hands. Peter laughs and his white teeth and bright voice are a momentary distraction from a growing tension between Lena and Dagfinn. Lena smiles painfully at Dagfinn and pockets her cell phone.

"Are you married, Oobamcee?" Pharaoh resents Hannah's question, even as she cloaks it in innocence.

"I am married," Oobamcee replies, expectantly.

"And do you have children?"

"I do," he acknowledges quickly.

"And are you *all* married?"

Sail shakes his head while chewing. It is not an impetuous gesture but an impolite one whose significance allows no escape. Everyone waits for his answer while Hannah crushes Amaryllis's food with the back of her fork.

"I am not married, but I would like a wife," Peter says. His eyes glide hastily over the women at the table, as if he is prepared to make a selection, finally settling on Inger Lise, crouched in her seat beside Knut. She drops her head toward her plate under Peter's gaze and rears it again as the doorbell rings. Sara is out of her seat and running to greet Santa Claus. Dagfinn announces after checking his watch and looking at Thor suspiciously that Santa has arrived at the wrong time.

Sara returns and shouts excitedly, *"Politi og Brannmenn er her!"* Thor pushes his chair away from the table and hustles toward the front door, followed by Dagfinn, Lena, and Hannah, carrying a reluctant Amaryllis over her shoulder. Oobamcee remains seated and continues to eat, completely ignoring the announcement. Perry, however, with a hushed finger to his lips, nudges Gawne.

Sail asks for more bread and Tabasco sauce and casually splatters the sauce atop his food. Anna does not go after her family, nor does she seem concerned that policemen and firemen are outside. Instead, she maintains a rigid pressure against Pharaoh's thigh with her leg.

Amid laughter and Christmas greetings outside, Thor learns that a neighbor who witnessed his efforts to extinguish Inger Lise's inflamed fur coat has summoned the fire department. The policemen had naturally tagged along.

"Our public authorities are very efficient," Knut says, leaning out of his chair.

"I would expect nothing less than efficiency from your public authorities," Oobamcee replies. "But they rely too much on technology. You have security cameras everywhere. I see them on buildings and at intersections in your city, and whenever I enter a kiosk, I can see my face—everywhere. Yet I have heard that your police cannot find the missing parts of someone who was found under the street, in a manhole, I believe. Perhaps your authorities should install cameras in such holes." Oobamcee's cordial smile is interrupted by Perry's abrupt departure from the table.

"The dude's got a weak stomach," Gawne says.

"It is not his stomach that is weak," Sail says.

"Ain't that the truth, homey."

Trine, who is confused by everything that has happened, begs everyone to eat as much as they want, especially the African students, who look much too thin.

"We will find the one responsible for that awful crime," Knut says. "They cannot hide from our police, and we are not too proud to ask for help from our neighbors."

"Ah, yes. The German dogs."

"You do not like the Germans?"

"I speak of their dogs. But Germany has placed a blemish on history. I do not feel sorry for her like some people because she is still paying reparations for her historical image. Because of Hitler, Germany can never escape its history."

"Y'all ain't got too much room to talk, homey. You seen *Roots?* Hell, ain't no one gonna forget slavery, holmes."

The African students look at Gawne.

"The Germans are respected here in Europe," Knut says. "We will find who did that crime."

"This is very good food." Pharaoh tries to change the subject and deflect a confrontation.

"Kjempegod mat, Mamma," Knut agrees, raising his small glass of aquavit in a toast.

"Perhaps we should await the man of the house and the rest of your family," Oobamcee announces.

Anna ignores his suggestion and empties her glass in one motion, her leg still attached to Pharaoh's thigh. Knut, Trine, and Inger Lise empty their glasses as well. Pharaoh shrugs at Gawne, and they both tilt their glasses until they are empty.

"Perhaps not," Oobamcee concedes, and follows suit, frowning as he swallows.

"Do you think it is too strong?" Knut asks. "I do not think you have this drink in Africa."

"Tell me, sir, have you been to Africa?" Oobamcee asks.

"No, but I do not think you sell this there. It is a Norwegian drink."

"You, my friend, will be surprised at what we have in Africa."

The firemen and policemen have left, taking with them the charred fur coat for proper disposal. Curious neighbors and children mill about their yards as if looking for incendiary devices. Inside, everyone has returned to the table, but the atmosphere is not how they left it. To avoid further discussion with Oobamcee, Perry has begun speaking only Norwegian and has found a friend in Trine. Knut continues to argue with Oobamcee. Lena and her mother are talking again, their frequent exchange of glances decreasing the pressure of Anna's leg against his thigh, but he can still feel her. Amaryllis and Baby Thor are on the parquet floor tugging at chair legs and ankles like mischievous pets. Dagfinn attempts to tell a joke he has read on the Internet, yet another jab at Americans. Pharaoh will never get used to these barbs. The joke involves a policeman who stops a female motorist and her passengers. He approaches the vehicle, unaware that his zipper is down, and the surprised woman yells, "Oh no. Not another breath test." Pharaoh, of course, has heard it before, but Gawne cannot stop laughing. Neither can Trine and Thor, after receiving their translation. Anna simply glares at her husband.

"Do you celebrate Christmas in Africa also?" Knut asks.

"Of course. We do not live on a different planet. But our Santa Claus has big muscles, for there is no snow for him to ride his sleigh or reindeers to pull him where he shall go. He must use a bicycle and carry his sack on the handlebars or his head. It is not such an extravagant ritual as you have in the West. His presents are mainly cloth, kola nuts, cashews, and palm oil," Oobamcee says, as if he is educating a child. Knut frowns. Sara, who is eager to open presents, tugs at Dagfinn's arm and points at the markings on Oobamcee's temples. Dagfinn lifts her and hugs her, but the child won't be distracted. She pouts for a moment, and then begins to play with her top lip, trying to imitate the African's appearance. She is seated across from Peter who blinks at her, turning the flesh pink insides of his eyelids back over his eyes. It is a frightening look that makes his pupils seem as if they are half covered in blood. Hannah places a hand over her mouth, aghast at the sight. Sara screams and begins to cry before Peter blinks again to return his eyes to their normal white.

"I am sorry, little one," he says to a terrified Sara. "It is a common trick we use to entertain the little ones in my country."

"Well, we don't do that here, especially at the dinner table," Hannah says in a scolding tone.

"It is because your kids have television to keep them entertained, madam. We do not have *The Little Rascals* or *Lassie* for everyone. I am only trying to do what your Buckwheat might if he was present," Peter says, aware that his explanation has become a subtle accusation.

"Can you do it also, brother-in-law?"

"No, unfortunately. I have other skills," he says to Dagfinn. Anna's leg returns immediately to his thigh.

"Yes, I have heard. My wife thinks you are a very good dancer, like me." Dagfinn laughs. "You must teach her—how do you say in America—some moves?"

"Hell, I can groove," Gawne says, peering at Anna from behind his plate. "I got all kinds of moves."

"I have heard that white Americans are not gifted dancers. No rhythm," Dagfinn says.

"Not this one," Gawne replies, and gives Pharaoh a questioning look. Trine rises from her chair quietly and begins to circle the table with her camera. After a series of flashes, most of which are directed at the African students and Amaryllis, Hannah disappears and returns with a light sweater. She hands the sweater to Inger Lise, who is completely unaware that milk has begun to leak from her breasts onto her bodice.

"Who will have more aquavit?" Thor asks, encouraging his guests to fill up. Glasses are held in preparation for a Christmas toast. Thor brushes a palm over his scalp, then stands and surveys the table like a short king surveying his seated but taller subjects. "To the guests at our table, I say welcome to our house and welcome to Norway. *Skål.*" He sits, shrinking from the spotlight, before the first clink is heard.

Dagfinn does not seem happy with Thor's salutation. Knut also seems disturbed. "Family is also important, too," he acknowledges, raising his glass to Dagfinn's.

"To guests and to family, then. Great bells!" Dagfinn says.

"It is a good toast," Peter says, smiling to Sara. "In my country, it is customary to perform a dance to the host and his family to express great appreciation when one is given food for free."

Sara blows saliva from her lips. Amaryllis finds Gawne's chair and is up in his lap before Hannah can retrieve her. She turns toward Pharaoh with a scowl.

"It's no problem. She's a cool kid, and I think she likes me," Gawne reassures Hannah.

"Be careful with her. Don't give her any aquavit," Pharaoh warns. He wishes that Meg and the other members of their class could witness Gawne's transformation when he and Amaryllis are at play. Meg, especially, would marvel at the change.

Oobamcee has made no further reference to Meg's deportation, and Pharaoh hopes it is all a misunderstanding. He feels a hollow, anxious feeling in his stomach, however, that keeps him from asking Oobamcee if he has heard anything more about her situation.

Dagfinn turns down a Norwegian version of "The First Noel" as the African students, humming at first, form a circle behind their chairs and begin to chant and clap their hands in unison. Pharaoh finds their spontaneous performance humiliating. He slouches in his chair and feels Anna's hand travel to his groin. Everyone stares at the African students, whose chants and stomps have become louder and more energetic. Trine and Thor fidget in their seats, not because they are uncomfortable, but because they too would like to dance. Dagfinn smiles at them, then at Pharaoh, and moves his head and shoulders from side to side in search of a rhythm, hesitantly at first, as if balancing heavy headgear at a parade. He cups one palm in the other and applies it to his mouth like a harmonica. Inger Lise, too, in her trancelike state begins to sway even as she tries to locate Baby Thor to place in her lap and dance the way she sees Gawne doing with Amaryllis.

"They are very good," Hannah says, snapping her fingers as if she is at a concert. Lena is already punching the keypad on her cell phone. He can only guess at the messages she must be sending to friends. Since Pharaoh cannot turn his eyelids inside out like Peter, Dagfinn assumes there must be *something* he has in common with the African students. With a gesture of his head while still pretending to play the harmonica, he attempts to get Pharaoh to join the dervish spectacle, and Oobamcee seeing everyone's enthusiasm motions toward him to participate. His rare smile suggests it is simple, nothing to it.

Pharaoh is aghast and begins to shake his head. His frustration is interpreted as zealotry by Anna's kneading hand between his legs. He cannot stand their nonsense any longer. "Get your fucking hand off my dick, goddamn it!" It is enough to end the chant and return the African students to their seats.

"What the hell is wrong with you, Pharaoh? Was that really necessary? It was rude," Hannah announces. "You should apologize to your friends. No one had their hand on your dick." He does not think she is sincere. Anna pushes her chair back, as if she is about to leave, but instead bends and picks up Baby Thor, who is playing at her feet. He is not happy and looks like a cherubic invertebrate writhing in her hands.

"We have embarrassed you, Mr. USA. For that, we are sorry."

"No. It is I who must apologize," Pharaoh admits. "I am sorry for my outburst."

"Perhaps it is an early stage of Tourette's syndrome. It is common among you Americans," Sail says.

"I can assure you I do not have Tourette's syndrome. I am not sure what came over me, but I must apologize."

"No more apologies. We must eat so that Trine can bring dessert," Thor says.

Oobamcee is silent. Beads of sweat appear on his forehead and above the markings on his temple, but Pharaoh cannot tell if it is from their exotic dancing or simmering rage.

* * *

Anna and Dagfinn have left the table to argue, leaving their children exposed to the kind of scrutiny children are subjected to when adults understand the potential for disaster that can result from a contentious argument. Pharaoh can hear them in the kitchen, though it is Anna who does most of the arguing. Their argument seems familiar, not only to them, but to Dagfinn's family around the table. Pharaoh's name isn't mentioned once, nor does he hear any accusations by Dagfinn toward Anna. From what he can understand, however, it is the husband who is in trouble.

"That's none of your business!" Hannah whispers to him as he strains his ears to listen. "Quit being so nosy! Worry about your guests! I think you've made them angry." His African guests have begun another round of discussions that have already escalated into entertaining political discourse. He is concerned that their frequent squabbles may ineluctably support this family's belief that, like Buckwheat, it is in their nature to entertain.

Knut, swollen with pride at Peter's admission that he is attending the university to learn how to build bridges and dams for his country, sees that pride return and clip him in the face like an errant boomerang.

"You should not boast, comrade," Sail says. "You have come here to study old, outdated technology. People are not building dams for power anymore. It is ancient technology the West attempts to pass off on the Motherland, and they are succeeding because you are here. It is like watching elephants gallop after a football in India because it reminds people that someone else was there and considered the natives primitive. Are they building dams in the West? Of course not. Their energy is advanced, nuclear, yet they have no problems promoting old bridges and dams as advanced technology to Africa and India."

"And why are you here?" Peter asks.

"I am here because my country is bleeding. I am here to stop the blood."

"Yes, comrade, but your country bleeds from within. They are not superficial cuts or abrasions or the like. One should fix an internal wound from within, by operation if necessary. You cannot use the same methods to fix an external wound as you would for an internal wound. One cannot apply bandages or tourniquets when transplants are needed." Peter flashes his white teeth at his audience and, using the handle of his fork, scratches his head.

"The wounds, as you say, comrade, are inflicted by the West. To better understand my opponent, I must see what he sees, hear what he hears, and read what he reads. Only then will I be able to heal Nigeria."

"But you are only one man," Knut mumbles.

"Oh, but you are wrong. It is true that I am one man in your country, but multiplied by Nigeria's pain, I am a revolution."

Lena's phone interrupts the contemplative mood at the table with its musical chimes to Rosenborg's fight song. She bolts from her chair and launches into a conversation with the caller on the other end.

"Why don't you say something?" Hannah whispers.

"She is not my child. She can behave how she pleases. I have no say," Pharaoh says.

"Say something about Africa." Hannah smiles, but it is a disconcerting smile. It is the first time in their marriage that he feels she is ashamed of him. He does not care. He must call his sister. Perhaps Gwen in her callous but direct manner was right: His marriage to Hannah has been nothing more than bullshit on the sly.

"I don't know enough about their problems to play Mr. Buttinsky," he says. "It is too presumptuous. Maybe you would like to contribute to their discussion."

Hannah frowns and shakes her head in disbelief. She initiates a discussion with Inger Lise from across the table, occasionally glancing at her parents, trying to get them involved.

"I do not think Norway teaches old technology to Africans and Indians on purpose. Maybe you mean the US and the United

Kingdom. We are only a little land with less than five million people," Knut says, finally coming to his country's defense. "We are not the cause of your country's problems. If there are millions of poor people in India and Africa without electricity and roads, why should we not help? Is it not our duty to help?"

"You have no duty to Nigeria," Sail says. "Perhaps you have a duty to India, I do not know. But you have no duty to Nigeria."

"What my comrade means," Oobamcee begins, "is that countries, no matter how poor, are still sovereign nations, often with proud citizens. No nation enjoys being treated as a child or exploited as such under the guise of humanitarian aid, especially by countries, one can argue, with similar problems of their own. A bag of cornmeal here or a bag of grain there does not justify secondhand technology. We would prefer no technology."

"Maybe India appreciates our help," Hannah says, scraping her empty plate with the underside of her fork and licking the residue with the tip of her curled tongue. It is a habit she has acquired since returning home. Pharaoh has since seen many Norwegians clean their plate in a similar fashion, intent on never leaving food on their plate after a good meal. Pharaoh has warned her against teaching Amaryllis that custom.

"Perhaps they do. But again, they have their own problems to solve. If your husband lived in India today, you may have been set on fire if he was unsatisfied with his dowry. Your beautiful daughter can also be torched because of the devaluation of her sex in Indian society. Forgive me if this is unsettling, but I only speak the truth. The decision by the government of a particular country to accept humanitarian aid does not always bode well for its citizens. I am certain that India appreciates your country's aid when it tests nuclear missiles along its border with Pakistan."

"Saber-rattling," Pharaoh says.

"Exactly!" Oobamcee replies. "Your husband understands me well."

Hannah is livid. Her eyes blink repeatedly, and she turns deep red from her face down to her neck. She looks to Pharaoh as if she is on the verge of choking, but he decides to let her stew in her own brashness as punishment for entering a conflict she does not understand. Knut would like to speak but holds his tongue, clearly intimidated by Oobamcee and his knowledge of how Africa is perceived by the West. Hannah rises from her chair and begins to clear the table, collecting utensils first, then plates and glasses, then bowls, stacking them in the kitchen sink with sharp, loud clangs. Trine and Thor join Hannah in the kitchen. Their research has not prepared them for the African students.

Peter returns to Sail's accusation about outdated technology, and the conversation takes on a more nationalistic tone. They spar over which country is considered the best in Africa, oblivious to the fact that their bickering is incompatible with their earlier claims about a united Africa. Peter believes that Ghana is the best African nation. He considers Nkrumah, a former president, to be a visionary, and Rawlings, the current ruler, to be a statesman and a patriot.

"We are considered the star of black Africa," Peter says, securing the loosening bandage above his eye. "The international community looks to us to help solve Africa's disputes."

"They look to you because you are in debt," Sail says. "How can you say no when the IMF or the World Bank comes calling?"

Peter is offended by Sail's remark. He looks toward Oobamcee, who has increasingly become the mediator between the two, for support.

"It is time to end this discussion," Oobamcee acknowledges. "Perhaps another time and another place, comrades. As you say in America, we have been airing our soiled linen for all to see. Perhaps now we must hide it again." Oobamcee smiles broadly, but his comments have done little to assuage Peter, who turns away when he sees Sail fondle the amulet around his neck.

"You brothers make me wanna go to Africa." Gawne gives the African students a thumbs-up.

"You are welcome anywhere in Africa," Oobamcee says, but Peter and Sail remain silent. It is a deferential silence, one that neither man is about to concede to Gawne.

Amaryllis's elf outfit sags as she wiggles her way across the floor toward Pharaoh's chair. When she arrives, he picks her up and rewards her with hugs for her effort. Even with her snotty nose, she is truly the most beautiful person he has ever seen.

Dessert is a hurried affair; everyone is eager to receive presents and put the dinner behind them. It has begun to snow. As the fluffy flakes descend on footprints and lighted candles outside, Pharaoh compliments Trine on her dainty teacups and saucers, and the tiny silver spoons that he has difficulty getting his fingers to handle delicately. Then he excuses himself to call his sister in LA. Anna has returned to the table. Although she avoids eye contact, he sees that she has been crying. He hurries away before he is compelled to make another mistake.

When Gwen answers the phone, Pharaoh gets a distinct feeling that something is wrong.

"The pharmacy has been robbed again. They have ransacked the store and blown the vault. Someone's having a very merry Christmas with my morphine and codeine, and they've even taken my vials of cocaine, all my Schedule II drugs. The state is investigating. They think it's an inside job. It's possible I can lose my license."

He does not know what to say, although they are not really her drugs. A Christmas wish seems inappropriate, and he has had his fill of being insensitive. "Do they think it's you?"

"No, but I'm in charge. And the thieves took all the expensive stuff. I'm not worried, though. How's my baby?"

"I'm doing all right."

"I don't mean you."

"She's okay. A little ear infection."

"Figures. It's too cold for that child over there. I hope you're reminding her that she has family here, too."

"All the time," he says.

"How you doing?"

"Fine."

"Liar. You want me to send you some black people?"

"A bunch of them. They don't have to be good, just black and good to look at."

"I'm on my way, honey," Gwen laughs. "They got sunscreen over there for all them white people, or they all rubbing up on you?"

"It's winter, Gwen; they don't need sunscreen. How's the gardening?"

"Boy, I got flowers you won't believe."

"You should send me some pictures."

"You, too, of my baby. I already know what you two look like. You sure Amaryllis is all right?"

"Yup. She's just getting away from me a little; that's all."

"I could have told you that would happen way the hell over there, Pharaoh."

It is nice hearing her voice. He does not have to think hard to talk to her. He doesn't need to dissect her words. It is probably why he found Meg so refreshing. Pharaoh tells Gwen about the African students, and she accuses him of being as afraid of them as Hannah's parents. He dismisses her accusation, and she warns him that the next time he calls for a dose of wisdom, she will give him only two milligram's worth. It is all she thinks he can swallow.

Upstairs Gawne eyes Pharaoh suspiciously, looking for any indication that he may have gotten stoned without him. The women are seated on a couch in a corner of the living room. Hannah appears more composed after dessert, but Pharaoh knows how skilled she is at suppressing her anger toward him—until she finally explodes. Perry and Knut are whispering by a window. From their intent bodies, Pharaoh suspects that they are discussing the African students, perhaps formally registering their dissent.

"Gwen says Merry Christmas," Pharaoh announces, and then kisses Amaryllis, who is sitting on Trine's lap, on the cheek.

"How's your dad?" Hannah's tone is flat but stinging.

"Don't know. I didn't bother to ask, and Gwen didn't say."

"They have a different family than us," Trine comments. He is not sure what she means exactly but knows that it is meant as an insult. Hannah says something to Trine in Norwegian that Pharaoh cannot understand.

"Brother-in-law," Dagfinn calls, "you must join us. Leave the women and the children. We are men, brother-in-law." Dagfinn, Gawne, and the African students have not left their seats, though. Thor is noticeably absent.

"I have invited your comrades to an underground jazz festival after the holidays. You must come also. It is only by private invitation. No one knows where it will be until a few days before it begins. Do not disappoint us, brother-in-law. It is important."

"He's there!" Gawne says.

"I must check—"

"—with my sister? Your wife? I will take care of it, brother-in-law." Pharaoh, aware that his embarrassment might be apparent, attempts to disguise it with a smile and a light pat on Dagfinn's back. The gesture, uncommon between adult males in this culture, disarms Dagfinn. He awkwardly adjusts the jacket of his German suit with rigid tugs at the cuffs of both sleeves. He crosses a leg over his knee, admiring the glassy shine to his shoes, and then slides his foot from side to side beyond the edge of the tablecloth as if its reflection can reveal bombs hidden under the table.

"I must check my schedule," Pharaoh says.

"Oh, *unnskyld*. I forgot. You are a working man soon."

"You have gotten a job, Mr. USA?" Peter, inserting a toothpick between his white teeth, seems surprised by this new information. "Doing what in this country? Delivering newspapers?"

Pharaoh's explanation provokes accusations from Peter regarding a double standard in the preferential treatment of Americans over Africans.

"I am not rich, Peter. I need a job. You, on the other hand, are a rich man from Ghana, with gold chains and diamond rings. You do not need a job."

"It is all a show," Sail interjects, "to pretend to the West. He is far from being a rich man in his own country. It is he who has delivered newspapers."

Pharaoh is tired of hearing about the West.

A knock on a window and then a ringing bell temporarily halt any further bickering. Trine and Inger Lise lead the way toward the knock, preparing Amaryllis and Baby Thor for their first introduction to Santa Claus, who is short, stubby, and sunk in the snow up to his knees. Everyone gathers at the window to wave and to laugh at Thor's costume. Sara is outside waving and tossing snowballs at Santa's back. He waves toward the others for a moment, then turns to retaliate at Sara with a quick, overwhelming barrage of snowballs. While she takes cover in the snow, he reaches into his coat and pulls out a miniature Norwegian flag, uncovers his mouth by lowering his beard, and sticks the handle between clenched teeth. Everyone laughs, and Hannah takes pictures of the kind of Christmas celebration she had pined for while they lived in LA.

Inside, Pharaoh has finally found a moment to talk with Anna, who has been drowning her embarrassment in wine and sorrow. They are downstairs at the entrance to the basement apartment, close to the storage room where he was dispatched earlier. He had just returned from placing Amaryllis in her crib and had recognized her legs descending the stairs.

"Amaryllis is now sleeping?" she asks. She is visibly shaking, and her uneasiness bewilders Pharaoh after her earlier behavior. The hum from a freezer prevents them from whispering. He notices the dank smell of Anna's perfume.

"She is sleeping like a log, a small log, maybe a branch," he says. Anna does not laugh, and Pharaoh realizes that he is nervous, too.

"It was not nice. You hurt," she says. This time she does not avoid his eyes.

"I am sorry, but it was wrong. I should have said so earlier. It is probably my fault. It is I who must take the blame."

"We only talk," Anna says. When he looks puzzled, she makes a syntactical adjustment. "We talk only." She has interpreted his nervousness as fear that they may be caught alone. He can still hear a faint chant and distant footsteps upstairs. Perhaps it is his imagination.

"Your Christmas present to Amaryllis was very nice. I can see that it will be a favorite."

"It is special to her? It is an import."

"Yes, it is," he says. He was not sure how to react to a black doll, especially from Anna. But when he saw her delight in presenting it, along with Amaryllis's only fleeting absorption with it before reaching again for the bright wrapping paper, he had relaxed his concerns. He is certain Amaryllis has no intention of playing with the doll.

"You do not speak truth."

"I try to speak the truth," he says, unsure of her reference.

"You enjoy it. It does not lie."

"Well." Pharaoh does not know how to proceed, and she does not allow him to.

"I love you," Anna says. He is certain that it is not what she has meant to say.

Pharaoh tries to assure her that she is overstating things, that she will feel differently in a few days.

"I will prove it. I will do anything. I will learn English."

"I like you also, Anna, and so does Amaryllis. Hannah likes you also," he says, struggling.

"I do not want her to," Anna replies immediately. "I want you to."
"I do."

"You must learn to love." She nervously fondles the strands of her hair. She reaches up and caresses the side of his face with the back of her knuckles, as if he were a pet. Her fingers feel suddenly damp, like plump earthworms slithering down his cheek. He responds to her touch by covering her hand with his own and gently removing it. As he does this, their fingers become entangled. She finds his other hand and places it on the front of her skirt between her legs.

"I do not lie," she whispers, squeezing his fingers in her clasp. She leans forward and strains toward his mouth.

Pharaoh isn't thinking of Hannah or Amaryllis as he hesitates and turns away. It is the ridiculous dance upstairs that saves him. He can still hear their chanting echoing in his head. Perhaps there is something to Gwen's claim that he is afraid of the African students. They are men with strong passions, and their passions, when provoked, fester into different forms. It is their passion that intimidates him. Gwen characterizes Africans as greedy. It is this greed by her people, she believes, which began the slave trade and decimated Africa's culture, resources, and people, for little more than brandy, tobacco, and guns. And it is the lingering traces of this passion and greed that force her to work today behind bars and bulletproof glass in her pharmacy.

Anna's meeting at his mouth becomes a torrid plunge of her tongue. Her nervousness has disappeared. She is soft against his hand and the pressure she maintains as she guides his movements between her legs results in groans he expects immediately before an orgasm, and not at a touch. He does not understand her desire. Her lips are warm and are not lips that belong to someone who is simply trying him out. He can feel her moisten gradually and relax her weight on his hand as she guides his fingers faster and deeper into the cloth. He does not think she needs his hand, really, and the thought elicits a chuckle from inside his throat that Anna responds to by biting his tongue. She is right. It does not lie, but he must not continue. It is what he tells himself, wills himself to do, even as her body continues to thresh against his hand. She removes her mouth from his and buries her face in his chest, stifling her convulsive groans while he makes a ridiculous plea, a faint plea for them to stop, even as he pulls her toward him for balance. He can no longer smell her perfume with his face covering her hair. Instead he smells sweat and must, and it keeps Pharaoh aroused. Anna, as if suddenly aware of him leaning against her, looks down at his erection, an intumescent bulge, as he awaits an opportunity to deflate his embarrassed ego.

"You touch my pussy. It is very okay to love," Anna whispers and smiles again, rubbing the side of his face with the back of her knuckles. She unzips his pants, maneuvering her hand past his cotton shorts and shirttail, until he feels her touch him. She closes her eyes, removes her hand, and licks the inside of her palm for him to see. She closes the zipper.

"You touch my pussy. It is very okay to love." She straightens her clothes before beginning her hurried climb up the stairs. Pharaoh follows her as if he is following her scent, but he can no longer smell her perfume.

As he ducks into the hallway lavatory, Pharaoh wonders what his sister would think of the mess that is brewing in his life. There is no more chanting, but Bruce Springsteen's rendition of "Santa Claus Is Coming to Town," accompanied by Dagfinn's mournful vocals, can be heard coming from the living room. No doubt, Gwen would remind him of her belief that there is no gray where race and sex are concerned. Then she would accuse him of committing more bullshit on the sly.

In college Gwen had gone through an identity crisis, first becoming a Rastafarian, then a devout Christian, and finally abandoning her religious beliefs to become an avid gardener. The laws of gravity, she had explained, couldn't hold up Jesus pinned to the cross with three nails. And churches in LA are all about money and politics, she claimed, even if you weren't supposed to mix the two.

"There were about three hundred and eighteen different gods, the last time I checked. Somebody is praying to the right one, but it is definitely not you people, even though you're the most revered worshippers around. I don't see how you people can cause so much ruckus during the week and then drop on your knees on Sundays." The words had been addressed to Pharaoh, who had never been to church or to Sunday school in LA. But that doesn't matter to Gwen when she is in one of her moods. She always calls it as she sees it.

Pharaoh flushes the toilet and washes his hands. The music has stopped, and he can hear raised voices in another discussion, as well as Thor's ringing bell outside, until these sounds are drowned out by the tones of Earth, Wind & Fire's "After the Love Has Gone." Only Dagfinn would make such a selection on Christmas Eve.

"I believe your brother-in-law is drunk," Sail says outside the lavatory.

"Which brother-in-law?"

"The one who does not like us," Sail says, hurrying in and shutting the door. But Pharaoh is more concerned about Hannah. It is at his own peril that he enters the living room.

"It's like listening to a black person with a British accent."

"Motherfucker, what's wrong with how I talk?"

"You sound like Vanilla Ice. That's what's wrong with how you talk," Perry says. "A fricking wannabe!"

"Some people would call it integration," Pharaoh says, surprised at Perry's disparaging comparison to a British accent.

"Hell, as long as the ladies don't mind."

"Grow up, Señor Gawne! Is that all you're worried about?"

"Hell yeah! We all know what you're worried about. And you're a beaner, motherfucker! You're not from Spain!"

"What's that supposed to mean?"

"Man, I'm down with the ladies!" Gawne grabs his groin with two hands.

Perry looks at Pharaoh, then turns away sheepishly. Pharaoh displays no remorse for Perry's predicament.

"Simply say what's on your mind, Señor Gawne."

"You a homo?" There is a sudden uncertainty in his tone.

"I am as straight as your little dick," Perry says. "However, you, Señor Gawne, sound like a man who is about to come out."

"Sure you right!"

"See? What the hell does that mean? Why can't you speak like a normal person? You hear Pharaoh talking like he's from the Bronx?"

"No, no, homey. You ain't squirming your way out of this one, man. We're waitin' for an answer. We can see right through your bullshit." Gawne curls the tips of his thumbs and indexes together and covers each eye, peering through the holes in his fingers at Perry as if he were using opera glasses.

"You Americans are funny people. I do not understand your interest in sex in your movies, where you show the world what you do in your bedrooms and your desire to keep it hidden from your friends," Knut says.

"Well, it's no one's business, really. We value our privacy. It's in our constitution," Pharaoh says, glancing at the women sipping coffee and Kahlúa as they make notes of who gave them presents.

"Yeah. It's not like we're in the jungle. We're civilized!" Gawne snaps.

"What do you know about the jungle? It is not so bad living in the jungle. Perhaps if you lived there, you would not be concerned about your friend's sexuality. He might be concerned with yours." Oobamcee smiles listlessly at Gawne, who seems confused about the insult.

"Yeah? Well, I can't survive on birds and chimpanzees and shit, man. Eating a chimp is like eating your own brother, holmes."

"Ah, yes. But some of us prefer a European diet," Oobamcee says, raising his brow at Hannah. This time, Pharaoh believes that both he and Gawne have been insulted. Peter removes his toothpick and laughs as he nods at Pharaoh.

"Mr. USA, it is clever how our jungle has come up again and again among the civilized. Very clever." Peter continues laughing.

"I didn't mean you fellas." It is the first time Pharaoh has seen Gawne back down with anyone.

"It is okay. We are proud of our jungles. It is part of our soil in Africa and it has seeped into our culture. We do not try to escape it, even when we are not there. The jungle to us is a great place to build noble warriors. It is truly difficult for you to understand if you have not experienced a civil war in our environment. It is not unusual, my friends, to eat insects, the barks of trees, flowers, cloth, even dirt, during war. Dogs and rats are delicacies when roasted. But birds are better eaten fresh, the way fish is eaten in Asian countries. Ask your Vietnam vets. They ate both in your war. One must eat to stay alive. I have proudly eaten the afterbirths of future warriors. I have eaten blood omelettes when there was nothing else to eat. Do you know how that tastes? Ask the Jews in your country. It is what some ate under Hitler. We have no weight problems where I come from. I have never seen an overweight African, nor an overweight Jew for that matter."

Like a vampire, Oobamcee's words have sucked the blood from the pale faces in the room. Pharaoh would not be surprised to learn that the eviscerated parts of animals are eaten or that Oobamcee has also eaten bats.

Inger Lise snuggles Baby Thor, asleep in her lap, closer to her bruised breasts. Meanwhile, Dagfinn, who has been singing along with Earth, Wind & Fire, believes that it is his singing that has soothed Baby Thor to sleep.

"You even eat the exotic ones, the exotic species of birds in your country?" It is difficult to tell whether Perry is genuinely interested or just trying to divert the conversation away from his sexuality.

"One does not have the luxury of being a vegetarian in times of war. Who has heard of a warrior that is so concerned about his diet that he refuses to eat what he must to continue to fight? It is absurd. I am no preservationist. The more exotic they are, the better they taste."

"I would think that self-preservation ought to be a priority among warriors," Pharaoh says. "Are you not encouraging the spread of diseases and viruses that can lead to dangerous epidemics for your people, including your warriors? Are warriors that careless and irresponsible?"

"An excellent question, comrade. Perhaps you speak secretly of AIDS and Ebola that frighten the West, and with good reason. You are a military man. Diseases and viruses can often be controlled. And often what your Western researchers learn about our diseases and viruses is never entirely complete. Let us just say that these are our secret weapons. They are our weapons of mass destruction. Think what can happen if it is introduced into a population like China's."

"Lotta Chinese food," Gawne snortles, but his attempted interruption goes ignored.

"I have seen your wars on CNN. Your weapons are impressive. They strike targets, and everything is no more when I turn off my television. When I turn it on again, you are on your way home. But our weapons take their time to destroy and can inflict fear and pain for a lifetime. They can strike anywhere. We do not need satellites, just people with passports. There is no defense if we wish there to be none, comrade. Like your weapons, ours occasionally err and strike innocent civilians. It is unfortunate, but we are never careless and irresponsible. In any battle there are always collateral damages and necessary casualties of war."

Perry shakes his head. "Hitler was a vegetarian. He would never eat exotic birds."

"People eat eggs, don't they? Chicken, turkey, even ostrich, motherfucker. Ostrich!" Gawne says, lifting his hand above his head to emphasize the bird's height. "What's the big deal?"

"Then, comrade, as vegetarians you and Hitler share something in common? Maybe that is not all you share. Maybe you both also have similar tattoos?" Oobamcee raises his brow but does not laugh. Peter does.

"I am happy to be in Norway. Here we have no civil wars, unless you count the Swedes," Knut says, his swollen bottom lip filled with snuff. "We are a little land and celebrate peace here. That is why we have the Nobel Prize for Peace."

"Maybe one day," Oobamcee says, clasping his hands.

"It is not for selfish warriors," Knut says proudly, as if it is his prize to award, "or for people who fight wars. It is not to encourage civil wars or any kind of war. It is to encourage sacrifices toward peace, especially if the sacrifice is war."

"Ah, yes. Perhaps it is a tradition among Scandinavians to make sacrifices. I have learned about your Odin who sacrificed his eye for wisdom. He is the Mighty Thor in American comic books in my country, the god of thunder with a hammer, but he has no home with the living. His home is with the dead. Tell me the wisdom in that. We do not deal in myths and fairytales when land is at stake. In my country, we shall never sacrifice our territory. Tell me, comrade, do you have warplanes? Why? Why are your men required to join the military? Will you go to war if your country is invaded by another?"

"We will defend ourselves, of course, but we will negotiate peacefully," Knut admits.

"Then, my friend, I do not think you are a true viking."

Knut clenches his teeth, then spits in an empty coffee cup on the table. It is not a clean spit and some of the spittle attaches itself to his brown tie. He rubs it away quickly, trying both to prevent a permanent stain and to keep others from noticing.

"Fire in the hole!" Perry mutters.

"Speaking of holes," Gawne says, "you best stay the fuck away from mine. I ain't from no land down under; so go get your Vegemite sandwich somewhere else."

Pharaoh and Perry laugh at him cautiously. Knut, still rubbing on his tie, stands and pushes his chair away from the table, then slaps his leg and beckons to Inger Lise as if she is a dog. She stirs and rocks her bottom on the cushion from side to side, as if it is a heavy carcass. The motion carries her closer to the edge of the couch. As she attempts to rise with Baby Thor still asleep in her arms, she stumbles forward in a fall. Peter rises quickly from his chair, catching them upright before there is cause for alarm or injury to Baby Thor. His swift and agile movements surprise Pharaoh, who becomes more skeptical about Peter's claim that he had been ambushed.

"I have got you and the baby, madam. It is safe," Peter says, grinning.

"They are okay. She is used to falling," Knut says, shuffling them out of Peter's embrace.

Oobamcee glances at Peter approvingly. "It is the African way," he says to keep Peter's actions honorable. "We must always look after a mother. They bare us warriors."

It occurs to Pharaoh that Oobamcee is apologizing for Peter's actions, not because it is the African way but because he does not believe Inger Lise is worth protecting. Her son is clearly no warrior.

Trine rushes forward in a show of false hospitality, with offers of more coffee, cake, and ice cream that no one accepts. Dagfinn requests more cognac and encourages the men to join him. He announces that he would like to see more dancing from the African students and promises to join them. Trine implores Knut to stay, at least until Thor returns, but he is already dusting snow from Baby Thor's stroller for their departure. Inger Lise steps outside without a coat, despite everyone's protests, and hustles to catch Knut, determined, it seems, to prove to everyone that she is willing to accept the blame for her coat going up in flames. Pharaoh thinks she has been underestimated. He has already seen how much she can drink and concludes that she must also have a high tolerance for pain. Her casual trudging in the frozen snow establishes for everyone that perhaps she is the true viking in her family.

"It is just as well. We must leave also. We have responsibilities at home, and it is not brave or wise to leave mothers and children at home alone in another man's country," Oobamcee says. "You are all invited to my home. We must return the warm greeting we have received in your house. We will have hearty meals and continue our discussions if you wish. Mothers are also delightful cooks."

"Man, I ain't down for no birds," Gawne whispers behind Pharaoh. "Think I'll pass on that invite, homey."

"Remember our underground jazz festival after the holidays. It is very important," Dagfinn says to each man as he shakes his hand. His invitation becomes part of a bargain when he also invites them to go skiing with a promise to teach them how to ski. Peter winces, as if the mention of skis has elicited a painful memory.

"I can see one of you do not like to ski," Dagfinn observes. "It is not for everyone."

"We are not comfortable on skis," Oobamcee says, putting on his coat. "But I agree with you, comrade, because here it is also like jazz. Jazz is not for everyone."

"I will walk them out to the trolley," Pharaoh says to Hannah, who is comforting Trine. Her son's abrupt departure has left her wandering about the kitchen in search of more treats for her American guests, whom she has convinced to stay.

"We cannot leave without my errant disciple, comrade," Oobamcee says, collecting Sail's overcoat. "Where is he?"

"He is in here," Pharaoh says, pointing to the lavatory. "He is a disciple who uses a lavatory?"

"You do not expect him to shit in a corner, do you?"

"I suppose not. It was only a joke."

"Ah, yes. Americans laugh at everything." Oobamcee raps his knuckles on the door. "It is time, comrade. He is my best disciple."

"And what does a disciple do?" Pharaoh regrets his question immediately. It was not a safe inquiry to make.

"Whatever he is told," Oobamcee says.

"Then he is your Man Friday."

"Ah, yes. It is true. You are a reading man. But my disciple is not in the pages of a book. He is real, comrade."

"Yes, I know," Pharaoh says. "He is taking a shit."

"If we are to continue to be friends. I would prefer that you do not insult me in front of my family or friends," Pharaoh says as they await the trolley's arrival. He has noticed that the Africans, despite their emphasis on unity, can be extremely divisive. On the distance to the trolley, Sail walks ahead while Peter maintains his steps a few paces behind. As Oobamcee and Pharaoh find shelter from the falling snow in a booth, Sail and Peter continue to stand apart in the snow as if they are proud members of different armies.

"That is fair, comrade. But I do not think you know them as well as you should know a family. Perhaps now you do. They still believe we are rustic people who resemble bush pigs, wear leaves as loincloths, and swing from vines as your movies show."

"Well, your portrait of warriors certainly did not help."

"But it is an accurate picture, comrade. What I have seen in movies has not been the truth about Africa. But it is what people here believe."

Oobamcee's accusation immediately places Pharaoh on the defensive. "Well, I don't think Hannah and her family believe it, and I have known them for a long time."

"You are not certain of that. But I am. It is because you are an American. You live in a rich country, comrade, where even your local governments have more power than humanitarian organizations or the Red Cross. It is not that way in our country. They tell our presidents what to do. Once they have arrived it is difficult to get them to leave, the women especially. They enter our countries, establishing churches, safe houses, and schools for our children because they think we are too poor and primitive to do it ourselves. And when it is time for them to retire in their country, they come back to us, without their uniforms with red crosses or flags, in short-sleeves showing loose flesh, and they settle in villas and resorts along our beaches. Some are in their seventies, but we can see them walking along the beaches with our little black boys, as young as fourteen or fifteen, who do not resemble bush pigs to them then. And the women are so in love, and the boys, too, barefoot and shirtless, are also in love with these grandmothers who will never fall in love with white boys or black boys in their own countries."

"These grandmothers, are they Norwegians?"

"Some of them. They are always offering our children their flags. So you see, I know about them. You, too, must be careful, comrade. Your sister-in-law sweats every time you are near. It leaves a smell she believes she can hide with perfume, but I can smell it. She does not wear a Red Cross or work for a humanitarian organization yet, but she has the signs. You should be very careful."

Pharaoh is not in the mood for advice. "I am married to her husband's sister. I am not foolish. I believe she has problems even I cannot solve."

"Perhaps you have already solved them," Oobamcee says, raising one brow.

"Yes, perhaps. It is one of the hazards of having one wife."

"Ah, yes. I see. But we have other matters we must discuss. Your friend, Meg."

"It would seem that she is your friend, too."

"Ah, yes. You are wondering how I know. It is by chance only. I know a comrade who works in the police building. It is his information, not mine. According to Norwegian law, you must declare yourself to the police if you are a visitor for more than three months. Apparently she did not. Then she must leave and return again to get a new stamp."

"But she is a student."

"She did not come here as a student. She came to travel and then decided to stay. They are very strict here. They do not let many people into their country, but she will be back. She will have no problems." The rumble from the oncoming trolley is felt underfoot before it is seen or heard from a distance. The car is well-lighted and Pharaoh can see stoic passengers shuffling through the aisles as it approaches, acting as if they are on tranquilizers.

"And the other matter?"

"Ah, yes. You do not believe my disciple. You think he is a villain. He is an honest man, comrade. Nothing will come back to you. I see our train is approaching, so we must go. But you are still welcome in my home even if the others do not come," Oobamcee says, offering a handshake as they emerge from the booth. Pharaoh thanks Peter and Sail for coming and wishes them a Merry Christmas. But his farewell is premature. The conductor draws a curtain around himself as the trolley gathers speed and rumbles by on its frozen rails, leaving a trail of blue electrical sparks as it disappears along the track toward the city. Pharaoh offers to drive them home, but Oobamcee refuses his offer, insisting that he will walk instead. The Africans begin their walk, three black figures in the snow making their separate paths along the tracks, leaving Pharaoh standing alone and humiliated as he stares toward the black dense forest.

"What's happening, homey? Look like you seen the gimp. You didn't bite down on no bird out there, did you?" Gawne and Perry are outside drinking cognacs and warming themselves around one of Thor's lighted candles. They have reached some kind of understanding and are friends again, perhaps even more than friends. Pharaoh does not care.

"Your mother-in-law is a wonderful host, but the music has driven us outside," Perry says.

"Yeah. We can only take so much Christmas music, even at Christmas."

Pharaoh barely nods then takes a swig of Gawne's cognac.

"You all right?" Gawne asks.

"I'm fine." But he is not fine. He begins to understand Perry's earlier frustration. At what stage does society begin its caricature of one culture by another? Perhaps it begins very early. Perhaps for Gawne it began after bitter feelings for his ex-girlfriend, the one whose Mexican husband does not know that she is a whore. It is time for Gawne to grow up.

"Which side you sip from?" Gawne's deprecating smile follows his stare as Pharaoh unzips himself, pulls out his dick, and pees on the candle, leaving an acrid smell, the wick now submerged in a buoyant mixture of wax, melting snow, and urine.

"How many times do you pull that thing out?" Perry says, clearly surprised.

"I don't know. How many times do you squat? Let me have another sip," he says, and then slides his tongue around the edge of the empty glass before returning it to Gawne. Gawne grins and then frowns.

"Good thing you're my bitch, holmes."

Perry stares at them as if they are children. "And what do you want to be when you grow up, son?" he asks Pharaoh.

"That's easy," he quips. "An American."

"You have to set your goals higher, son. Your friend won't have to worry, though. He will never grow up." Perry grins.

"Man, fuck you, bitch!"

"So what's the verdict? You hear anything from them?"

"We don't have anything to worry about."

"Sure you right! I told you," Gawne says, sticking an index finger in Perry's face.

"You sure? Did he say it wasn't the same guy?"

"He didn't have to. I believe him. He doesn't lie," Pharaoh announces sharply.

"Hell, I won't go that far, holmes. Those boys are hiding something. You seen all that jewelry on Peter? They ain't starving and they ain't poor, if you ask me."

Perry nods his agreement. "I'd like to be sure," he says. "Only way to do that is to come forward. Tell the police that they assaulted Peter and we came to his rescue. That would clear our names, and if they're lying, then that's their problem."

"You mean like self-defense?" Gawne says.

"Exactly!"

"I'd prefer you didn't do that," Pharaoh says.

"Boy, you definitely ain't from the hood. I'ma have to school ya. You don't rat on a brother, man."

"I am a beaner, remember? They are not my brothers. They are not your brothers either. And this isn't high school. You don't have to school me on anything unless you're more knowledgeable about the Pythagorean theorem than I am." Perry grins mockingly at Gawne.

"Bitch! Don't let me get started on you again."

"It's getting late," Pharaoh says, "and cold. I should go inside."

They look at each other, sensing something has changed among them. Pharaoh closes his eyes, opening his mouth wide as if to scream, but only inhales cold air. When he opens them again, he realizes that there is no one to whom he can confide about what he is at a loss to explain and still cannot understand. He thinks of Amaryllis. He does not want this society to have her. It does not deserve her. It has not paid its dues. He will talk to Hannah about moving. He does not wish to grow old in a country that used to cast its infirm citizens from cliffs to get them to heaven. Such acts are now celebrated as fantasies and fairytales in bedtime stories, not condemned as the behavior of fanatics. He has heard Hannah reading them to Amaryllis, who does not seem all that interested in whether three princesses outwitted three Trolls on three successive Thursdays. Everything occurs in threes. Perhaps he should await a third sign.

"How about something for the road, man? Let's see if that pipe works."

"Not tonight," he says, and turns to go inside.

Pharaoh enters to whispers and hushed voices, with Hannah as the ringleader. Trine clutches a photo album to her chest, and Hannah gently coaxes her to release it. Pharaoh can smell Anna's perfume. He tries to steer away from them, and then hears Hannah's voice directed toward him.

"My mother wants to know if you have seen her camera. It has been stolen." Trine points to a spot where she is certain, according to Hannah, she had left it.

"Really. Perhaps she has misplaced it somewhere."

"No, she hasn't. We've looked everywhere."

"Well, I have no idea where it is, Hannah."

"Maybe you should ask your friends."

"How would they know?"

"Maybe one of them borrowed it."

"They're about to leave. You'd better hurry. You're right. One of them probably borrowed it," he says upon reflection.

"Not them," Hannah says, as Perry and Gawne enter behind him. "They've been here the whole time."

"Ah, yes. I see," he says, smiling to hear himself use Oobamcee's phrase.

Hannah immediately rushes at him and pushes him into a corner. Pharaoh looks past her to Anna, still seated on the couch. "You just fucking sat there and agreed with them!" she says between clenched teeth. "Don't ever do that to me again, especially in front of my family."

"They were guests. I was being polite."

"Like hell!" she says, glaring at him.

He believes that her reaction has been rehearsed and is now on display for Trine's benefit. "You shouldn't need me to support your argument, if it can't support itself."

"It's not my argument I wanted you to support. It's me! It's us!"

"Hannah, his discussion had nothing to do with you or us. What makes you think it did? It was not a personal discussion. It was a political one."

"I know that," she says, still hurt. He doubts that she can explain exactly why she is hurt. "I'm not stupid!"

"I'm not saying that you're stupid, Hannah. Just that sometimes you tend to take matters personally, even though they have nothing to do with you."

"And it wasn't personal for you? You made it personal when you sat there and agreed with them. You took their side. I'm not an idiot. I saw what was happening."

"There was no side to take, Hannah! Just let it go."

"Like hell! And eating animals? At the dinner table? Disgusting! After we fed them? Not you guys," Hannah says, looking past him to Perry and Gawne, who by now are looking for an opportunity to escape.

"I can pay for what they ate, if you like."

Hannah blinks and rocks backward as if she has been pushed. Pharaoh can feel a slight heat in his chest from the sips of cognac. Or perhaps it is anger.

"Excuse me?"

"I said I can pay for what they ate."

His insolence stuns Hannah, who turns to look at her audience. "I heard you! I just can't believe what I heard."

"I can repeat it if you like."

"You're beginning to act just like them. Did they place you under their spell, or is it some black thing that we can't understand? Is that the reason?"

"Hardly."

"My mother thinks it is."

"And what do you think?"

"It must be. I've never seen you act this way before. They're poisoning your mind."

"Is that what your mother thinks?"

"No. It's what I see happening. They're angry niggers, and they're turning you into one. I don't like it."

"Are you sure it's them?"

"Oh, so you agree that it's happening? And who else can it be?"

"Well, it's not them."

"They're not welcome here ever again," she says. "And I hope they hurry up and get out of my country!"

"You didn't think they were angry and disgusting when you were snapping your fingers to their dancing earlier."

"That was different. They are not welcome here," she repeats.

"You should tell them, then, Hannah."

"I don't have to. You're the one I am telling. Why do you always have to be around people like them?"

Pharaoh wonders why her opinions about his friends in LA are only surfacing now that he and Hannah are tucked away in her native land. He feels suddenly betrayed and angry. They stare at each other like lucid opponents before a match, looking for weaknesses, anticipating strategies, until Thor enters, ringing his bell and stamping out snow from his boots.

"I want my mother's camera back," she whispers threateningly.

"I can buy her a new one, if you want."

Thor's presence and Hannah's acknowledgement of it further infuriate Pharaoh. Anna smiles at him from the couch, and he notices an expression of awe on Trine's face. She is impressed with either her daughter's ability to argue in English or with the obdurate stance that she has taken against her American husband. She glares at him, as if attempting to continue what Hannah has begun, and he sees, though only for a second, a glimmer of something in her eyes. He can't believe he hasn't seen it before now. It is a look of resignation, tinged with fear. It is all he needs.

Perry and Gawne say their goodbyes, surprisingly receiving hugs from Trine and Hannah and handshakes from Thor. For a moment, the jovial spirit of the season is rekindled. Dagfinn is nowhere to be found, but Anna offers his goodbyes as well. He has gone in search of Sara, who has a neighborhood boyfriend.

"I apologize for my wife's behavior," Pharaoh says when they are outside, but neither of the men seem to think that her behavior has been unusual. Gawne turns up his collar, stuffs both hands in his sagging pockets, and rolls his shoulders forward. Perry looks at Pharaoh sheepishly. His look reminds Pharaoh of the look he had once seen on the face of a black boy who had been caught by his mother lifting up the skirt of a female mannequin in a department store.

"Hell, you got a cute kid, man, but I ain't never getting married," Gawne says.

"Me neither," Perry agrees.

"Yours ain't legal no way."

"Talk to the fucking hand!" Perry says, raising an open palm in Gawne's face. They laugh and hurry to catch the approaching trolley.

"Be cool!" Gawne shouts. Pharaoh waves, and then watches as they sprint away. He is not concerned that the trolley will fail to stop as they disappear around a bend. He hears the trolley screech to a halt and its hydraulic doors disengage.

Pharaoh tries to call Clint and Tim in LA to get redemptive therapy for his self-imposed isolation, but there is no answer. He checks on Amaryllis, then sits down to write his friends serious letters with texts that end up reminding him of Hallmark cards. He contemplates leaving to send them emails from the university, believing that his catharsis will be more immediate, but he is interrupted by Hannah's entrance into the living room. She is drunk and engorged with wildness. She brushes aside the pad and straddles his thighs shamelessly, sliding back and forth on him as if she is on a banana bike seat. She forces her tongue into his mouth.

"Take off your pants. I am ovulating." Swaying as if she is not quite sure of her balance, Hannah sticks both hands in the elastic band of her slacks and cups her abdomen like an expectant mother feeling for a baby's kick. It is meant to get him aroused, but instead it causes her to tilt too quickly to one side and fall against a lamp with a loud crash. He cannot react in time to prevent her fall or save the lamp. It is a pathetic display and conjures up images of Hannah's departed sister. She remains on the carpet, laughing perversely, before rising in a stoop.

"You still love me?"

"Not when you're this drunk," he says.

"Jeg elsker deg," she says.

"You're too drunk, Hannah."

"I am supposed to be drunk on Christmas Eve! Let's go into the bedroom."

"Be quiet or you'll wake Amaryllis."

"I'll be quiet once we're inside. I promise."

He tries prodding her to explain their earlier argument, to get more insight into her comments about his friends in LA. Often, in this state, her tongue can be a mirror to her mind. But she has no time to answer questions, especially when her ovulating window is about to close.

Hannah collapses on top of him, and her warm, stale breath tickles his ear and neck as she enjoys her orgasm. He is still erect but cannot bring himself to ejaculate into her vagina. She belches as if she has just been fed. He smells the rancid odor from the Kahlúa and hears her swallow whatever she has regurgitated. Her white panties lie discarded at his feet, and he can see a discolored streak that begins at the crotch and ends at the seat. Her breasts and soft stomach blanket his. Pharaoh caresses her back and massages her wide behind. He tries to penetrate her further by lifting and releasing her groin like a tractable device, but his erection abandons her vagina like a slippery harpoon. Quickly he rolls her off and places a pillow under her head. He straddles her breasts and tries to place his limp erection in her mouth, but it is no use. She is fast asleep. He tosses the blanket over her and listens to her idling snore. Her toes protrude from the broken saddle stitches at the bottom of the blanket. It is just like her to sleep soundly after an argument of such proportion. He remains wide awake, listening to the discordant sounds of winter birds that resemble penguins outside of his window and thinking of Meg and Anna and warriors and roasted penguins. He does not fall asleep until dawn.

Tomorrow will be a better day for Hannah, but not for him. Their arguments are rare but usually intense. It is a cycle of anger, fatigue, and resolution after a burlesque performance. This time, however, Pharaoh experiences an epiphany. He realizes that their sex afterward is actually an extension of the same argument. It is Hannah's humiliating way to satisfy her need for his virility, as well as her need to control the final outcome. He resents her for it, and it is becoming increasingly difficult for him to offer her his sperm.

CHAPTER 15

THE RELATIONSHIP BETWEEN Pharaoh and Hannah's parents goes quickly south. Like his wife, Thor is no longer objective or diplomatic. He no longer speaks with pride about his country to Pharaoh. He looks to Pharaoh like a confused amphibian, especially when Trine is in the room. He no longer volunteers his services regularly but continues to clear a flat path around the house after heavy snow. Thor and Trine pace the path on occasion, as if they are inspecting the pitch after a cricket match, and Pharaoh tells Hannah that he will no longer shovel their snow. He keeps only the entrance to the apartment clear and digs the SHO out as often as he has to.

A few days before New Year's Eve, a strange event occurs that is baffling to everyone except Pharaoh, and does nothing to reduce his alienation from this family. Summoned from his bed by Thor, he grabs an apple as a substitute for brushing his teeth, leaving Amaryllis asleep in her crib, and follows his father-in-law and his flashlight into the early morning darkness toward his garage. Trine stands with her back toward the street, staring into the garage with disbelief at Stig, the coughing affenpinscher, who has returned to the garage like a homing pigeon. The dog is thin, haggard, and scared, but there is no mistaking its identity. Thor's anger is visible.

His invectives and vituperative gestures bounce off Pharaoh like rubber arrows. Trine is distraught as Stig approaches her playfully. She points accusingly at Pharaoh, as if he is responsible for reincarnating Kjersti from the dead. Stig's excitement at returning home has caused him to produce round black droppings the size of small kumquats scattered in corners of the garage. Trine grabs a trowel, scoops up sand from a nearby wheelbarrow, and dusts Stig's droppings as if she is sprinkling sand on a kill to cast off spirits or to prevent them from arriving in the first place. Her manner suggests that it is already too late. The dog whimpers in the corner.

"*Du er en svarting!* You are a black devil! This dog is not dead! It is a terrible, terrible thing!"

"Take it easy," Hannah whispers, then turns to Pharaoh. "Never mind him. He is only upset. You must understand that this is a shock to them."

"Tell him that I am not here to do his bidding. He is not my father. If he wants the stupid dog dead, let him take it to the vet himself or kill it here. It means nothing to me where he does it."

Hannah looks sharply at him, and then thinks of some other excuse to tell. "I thought you took him to the fucking animal clinic," she says, puzzled. She is in a knee-length windbreaker, pajamas, and boots, still disoriented from Thor's frantic pounding on the front door. Pharaoh is in a sweater and shorts, sockless in his unlaced Caterpillars.

"I changed my mind. It was not fair to put a dog to sleep under those circumstances. Stig was not responsible for Kjersti's suicide."

"What have you done with the money? You have taken the money? You have robbed us? We shall call the police." Listening to Thor's tirade, Pharaoh can feel his toes curl into fists in his Caterpillars. He turns to leave and continues eating his apple. It is too early for him to unscramble Norwegian tantrums.

"Do not leave, black devil, or I will get my pistol!"

"Stop that, Pappa!"

Pharaoh stops and turns to see Hannah attempting to block her father's advance.

"Leave him alone. Let him come," Pharaoh says, and begins to retrace his steps in the snow. He does not understand what is happening between him and this family, but he knows that whatever it is, it is already too late.

Trine sees Pharaoh approaching and yells, *"Nei! Nei!"*

He stops and tosses the apple in the snow but cannot continue on. He savors the last bite while he studies Hannah and her parents. They look on expectantly, waiting for him to speak, but instead, he closes his mouth, lowers his jaw, and, with the tip of his tongue, cleans the surface of his molars before turning to go check on his daughter.

Amaryllis is still asleep in her crib. She is propped awkwardly on her elbows and knees. Pharaoh is tempted to rouse her to make her more comfortable but decides not to interrupt her sleep. He cannot picture himself without her nearby. He hovers around her crib observing her from different angles. Her hair has gotten darker and softer, and for a moment he is frightened at the prospect of not seeing it grow into various shades. Thor's threat hovers in the back of his mind, but for Amaryllis's sake, he cannot take it seriously. He has caught her more than once chewing on the laces of his Caterpillars. He does not want her waking up one day to just his boots and old pictures. His home has become hostile territory, and he is concerned for her safety. He considers raiding Amaryllis's war chest and returning to LA. But Pharaoh does not want to leave anyone, especially not his daughter, with the image of a horse returning from a battlefield without its rider. He is no fallen soldier.

He does not regret his compassion toward the dog. Thor and Trine's odiousness toward both him and the animal is simply misplaced guilt. Stig's absence has allowed them ample time to ponder their sorrow over Kjersti's suicide, but instead they still morbidly associate Pharaoh's arrival with their tragedy. And it is ridiculous for them to believe that Stig's return after Christmas is an imminent curse. He attributes it to firecrackers more than anything else. That's probably what kept Stig on the run since he received his freedom from Pharaoh on a farm at the outskirts of the university. Pharaoh had struggled at first with the decision to release Stig because of his sympathy for his new family and his desire to help and please them. Once he had decided to turn Stig loose, however, he had done so quickly and without anguish. He had driven back listening to loud music and toying with the idea of beginning his own animal-disposal business here. He had even imagined a business card with a rainbow in one corner and a picture of him chasing frightened animals with a pitchfork as a background. Suddenly repentant, he had turned the car around immediately and driven back to find Stig. He would dispose of the dog after all. But Stig must have sensed that his freedom was a fragile thing that day and had completely disappeared. Pharaoh imagined Stig stumbling ironically and fatally into the SHO's path as he drove home.

With these memories in his head, he lifts Amaryllis out of her crib, no longer concerned about interrupting her sleep, as Hannah enters the apartment.

"Did you wake her?"

"No. She's still asleep." He cradles her into the living room.

Hannah's face is red from the cold and she has been crying. He can hear her sniffles as she follows him. "You should put her down. Let her sleep."

"She's asleep," he says irritably, as he stretches out with Amaryllis on the couch so that Hannah must sit elsewhere.

"I can take her if you want to do something else or go back to sleep," she says, unconvincingly.

"This is all I want."

"Okay." Her response is quick and evasive, as if to appease him. He wonders if she and her parents have reached some agreement that will allow them to stay.

"He really didn't mean those things. He's already sorry."

"It doesn't matter, Hannah. I've already forgotten all about it. Water under the bridge."

"No you haven't. You will never forget this. It's that stupid dog." Hannah rubs her eyes, then prepares herself a cup of coffee. He says that he does not want coffee, only to enjoy Amaryllis's weight on his chest peacefully. She continues to blame Stig for Thor's outburst, stopping short of actually blaming Kjersti, perhaps realizing how morbid that might seem. He can already feel himself sinking deeper and deeper into a quagmire in this little land carved out of rocks and fjords.

"We should think about moving back, Hannah."

"Like hell! We just got here. I mean," she continues in an appeasing tone, "this is just a passing thing. Don't let his talk bother you. He was just angry, hon. He'll be fine tomorrow. You'll see. Just let it go. He'll be fine."

"Too many things can go wrong, Hannah, if they haven't already." He sees her lick the tip of her cup to avoid scalding her tongue on the hot coffee.

"Okay. Let's think about it. But it might be awhile. I've just missed my period." She is clearly pleased and expects a similar response from Pharaoh. But all she gets is absolute silence as he strokes Amaryllis's hair.

New Year's Eve arrives, filled with longing and uncertainty for Pharaoh. Each day that Hannah's period does not arrive feels like a harness tugging him by the throat. He feels trapped and uneasy. He attributes his unfortunate circumstances to a malevolent spiritual power. Overwhelmed, he considers rushing to a confession chamber for reprobates before the new year begins. Hannah begins to make future plans, while he secretly hopes for a miscarriage. Her eyes wide, she and Trine prance between apartments like participants in a cavalcade with colorful childhood items held up for display before him. He has refused offers to celebrate the arrival of the New Year with Hannah and her friends in the city so that he can call his friends in LA. Pharaoh encourages her to have a good time and to drink as much as she wants on his behalf, but he stops short of actually telling her to abort the kid.

Hannah and her father have grown closer, though Pharaoh fears that their renewed closeness is achieved at his expense. Stig has also benefited from Thor's changed mood. The dog now has a wooden box and blanket to complete his reprieve. The sounds of weak fire-crackers outside remind Pharaoh that it is indeed the last night of the year, and he decides to smoke his last joint by himself in the living room. Amaryllis is fast asleep and Trine and Thor are somewhere in the city. Pharaoh's melancholy becomes too much for him after the first few hits. He reaches for the phone, unaware that he has already begun to talk to himself. After leaving messages on several answering machines in LA, he rings Oobamcee, who is clearly surprised to hear his voice on New Year's Eve.

"Comrade, you are home alone on a night of Western extravaganza! Did something happen? Did you miss your train?" Annie Lennox's "Whiter Shade of Pale" can be heard faintly on a radio in the background.

"Just thought I'd call to say Happy New Year! Nothing has happened."

"It is not my music. It is my wife's music," Oobamcee explains.

"Wish her a Happy New Year also," he says.

"She is here washing my feet. I have been walking with the children all day, and my feet are tired and cold. It is very soothing and sensual to have them washed in warm water. It is what they did to Jesus."

"Jesus had to go barefoot, Oobamcee. You have the luxury of wearing shoes. Perhaps you have been away from your country too long." Pharaoh smiles into the receiver and takes a stilted drag off his joint, letting the smoke escape through his nostrils.

"Perhaps. But Jesus was never in Norway in this cold, and he wore sandals wherever he went." There is a whisper beneath the receiver, and Oobamcee laughs. There are more whispers, and he bellows. "Excuse me, comrade, but my wife is very funny tonight. She suggests that Jesus's sandals were made by Nike. It is a capitalist joke. It seems she enjoys purchasing items manufactured in your country. I think she is here only to taunt me."

"Well, it is okay to hate the sin and still love the sinner," Pharaoh says. The popping of firecrackers outside has become louder and denser in the final moments before midnight. From Oobamcee's playful mood, Pharaoh suspects that he has interrupted an intimate moment between the warrior and his wife. He doesn't want to ruin their mood with any reference to the incident on Christmas Eve.

"You are quite right. My wife believes that walking from your home has blistered my feet and that I should have accepted your offer to drive us closer. I have told her it is too late, however. I am already home." There is more laughter in the background and Pharaoh recognizes Peter's scratching. He does not appreciate their lightheartedness, and because he cannot see them, he assumes it is personal and that they are ridiculing him.

"I did not call you to hear jokes." It is his turn to speak in earnest. There is a sudden silence on the other end, as if everyone is listening.

Finally, Oobamcee speaks. "Now we are alone, comrade. I sense that there is something we must discuss. I hope you are still not concerned about other matters."

Pharaoh begins by describing the family's reaction to Kjersti's suicide and the lambasting he received from Thor after Stig's return. He smokes the entire joint during their conversation. Although he feels more relaxed and cleansed after his declarations, he does not mention what has occurred between Anna and him, or Trine's missing camera.

"My wife is pregnant." It is the first time he has uttered the words since her announcement. As high as he is, it comes out as clear and filled with theatrics as if he has announced it from a rostrum.

"Is it official?"

"My wife thinks it is."

"Well, we must wait. Perhaps she is mistaken. Meanwhile, we must put our heads together, comrade, to help you solve your problems. Your life has been threatened, you say?"

"Not really. I don't think he meant it," Pharaoh answers, feeling his inadequacy surfacing again. "Perhaps I should leave matters where they stand."

"Quite the contrary, comrade. Your father-in-law must realize that he is flying too close to the sun. We will introduce him to a black devil, comrade."

Oobamcee's statement makes Pharaoh uneasy. They hang up with Pharaoh accepting a lone invitation to Oobamcee's home.

With the advent of the new year, Pharaoh's paranoia intensifies. He believes that Hannah and her parents are secretly conspiring to take Amaryllis away from him. There have been too many invitations from Trine and Thor lately for coffee and cake, their furtive eyes peeking from behind newspapers while Pharaoh channel surfs between CNN and MTV. Hannah crouches close to photographs in the wedding and new-birth sections of the paper, recalling that in spite of recent events, he is not expendable. While Trine looks at the obituaries, Thor is making notes in his tablet about bankruptcies and public announcements, then handing them to her so she can match the names. Pharaoh does not know how much longer he can endure their feigned hospitality. His first day of employment at the Folk University is now almost here and is mentioned so often he feels like an old Negro entertainer held up for exhibit. His growing paranoia makes him more and more dependent on Amaryllis's affection, and he finds himself embracing her more and more frequently. He observes her while she is asleep and while she is at play, sensing that his time spent with his daughter is measured. And when Amaryllis looks at him lately, he believes that she, too, can sense it. Forces are pulling them apart.

Pharaoh can hear voices outside the living room window after each lull in the sounds of explosions from firecrackers outside. Occasionally a rocketlike contraption shoots up into the sky, leaving trails of sparks and smoke before exploding in the distance. He considers stepping outside to watch the lights, but instead picks up the receiver, reluctantly, to call his father. He is tired of their quarrel. It's time for them to abandon their old resentments and cherish each other.

A flat knock on the living room window disturbs his musing. Anna is waving a gloved hand and pointing toward the front door. She is dressed in black and has covered her hair with a black plastic hat. He stands at the window and tries to wave her away. "Happy New Year!" he mouths.

She points at her wristwatch, withdraws a folded piece of paper from her coat pocket, and waves back. He unlocks the door reluctantly, and her perfume hits him before the cold air does.

"*Godt Nytt År!* You are hiding from me?"

"Not at all. I am hiding from myself." She does not understand, and he does not feel like explaining anything to someone who is interrupting his high. Her lips are bright red, and the skin around her eyes is dotted with blue sparkles. She sees him looking at her covered head disapprovingly and smiles.

"It is there," she says, and hands him the folded paper. He takes it uncertainly and does not know how to receive the pencilled drawing of her lips and left hand. The details are fine. The drawing was clearly done with precision and patience. The lips are full and closed, and the fingertips are raised in a crawl like a hand that is about to strike the keyboard of a piano. Though Anna's drawing expresses little more than her boredom as a housewife, it evokes a sense of eroticism in Pharaoh. He is certain that is what she intends. He can tell by her impish smile that she will bring him more drawings, revealing more and more of her anatomy.

"You are smoking hash?"

"No." He is surprised that she can smell it above her perfume, and he opens the door to let in cold air.

"I smell hash," she says. "Have you some?"

"No."

"You are sad tonight. Amaryllis is okay?"

"My daughter is fine. She's asleep."

She reaches into her pocket and pulls out another piece of paper. "I have been practicing my English on this paper. I write everything on it." She begins to read to him. *"I miss you and have you in my head. When I think of you, I draw a piece of me so you know I think of you. I would like to do stuff to you and want the same. I promise I will never call you nigger and other bad language. Dagfinn and I are going to the city. Happy New Year!* How's my English? Don't worry. I burn everything I write on this paper." She gives him a warm hug and then departs, waving and skipping like a teenager. Pharaoh remembers Oobamcee's warning and sticks his nose out in the cold air, sniffing after her hidden scent. But his sense of smell has not been refined in the jungles of Africa. He can only smell her strong perfume.

Chapter 16

O N THE FIRST DAY of his job, Pharaoh enters the classroom and is greeted by absolute silence from the astonished students. Not all of the twenty-five people enrolled are present, according to an official form he found Scotch-taped to the blackboard in a sealed envelope. Six students are absent, and during the first hour before Pharaoh allows an intermission, five students casually clear the tops of their desks and walk out of the room. Most of the names on the form belong to adult women. Some of the students grin condescendingly as he attempts to pronounce difficult names. After introducing himself, Pharaoh randomly places the students into small groups to practice simple introductory dialogue in informal situations. He learns that most of them are neighbors and that a few of his students, although they are not seated together, are married couples. Occasionally he interrupts glances between the students who know each other. At the end of class, Pharaoh says goodbye to the nine remaining students. Without being asked, they arrange all the desks in rows and place a chair on top of each desk.

"There have been complaints from your students."

"Oh?" Rigmor's announcement causes him to shudder uncomfortably in his seat, and he suddenly feels himself in a forward slide.

He encircles the top of his hot cup of coffee in his left hand with the tips of his fingers and his thumb outward to prevent it from spilling onto her new floor. Her office has been closed since his interview, and he can smell the arid air from weeks of automated heating. He manages to get his index finger in the cup's handle and, adopting the custom of his wife, licks the tip of the cup before sipping the bitter coffee.

"I am sorry. Our students are angry. They have signed a letter to have you removed." Rigmor is sitting at the edge of her leather chair. Her back is rigid and conveys a professionalism he remembers from their first meeting when she turned toward the sun to read his CV.

"Are you sure?" It is a ridiculous question.

"I am sorry. We will pay you for your time. They are difficult students and older," she says, but it is no consolation. He stares at her with a dumbfounded look, expecting her to at least share in an official capacity the reasons for his dismissal, but she will not disclose the letter's content. He drains the last of his coffee. His face tingles, as if he can feel his facial hair grow in spots, and the room seems to get brighter in blotches. There is no offer to refill his cup. He fiddles nervously with the handle.

"How many students have signed the letter?"

"Most of them," she says, annoyed. The deep imprint around her eyes and her tanned, taut skin suggest that she has made a special visit to the city, interrupting her ski trip.

"Well, I suppose they had someone else in mind." He sees her look at the telephone, then her watch.

"I apologize, but we will pay you for your time."

He realizes that she has nothing further to say and he is being dismissed by her silence. Pharaoh places the empty cup on the table and rises on legs that feel as if they have just dismounted a rocking horse. He had arrived, at Rigmor's request, expecting to sign a contract, but had been greeted with this mysterious letter instead. As he now prepares to leave Rigmor's office, he promises to mail her the key and the cassettes, and they shake hands awkwardly. She points him toward the elevator, though he assures her that he can find his own way out. He hears her shut and lock the door behind him before he can press the elevator button.

The short walk to the SHO, parked on a sunny street near Rigmor's office building, does not allow Pharaoh sufficient time to process what has happened. He enters the car and places the key in the ignition, and then sits there quietly, staring at the digital numbers on the parking meter. The sun is almost overhead, and he tilts his head back to absorb some of its heat. A fisherman in a heated, makeshift booth on the pavement brandishes a long, glittering knife that gets the attention of pedestrians on the opposite side of the street but hardly disturbs three loquacious old women at his counter. Pharaoh closes his eyes and feels the sun's heat warm his eyelids, creating multicolored images behind them. Perhaps the sun's warmth will help him resist the mysterious forces that are now manipulating his life as if he is a puppet. He opens his mouth to allow some warmth to escape, but the words *bullshit on the sly* escape instead.

The fisherman's knife is still glittering in the sunlight when Pharaoh opens his eyes. He wonders if the knife is sharp enough to sever the head and hands of a body. There's been a lull in media coverage about the still unidentified body, relieving some of the tension and suspicion throughout the city. No one has come forward with accusations or tips about the assault on the three Norwegians, and it looks more and more as if Oobamcee has told him the truth. But Pharaoh cannot relax and relinquish himself to the calming sun. He considers sitting in his car, despite the cold, as self-imposed punishment for losing his job even before it had officially begun. In a strange way, he relishes the moment when he will tell Hannah and her parents. Perhaps he will invite them to dinner and then surprise them with the news of his dismissal. That is what he will do. The fisherman's antics continue to fascinate the pedestrians and eventually beckon Pharaoh toward the booth.

Up close the fisherman resembles a walrus. He is a coarse, round man with a plump face and an overbite that broadens beneath his whiskers when he grins. His forearms remind Pharaoh of Popeye, whose bulging forearms he and Billy often ridiculed in the past. A sure indication, they had laughed, that Popeye spent too much time playing with Brutus and not enough time playing with Olive Oyl.

"Fresh fish, my friend," the man says. His words are filtered through sharp strands of brown hair. Despite the overwhelming smell of fish, Pharaoh also gets a direct whiff of snuff.

"What do you recommend?"

"For you, my friend, big American tourist, we have a special fish. Very expensive." He points at a reddish specimen.

"It looks like red snapper. We have that in the US." The knife no longer glitters from where Pharaoh is standing, but the fisherman's showmanship has attracted more customers who wait stoically in line as he buys fresh fish from the tourist trap.

"*Nei! Vi har ikke* red snapper *her. Laks!* my friend. It is out of the North Sea."

"Way out there, huh. I'll have two, then." The knife slices smoothly and adroitly through scales and bone, and Pharaoh estimates then that it could easily sever the head and hands of a body. He pays the fisherman, who wishes him a pleasant stay in the city before dangling his knife toward the next customer.

On his way back to the SHO, Pharaoh stops at a phone booth to call Hannah and tell her that he has bought fresh fish for dinner and that she can also invite her parents. But he changes his mind at the last minute and dials Oobamcee's number instead.

Oobamcee's home is in one of two large apartment blocks visible from the center of the city. They are identical structures built on flat land, and each apartment has a small, concrete balcony surrounded by thin metal rails. Some of the balconies are decorated with Christmas lights that reflect tenants' personalities more than any religious devotion to Christmas. Others seem only to support the weight of summer furniture forgotten outside and now buried under layers of snow. The residents are both lower-income Norwegians and immigrants of different nationalities.

Pharaoh parks the SHO where he hopes it can be seen from Oobamcee's apartment and walks past a group of children kicking a large empty Coke bottle in the snow. Two women whose faces are covered in veils stand watch over the children. Pharaoh, unfamiliar with the protocol for greeting women in veils, nods and lowers his eyes in deference to his own ignorance. He can already feel a different atmosphere from where he lives as one of two men emerging from behind a glass-door entrance to the building holds one nostril and does a farmer-brown blow. The man's snot lands heavily off a path in the snow and disappears, melting the first layer. The buildings remind him of high-rise projects in poor cities in the US. Although they are kept clean, they are not without scrawled graffiti. The lobby is dimly lit, with signs in English that forbid loitering or parking bicycles. Another sign points to two small elevators behind wide concrete stairs. Banks of copper mailboxes sit on either side of the lobby, and a black boy on a canvas stool behind a small table with items for sale grins at Pharaoh expectantly. The boy is dressed stylishly in a brown, oversized corduroy jacket, black leather gloves, and faded black jeans. His eyelashes are long and black, like the bristles of a new paintbrush, and an oblong afro that Pharaoh believes would not survive the teasing it would draw in LA makes him look like a slight girl reincarnated from the sixties. A few afro combs, stainless steel bracelets, and chains with painted black wooden fists are on display next to a hollow enamel plate with Norwegian coins. Pharaoh eyes the display on his way to the elevator and considers telling the boy that he is dreaming; his idea might be a good one but his location is impractical. It is simply the wrong time and place. But he refrains. He does not want to shatter a child's dream.

The elevator opens to loud music and scampering kids on the fourteenth floor. Terrence Trent Darby's "Dance Little Sister" can briefly be heard coming out of an opened apartment door, before it is slammed shut. Another door opens, and a stout, jingling black woman with a baby in her arms, dressed in a dark, flowered dress, big-framed glasses, and a multicolored head wrap, steps out into the hallway to greet him.

"Ah. We meet," she says. "I am Bariti. So you are the man responsible for my husband's sore feet. Come in! Come in!"

Pharaoh removes his shoes and coat and enters before shaking her hand, surprised that it is Oobamcee's wife who greets him at the door. Both her wrists are covered with silver bracelets and produce a spirited jingle with her arm movements.

"I hope his feet have healed. I apologize."

She looks at him from head to toe, patting the baby's back as if she is coaxing him to burp, and shrugs her glasses down the bridge of her wide nose. It is a serious look.

"Oh, I am only jiving, as you say in America."

Her jocular tone also takes him by surprise, and he now understands how she could have held her husband in stitches a few days before when he called. He laughs, watches the baby drool over her shoulder, and then drops his eyes to Bariti's behind and its undulating roll as he follows her into the apartment.

It is a dusty place, with thick matted rugs covering circular sections of the concrete floor where Pharaoh is led. He can feel the grating of fine sand when he steps on the concrete. It is not a lavish apartment. There are four armchairs and a sofa made out of bamboo with thick cushions covered in matching brown sackcloth. He is seated in an armchair to wait for Oobamcee to conclude his business while Bariti and the baby disappear into the kitchen. He notices pictures of Oobamcee and Bariti in elaborate African clothing at their wedding ceremony, where some of the guests are dressed in green military uniforms. There is no stereo or television in the living room, but the top two shelves of a bookcase contain unlabeled videocassettes. Bariti returns without the baby and carrying a tray of glasses and a plastic jug filled with orange juice.

"Enjoy a beverage while you wait," she says, smiling. "He knows that you are here."

She again moves jingling to the kitchen but not before placing the tray on a rug on the floor in the center of the room. Pharaoh settles back on the armchair's cushion as the front door opens and two statuesque teenage girls and a lanky boy, about eleven, enter and walk hurriedly past him without any greeting. Minutes later, two younger boys appear, lingering inquisitively around the living room. A small green blanket trails the smaller boy, but he never leaves the other to stand or sit by himself. They look at Pharaoh cautiously.

"And what are your names?" Pharaoh forces a smile. He does not feel like being friendly and would prefer to deal only with adults. The younger kid, chewing on a piece of string attached to his blanket, stares at the other as if daring him to answer first before they leave the room. Instead they quietly disappear.

"Comrade, it is good of you to visit. I am sorry if I have kept you waiting. I am very busy today," Oobamcee says, entering from the kitchen. He is in his usual attire, but his bare feet are in soft white bedroom slippers that clash with his flesh-colored heels.

"I can come back another time, when you are not quite so busy, if you like."

"Absolutely not! You are here now, and I welcome you. We will eat lunch and discuss strategies, but first I must be a good host and show my guest the home I am allowed to have in the West."

In the kitchen, Pharaoh expects to meet the children he had seen earlier, but only Bariti is there, preparing lunch.

"You have met my wife. I hope she has been kind."

"She has been very kind," Pharaoh replies, uncertain whether Oobamcee's statement is a show of endearment for his wife or casual interest in her behavior when he is not present. Bariti smiles at him behind her glasses, then asks for his palm. Pharaoh looks at Oobamcee, then at Bariti, puzzled.

"You must obey, comrade, or we will have a bad lunch. My wife also reads palms. I often go to bed with secrets and wake up with disclosures."

Pharaoh offers her an opened hand that she touches lightly before rolling up her bracelets and beginning her examination. She hefts it with the full face of her palm and then blushes suddenly.

"You are not afraid of flying," she says. He is about to withdraw his hand, but she clamps a thumb over his palm like a trap. "You have a good soul, but a troubled one." Her claim reminds him of the generic predictions of fortune cookies, and he wonders if she arrives at the same conclusion with every palm she reads.

"We knew that all along. Isn't that so, comrade? We shall fix your soul." He is led away before he can thank Bariti for her services.

"So your new job did not go well?" Oobamcee whispers as they walk through a lighted corridor with boxes stacked along the floor.

"Not as well as I had expected."

"I cannot say that I am surprised, comrade. In this society, we are either villains or invalids, never both. We must know when it is advantageous to be one and not the other."

"It is the first time that has happened to me, but I suppose there will be more jobs." At the end of the corridor, he can hear a baby crying. Multicolored bulbs strewn along a door in a zigzag fashion suddenly begin to flash.

"This is my daughters' room, but we cannot enter when these silly lights are flashing. They are teenagers, and my wife has begged me to obey their request."

"I saw them earlier while I waited in the living room. You must be proud of them. They are beautiful girls."

"They lack manners and respect, comrade. But I blame outside influences, like your MTV, and not my wife. She will get them in line for me." Pharaoh does not want to encourage more bashing of the West, so he swallows his urge to defend Western culture, instead reassuring Oobamcee that his daughters' behavior may only be temporary. They approach another room with a life-sized poster of Michael Jordan in his Bulls uniform taped to the door.

"Here is my son's room. Here we can enter." Oobamcee knocks softly, then goes in. The lanky boy who had walked past Pharaoh earlier is lying in bed, fully clothed, leafing through a magazine. His headphones are the size of kidney beans, and the dangling cord is attached to a silver briefcase under his bed. A small, rotating fan on a dresser ruffles the magazine's pages like a tropical breeze but does not disturb the boy's concentration. Oobamcee barks at him in a language Pharaoh does not recognize, and his lanky frame responds by slowly becoming upright, making a foppish show of straightening wrinkled clothing. The boy continues leafing through his magazine and seems to move toward Oobamcee only when he remembers to place one foot in front of the other. When he stops, it is because the headphones will not permit him to go further. One arm hangs loosely at his side, with a bony index finger as a bookmark, while the other arm, crooked behind his back at the elbow, grasps the straight arm like claws. It is a familiar stance in the military, through which soldiers stand at ease, but on his frame it looks slack and suggests that he does not care for their interruption. He has a long neck and eyes that make him appear drowsy and not interested in what they have to say. The boy is a full head and neck taller than Oobamcee, but it does not seem to matter. Oobamcee slaps him in the face with an opened hand, and the boy, startled and wide-awake now, stumbles backward, losing his headphones.

"Hey! Be cool, man!" the boy says.

"Be cool? Be cool?" Oobamcee swiftly charges at the boy, who shields another blow with his magazine before running out of the room.

"My son believes he is a twelve-year-old man, comrade, because he reads sports magazines and is interested in girls. When he decides to stay and fight me like a man, I will think of him as a man. Right now he respects his magazines more than he respects himself. He cannot grow that way." Oobamcee kicks the noisy headphones under the bed, loses a slipper, and bends to retrieve it.

"He is very tall," Pharaoh says. "He can be an athlete someday, at least one that can read. Sports is a very lucrative business."

"In your country, comrade. Not mine. There are bigger issues to deal with in my country than sports. I have no time for a son who wants to be an athlete. Look at his room. It is like a shrine to strangers in uniform. I do not want any son of mine to grow up to be an athletic supporter."

"I understand," Pharaoh says, feeling as if his life has no purpose unless he can also find something to support.

"I do not think so, comrade, for you have missed my joke. But perhaps it was insensitive of me. It is you we must focus on today." Oobamcee removes a key from his pocket and unlocks a small door, also plastered with posters and pictures of athletes. They enter a fluorescent-lit room with one window hidden behind venetian blinds and thick curtains. Pharaoh closes the door behind him. From its size and uneven hinges, he can tell it is a recent addition to the wall.

"This, comrade, is my office. It is where I spend most of my time. It is our Donation Room."

The Donation Room is the most extravagant room so far in Oobamcee's apartment, but it has a rancid odor. It is a back bedroom that has been converted into an office, with a small closet that is now a darkroom.

"Do not look so surprised, comrade. I am not a man who only speaks to hear my own voice. After I have explained what we do here, I hope that you will consider joining our cause."

"Your cause?"

"Yes, our cause. We are an organization that helps people stand up to technology and capitalism, comrade."

"But who in their right mind would not want technology and capitalism?"

"Ah, yes. I can see that you are a challenge."

Pharaoh begins to regret his decision to visit Oobamcee's home. He wishes he had more than just the fish lying in his trunk to look forward to at home. He tries to think of an excuse to leave, but Pharaoh senses that this may be a difficult introduction from which to extricate himself.

It is a paneled, carpeted room with two television sets on a wooden table in a far corner and two video players stacked between them. A video camera on a stand points to a small refrigerator next to the table. Pharaoh follows Oobamcee to a cot that is surrounded by scattered newspapers, a laptop computer, a printer, a scanner, and a fax machine. The room is filled with a rancid smell that Pharaoh cannot identify.

"You can cover your nose if it helps, comrade. I am used to the smell."

"Jesus Christ! I thought you were against technology!"

"It does not mean that I cannot use it to defeat the capitalist."

"How can you afford all this, this technology?"

"Donations, my friend. Donations from the West."

Pharaoh does not understand, but still nods approvingly to Oobamcee.

"So you've misled us. You're not just a simple warrior." Pharaoh clutches his nose. Oobamcee offers him a seat on the cot by gesturing toward it with an opened palm, then crosses the room with quick strides and opens the window.

"Quite the contrary, comrade. I have misled no one. Perhaps you agree that Africans are simple people. We are not all that simple. We are more than white teeth, dark complexions, strength, virility, and dance. We are a resilient people. You, comrade, should know that, given your country's history. At a donation seminar in the city, an old woman once asked me how I can expect people to offer their hard-earned money to help African children when it is the children that they see carrying guns and fighting wars. It is the children's bodies they see piled in dirt streets on CNN. How can they afford guns? Those are legitimate questions when one considers how people in the West see Africans. But without the guns, there will be more bodies and more bloodshed. I am here today because I carried a gun as a child. My own son, who was born in Uganda and has known hunger, thinks that the starving African children he has seen on television cannot be real. He has sworn he has seen the same children in a bubble gum commercial. Even by our own people we are seen as a contrast in colors, comrade. A pink tongue in a black face in the middle of a desert is no longer an effective plea for a drop of water or a morsel of bread, but the illusion of bubble gum."

The hostility in Oobamcee's tone no longer surprises Pharaoh, but he has begun to resent these diatribes. The more he listens to them, the more he believes that hidden in Oobamcee's words are daggers that are directed squarely at him. He realizes that his own depiction of the African students is just as Oobamcee has described. Oobamcee's incessant talk of his countrymen, capitalism, and his aversion to technology cannot diminish his stature as a warrior. Oobamcee's desire to make Pharaoh see Africa with the clairvoyance of a compatriot is admirable, but it cannot dispel Pharaoh's sudden awareness that he is sitting on a bed in a private room with another man. He is close enough to notice strands of hair growing out of Oobamcee's ear. Pharaoh moves over to the window, where it becomes easier to breathe, but he still cannot identify the rancid smell. He cannot see his parked car from the window. As he stands there awkwardly, it suddenly occurs to him that there are no chairs in the room.

"Rest assured, Oobamcee. I don't see Africans the way you've described. Perhaps your argument isn't with capitalism or technology but with the multinational corporations your elected governments invite into their own countries."

"Ah, yes, comrade! You defend your country well. It is as I expected." Oobamcee speaks as if this is an admission he does not want to make. "Your suffering and apathy have made you very charitable people."

"Well, then. That should be enough. I have nothing else to give."

"You were a military man. You have loyalty. Tell me, comrade. Have you heard of Gresham's Law?"

"No. I'm afraid I haven't."

"Well, comrade, here you and I are examples of Gresham's Law on a human scale. In my country we have begun to stamp out what the colonialists have left behind. We do not care for shillings and pence anymore. So my government has introduced the Ugandan dollar, a most beautiful design. But my people have shot themselves again. Their pride has led them to hoard our currency. Because of this, the old colonialist money is still in use, while it is difficult to find our currency anywhere in my country. In some respects, you and I, comrade, are suffering the same fate. We have the same racial value in this country, but as an American, your value is higher. They like you more. I have seen it in the classroom. Hans does not speak to you as if you are a child or as if you are from a Third World country. He speaks to you as if America has the right-of-way in the world. It is only a matter of time before you will be hoarded and integrated. I, however, cannot embrace a language whose people use it to negate me. And I cannot accept that I must use their language to make changes in their attitudes when language is, by its very nature, resistant to change. A warrior must travel on many roads. You, comrade, because of your high value to these people, can make inroads for our cause."

"And what is your cause?" Pharaoh resents Oobamcee's comments about his racial value. It reminds him too much of the auction block during slavery. He wonders if Oobamcee's adamant stance against capitalism and technology is, at least in part, a response to the role capitalism played in Africa's early history. His mind drifting from Oobamcee's words, Pharaoh examines the expensive video camera like a customer who is more interested in the product for sale than the salesman's presentation.

"We are a private organization that attacks technology and capitalist ideas to promote and distribute wealth equally to underdeveloped countries. It is that simple. That is our cause. The IMF and World Bank must restructure our loans without penalties, or we will not pay. We are opponents of free trade because capitalists simply keep getting more powerful and our people continue to get only what they are willing to give us. We cannot provide education or alleviate poverty with their scraps."

"So, how can I help?" Pharaoh is impressed but impatient. This is not why he is here.

"We need more donations to help stop the war in my country, so that our children can return to school without guns."

"But you seem to receive more donations than you need."

"We need more, comrade. We always need more. Our organization must also support forces out in the field. Do not be alarmed, but we must fight the capitalists with their own weapons. They leave us no choice. We must also protect ourselves during peaceful demonstrations with bombs, grenades, masks, helmets, and padded clothing. The capitalists' gestapo will use everything in their arsenal to protect the rich corporations."

"I am still not sure how I can help, Oobamcee, especially since your cause isn't as close to me as it is to you."

"That is disappointing to hear, comrade. Even after receiving information from our pamphlets and web page, people are skeptical about our cause and are understandably reluctant to send us their contributions. Through private seminars in the city, we must therefore convince and solicit them in person. That is where you can help. You can speak to them directly. They will listen to an American who has been in the military, especially if you address them in your military uniform."

"What uniform? I am no longer in the military. I don't have a military uniform."

"That is not a problem, comrade. Leave that to me. I can get one for you."

"I'd like to help, Oobamcee, but I'm not sure that is the right way."

"You will be paid well. It is better than delivering newspapers," Oobamcee says, and produces a small pamphlet from inside his jacket. Pharaoh recognizes the Norwegian Monarchy insignia on the front. Below it in fancy calligraphy are the words, *The African Knights Economic Advisory: Peace and Understanding Serving Earth.* Inside are graphic pictures of children in various stages of starvation. The photos are disturbing but effective. Pharaoh recognizes the baby he had seen drooling on Bariti's shoulder and the young boy who had entered the room chewing on his blanket.

"Jesus Christ, Oobamcee! Those are your kids!"

"Ah, yes. That is why we only seek donations from strangers, comrade. As you have seen, my children are quite healthy. I am also amazed at what technology can do. It is all done right here, orchestrated in the West and distributed in the West."

"But those are *your* kids!" Pharaoh says, surveying the Donation Room as if its sanctity has been destroyed.

"We are all refugees, comrade. For us war has no conscience, but you will be well paid. It is a first step toward the solution to your difficulties at home."

Pharaoh's problems with Hannah and her parents seem suddenly insignificant as he reads the pamphlet about Oobamcee's organization. He does not know anyone in LA with such fortitude and purpose. According to the pamphlet, Oobamcee's anti-capitalist organization definitely means business. There are instructions for digging up cobblestone sidewalks to use the stones as missiles. Drawings of defensive and offensive formations are listed, and members are required to learn certain commands. There are even suggestions on how to become familiar with the routes and movements of the police. The pamphlet includes a brief section on the decimating effect that AIDS and Ebola have had on Uganda, Sudan, Liberia, the Ivory Coast, and the Congo. Pharaoh learns that Ebola is transmitted through blood and saliva and that its victims crash and bleed. It produces such massive internal and external bleeding that it is like watching a human being dissolve.

It is after reading this woeful information that Pharaoh and his hosts prepare to eat.

Bariti has set a meal of broiled chicken, rice, bread, and thick gravy before them on one of the circular rugs on the floor. It unsettles Pharaoh's stomach to remember what Oobamcee has eaten for survival. Everyone is quiet until Bariti begins to eat. She kneels, sits back on her heels, and eats with her hands, noisily rolling her food into a ball and dipping it in a large white bowl with gravy. She loses the ball of food into the gravy. It makes a plopping sound, like shit dropping into deep water. Her head wrap makes her seem tall and stately. Oobamcee, too, dips his chicken before leaning forward from his yoga-style position to place the food in his mouth. Pharaoh tastes, then nibbles at his bread.

"It is good food, comrade. In my village, my wife was known for her cooking."

"You want a spoon?" Bariti's chewing and jingling bracelets muffle her offer.

"No thanks." He does not want to insult them further.

"The children will eat later," Oobamcee says.

"I have heard about your American friends," she says, dipping a piece of bread in gravy and tossing it in her mouth. "Are they on holiday back in the States?"

"They're around," Pharaoh replies, catching his impetuous tone too late. He has not spoken to them since the Christmas dinner.

"Tell them I am a good cook and they will not end up in a pot surrounded by dancing natives if they accept my husband's invitation next time." She looks at Oobamcee and laughs, slapping her thighs. She holds her arms upright at the elbows and twists her closed fists to stack and support her bracelets.

"I have told my wife about our dancing, comrade. She believes it may have frightened away your friends."

"I don't think there will be a next time," he says to her. "My friends and I are at crossroads."

"We all arrive at crossroads sooner or later," Bariti says. "You, I think, will make the right choice."

"Perhaps it is my turn to get up and dance," Pharaoh says in response to the free advice and hospitality he has received from them so far.

"You have lots of room," Oobamcee says, nodding toward his sparse living room. Everyone laughs.

It is a delicious meal. Pharaoh finds himself reaching for more than he had expected to eat in this comfortable atmosphere, saddened only by the fact that he has yet to experience this level of comfort in his own home.

Bariti offers him a fragile wishbone, intentionally holding on to the shorter end. "We must make a wish," she says. They snap the bone in two, and Bariti holds up the longer piece with a loud, ostentatious display of her bracelets. "When we are free to travel again, I will go to the States, New York City. That is my wish."

"I will help your organization," Pharaoh announces suddenly to Oobamcee. They have been forced to surrender a freedom that he has taken for granted. He feels a special empathy toward Bariti, one that he cannot completely understand. He is no warrior, but he believes that he can learn much from these people about expediency and purpose.

Bariti gathers up her plates, and in an instant she is gone, leaving Oobamcee to explain her swift departure. "My wife must prepare meals for the children. She will return."

"You were right. Your wife is a good cook . . . and a good hostess," he adds graciously.

"She will be happy to hear you have enjoyed her meal, but there will be no dessert. You and I have much to discuss."

Bariti returns and hands Oobamcee an envelope before collecting their plates and departing again. Pharaoh has gotten used to her bracelets, which sound like wind charms. It strikes him how little he and Oobamcee have to say when they are not discussing Africa.

"This is for you, comrade. It is only a beginning."

Pharaoh accepts the envelope, aware that it is a kind of gratuity. He is surprised to find $500 in crisp US currency. He questions its propriety, he suddenly feels weak at the knees.

"This is too much money, Oobamcee. Shit."

"Trust me, comrade. It is not enough. Do not worry; I am not your benefactor. You will earn it. Now, about your difficulties at home. There is a simple solution. They are afraid of you. We must let them continue to think that one day a crow will fly into their home and attack them. Their fear is not a physical one, comrade. It is a psychological one. It is the best kind of fear to have on your side when the battleground is unfamiliar territory. But we must proceed with caution, for we do not want any harm to come to your child."

When Pharaoh arrives home, Hannah is on the phone speaking to someone in English. He rushes around the apartment searching for Amaryllis. When he doesn't find her, he charges upstairs.

The child is in Trine's lap. She wriggles free when she sees her father, but Trine restrains her gently with a one-armed embrace, cooing and pointing toward the television screen with her free arm. He has interrupted their viewing of a children's nature program. The program was filmed somewhere in South America but has been dubbed into Norwegian by what is obviously the voice of a little Norwegian girl pretending to be the brown-skinned child on the screen. South American skies are blue with clear white clouds suddenly bursting with rain. When the rain has stopped, butterflies flit about and a rainbow appears to protect everything underneath with its bright colors. Even things that are far away and in the dark seem to be under its protection. A bird takes flight from the branches of a lone tree on the horizon at sunset. Finally, the sun rises behind a forked cactus in the desert and the words *"Color by De Luxe"* fill the screen. Pharaoh takes his daughter from Trine and is about to leave when he remembers the fish he has left in the trunk. Trine abruptly removes her glasses and moves closer to examine his neck.

"Jeg har kjøpt fersk laks I dag. I morgen må du og Thor spise middag hos oss. Kanksje klokka seks."

"Tusen takk," Trine says, as if she no longer recognizes him. *"Det skal bli koselig."* She grabs him by the arm, tilts her head to one side, and, with one eye, stares pensively at the amulet dangling around his neck as if she is a skeptical bird about to pounce on a worm. *"Herregud!"* she says, releasing him. "What D fuck!"

"Where did you go? Your sister is on the phone."

"I went upstairs to get my daughter back. Say hi to Auntie," he says, placing the receiver next to Amaryllis's ear, but she is busy playing with his amulet. "By the way, I invited your parents for dinner tomorrow at six."

"That was nice of you," Gwen comments over the phone line. "Child, you cooking over there now?" She seems to have grown into his *older* sister since his move from LA, but he does not mind her attitude.

"Something like that. What are you doing up so early?"

"I'm getting ready to hit the shower and water my flowers before I go to the Drug Zone," she says with a yawn.

"Nice of you to call. They let you keep your license?"

"Oh. You remembered? It was an inside job. Now I have to go to court to keep them from locking him up and throwing away the key. He was one of my best workers."

"I guess you're just too damn nice, Gwen."

"Yeah? Well I got your letter."

"Don't give me any of your 'you people' about that," he warns.

"What are you so cranky about?"

"Nothing. Bad day, already. What's up?"

"You all right over there?"

"I can't go into it now," he says, looking around to see if Hannah is within hearing distance. "Maybe later."

"Your father is moving back," Gwen says.

"Where?"

"Where do you think?" she snaps. "Where he was born. Where his heart has always been."

"When did he decide this?"

"It's been coming for a while, child. I don't know what took him so long."

Pharaoh realizes that she is offering him an olive branch by implying that their father has been awaiting a conciliatory move from him. He does not accept it. "Is he taking anyone with him?"

"You know how he is when it comes to his personal life. He isn't saying anything about that, child, but one of you needs to make a move before somebody dies. You can't make up with the dead now, unless you're gone, too."

"What's that supposed to mean? What else is wrong with him?"

"I don't know. Maybe that's something you should be asking him, Pharaoh." He can tell that she is angry with both of them. But he also realizes that without either of them in her life, she will soon be alone. Her phone call may be an unspoken plea for him to come home.

"Tell him I said hello when you talk to him again." It is all he is willing to give.

"Yeah? That's a good start. Now what was it you couldn't tell me a minute ago? Hurry up, 'cause I don't want to end up sitting on the freeway longer than I have to."

He gives her a quick report on his dismissal from the Folk University and his admission into Oobamcee's organization. Her frequent "umm hmm's" sound disapproving but are also oddly therapeutic. When Pharaoh mentions his confrontation with Thor and Hannah, she becomes completely silent. He barely hears her breathing in the receiver.

"What do you know about Ebola?"

"Pharaoh, come on now! You're scaring me. We don't have anything for that in the States," she answers.

"No. It's not that," he says to assuage her anxiety. "Donations to the cause will help people with AIDS and Ebola in his country, too." But he barely convinces himself.

"Child, you don't have to sell it to me. I've already told you drugs can't fight that, and we still have our hands full with AIDS. Sounds like you got enough going on in that house. I don't see why you have to go out and join somebody's organization. First it was a European, and now it's an African. Boy, you best grab my baby and hop on a plane home."

"I can't come home. I need some direction to my life first, a little purpose, a greater cause, all that," he explains to Gwen, frustrated that he can't express what he's feeling.

"Honey, what's happening over there? What are they doing to you? I *know* you. Sometimes you just let a thing fall in your lap, and before you know it, it burns right through."

"You don't understand," he says. "This guy has probably been fighting wars in his country since you and I were in high school, Gwen. Now he and his family are living in limbo, and he's still trying to clean up the mess in his country. We don't have that kind of loyalty and patriotism over there anymore. We're short on warriors. Nobody wants to pay their dues."

"Honey, I'm paying my dues every day. Some of us don't run even if the opportunity presents itself. I'm in the middle of a war here, too, child, and I ain't about to surrender. And I ain't about to retreat neither. Bring on the gangbangers and the robberies and the riots and the LAPD. We're taking them all on, and we're winning. I know we're winning. You come on back, Pharaoh. That ain't your war over there, honey. Let them little pygmies fight their own war. We could use you."

"I'm needed here," he says.

"All right," she says with resignation. "You take care of my baby, though, and think about what I said. My flowers are calling their mama out there. Pinch my baby for me. And I'm still waiting for a picture."

They hang up, and he turns around to see Amaryllis darting through the room without a diaper.

"Get back here, Amy! Can you bring her back here to me? I need to finish cleaning her bottom," Hannah yells from the bedroom. He does not appreciate her shortening his daughter's name. He still feels her slipping away from him, in spite of his efforts to prevent it. He chases her around playfully on his hands and knees. He corners her in the little shower room in the kitchen. With nowhere to go, she turns and rushes toward him on naked legs, giggling and screaming excitedly. He is overwhelmed with love for her and the intense desire to protect her.

"What is that?" Hannah is standing behind them with a clean diaper and baby wipes.

"What?" He stands and picks up Amaryllis.

"Around your neck."

"I bought it in the city," he explains, gently tugging the amulet out of Amaryllis's grasp.

"You don't need that shit around your neck," she barks. "Amy, don't put that in your mouth! Take that out of her mouth!"

"Don't call her that! That's not her name."

She sees the bracelet on his wrist and tries to look away, but it's too late. "Only women who aren't virgins wear bracelets over here, in case you didn't know."

He tries not to respond. It is the right thing to do. He does not need her permission to adorn his body with whatever he sees fit. But he is not about to do the right thing today. "Well, I don't have to worry about that. I can wear whatever I want, Hannah."

"Like hell! Every man is a virgin until another man gets ahold of him," she says bitterly. Her remark silences them both until spitefully she reveals to him that she has gotten her period. His sperm didn't take after all.

"Ah, yes. A false alarm. Perhaps the gods are smiling. They are on my side."

Hannah looks at him as if she has no idea who the fuck he is.

PART IV

Chapter 17

OOBAMCEE IS RIGHT. Anna has a scent. The more Pharaoh becomes accustomed to her perfume, the more he can smell it, especially after sex. He and Anna develop an insatiable appetite for each other. The tablets she occasionally provides make their meetings more daring and risky, sometimes even frivolous. She begins to share with him elements of her life that involve more than quick copulation when they are alone together during the day.

"I can be afraid of people with white skin," Anna says.

He has locked the doors and drawn the curtain in his living room. They are on the floor as her hand moves from his amulet to his pubic hair to his bracelet.

"Your English is much improved," he says, as she burrows her flat fingers repeatedly and playfully through his coarse hair.

"I can thank you for teaching English. I like it when you talk. Please talk more."

He is surprised at the heavy weight of Anna's head on his arm as he caresses her hair and stares at her breasts. They are small breasts, but the nipples are raised high and protrude above them like thimbles. He has told her that he enjoys sucking them, but he has yet to receive a drawing of them. He assumes that they are too bruised after their meetings and that she may be ashamed of them.

"You are welcome. I enjoy teaching you English."

"I love to be your student." She rubs the side of his face, and he smells their mixed fluids on her hand.

"My children think English is very cool. But they love only bad words. We say them sometimes."

"Perhaps I should begin charging you," he says playfully. "I am an expensive teacher."

"I can pay. I pay with love and my pussy." She combs his pubic hair with her fingers.

"Why are you afraid of the color of your own skin?"

"Not me, very white skin, like rabbit on people. They shall see even when eyes closed."

"Albinos, you mean. With strange eyes?"

"Yes, and giants and roller coasters and flies. I hate flies."

"Very good," he says, as she fondles him until he is erect. "Your English is improving very well."

"And you. I was afraid."

"Why?"

"Because I love you when I see you, and you belong to Hannah. And you are giant." She curls her fingers around his erect penis. Pharaoh laughs.

"I belong to no one but Amaryllis."

"It is warm. It is nice in my hand, no?"

"It is very nice in your hand," he says, caressing and squeezing her nipples. His eyes follow her hand, and he watches as the tip of his penis becomes so engorged that it looks like the head of a mushroom around her flat fingers.

"You belong to me, no?" She moves toward his erection as if to convince him, kissing his chest and nipples while still holding him in her hand. Her hair has been hurriedly wrapped in a bun, and she drags the ends of it slowly and delicately along his chest like an artist with a paintbrush. Pharaoh giggles with excitement while she scolds him with gentle pressure to keep still.

"Why are you afraid of albinos? They are harmless, and cute sometimes."

Pharaoh tries to avoid answering her question but finds it difficult to come up with questions of his own. She bends over him, covering her hand and his penis with her hair as she takes him into her mouth. Pharaoh feels as if he is about to lose his bowels.

"They give me nightmares when I was young and in Denmark. But you belong to me, no?" She pulls back and straddles him, grasping him tightly in her hands as she prepares to guide him into her vagina. With the tip of his penis inside her, Anna shifts her weight to her knees and leans forward with her flat palms on his chest, the bun hanging to one side of her neck. She stares at him and he can see the intense desire in her eyes. She remains suspended over him, and he strains his back to enter her further. But Anna raises herself to stop him.

"You belong to me, no?"

"All right, I belong to you."

She smiles, lowering herself all the way onto his penis. "You love me also, no?"

"I belong to you," he repeats, as she slows her descent.

Her convulsions are immediate. When she has finished her orgasm, she climbs off him unsteadily, her legs still shaking, and places his moist penis in her mouth.

"You are gross," she moans in the middle of his ordeal. She spreads his legs further and lifts his thighs by rolling him backward. He feels her tongue searching, invading his holy of holies, his *sanctum sanctorum*. Pharaoh ejaculates immediately.

"All right, I love you also," he utters, gripping her hands and tugging at her as if he wants to pull her through him. With those words, he realizes that he has nothing to offer Anna that she has not already taken.

"I know. It does not lie. I cannot get too much of you," she says, and climbs on him again, trying to get his now limp penis erect.

He suddenly finds their lovemaking humiliating as he realizes that Anna's perception of him is not unlike his perception of the African students.

"I love you first. But I know. I know," she says, staring down at him.

He can no longer look at her. He forces her around hurriedly, his erection again pulsating, and enters her on the sly.

"Hannah has found one of your drawings," Pharaoh says to Anna while they sit in the frozen Volvo. "We must be more careful." He had forgotten and left a drawing of Anna's left ear and chin in one of his new dashikis. They were beginning to get careless.

"You keep them in here," Anna says. "No one can find them. I have a key alone."

"Where? In the glove compartment?"

"*Nei!* Under here," she says, offering him a frozen piece of gum that had been left in her Volvo from their last encounter. It is the one meeting place where he constantly worries that they will be caught, even with her repeated assurances of absolute privacy. He is worried about the footprints to the parked car that they leave in the thick snow. But Anna insists that no one will disturb them, even if there are footprints.

"You are afraid today? It is my favorite pills working, no?"

"Perhaps."

"We have radio and music here. I am better with music," she says, and settles the dial on a classical station. He is having difficulty becoming erect. He is too nervous and paranoid about getting caught, and the dim light inside the Volvo does nothing to relieve the cold.

"You and Hannah fight every day. It no good for Amaryllis."

He does not like discussing Amaryllis with her.

"Everyone is worried. They say you change to African. You have chain and band already, but I like it."

"Who is everyone?"

"Dagfinn, Knut, Mother, and Father."

"You're not worried?"

"I never worried. I like it."

"How about afraid? Are you ever afraid?"

"*Nei,* I trust you."

Pharaoh has grown tired of her obsequious nature and worries that she is becoming his disciple. But when they are apart, he goes out of his way to steal glimpses of her.

A Norwegian singer's lyrics cause her to giggle and sing along. *My dick is limp and my nose is bleeding.* "A very bad singer. Swedish singers are good."

"I am sure there are bad Swedish singers," he says.

"Like?"

He is unable to name any. Correcting her English, too, has become a chore. Her cultural naïveté as far as his blackness is concerned fosters a kind of loathing in him toward her. She has become disposable. He watches as the windshield fogs up from their breathing. The mournful lyrics of "The Night They Drove Old Dixie Down" on the radio remind him that they are taking other risks. She kisses him deeply.

"I want to now before I make dinner," Anna says, already poised over his zipper.

"You don't have to, Anna. We can just talk and listen to music and work on your English words." He is uneasy. His erection is still not forthcoming.

"I must. I like to please," she insists, and he allows her to unzip his pants. He rests the back of his head against the frozen window while she struggles to bring him to orgasm. Her lambent tongue flickers back and forth along the length of him as if sucking his dick is the only way she knows of showing obeisance. Pharaoh stares down at her, and their eyes lock. He cannot understand her submission to him. Still, he grasps her head and pushes down. Her nose flares. He maintains his grip on her as if he is trying to comfort a patient's suffering. No one blinks. He sees wax in her outer ear as tears escape the corners of her eyes. His eyes, too, feel wet. He does not deserve such intense love, and he knows that it will only lead to pain.

With each sexual encounter, Anna and Pharaoh have become collusive confidants. Anna's English is still primitive, but she is not as ignorant as Hannah believes. She is a physical person and places more stock in sentiment than reason. Her marriage to Dagfinn is one of pity and regret. He is like a fungus she can never completely scrape away. After years of burdensome efforts, she has finally given up and decided to let him grow on her. Her options were limited because her parents were eager to marry her off quickly so that they could nurture her younger brother to become a professional soccer player. Dagfinn seemed safe at the time, and turned out to be a practical choice, especially after her gifted younger brother became a bus driver instead of a soccer star. Besides, he was all that was left. It is the last time she will use reason for love, she tells Pharaoh. She also tells him that Hannah's family made jokes about him, and that Hannah warned them against making jokes in English during his first visit. Everyone expected him to be a temporary boyfriend, even Hannah. But Anna had been infatuated with his complexion from the start and had longed to touch his skin.

"Dagfinn was almost born a girl," Anna says the next time they meet, as they cuddle in a sleeping bag among old skis and summer shoes. "His balls were the big problem. They did not drop into his bag like they should, and the doctors did not know what to do."

"Was he in pain?"

"Oh, no. The rest of him was normal, but not his balls. When they grow out, he was eight years old. It was no secret, and everyone know he would soon have an operation to make him a legal girl."

Pharaoh does not believe her, but she insists it is true. She tells him that she has also had an abortion.

"I am very sorry," he says. He is not sure how to respond to such a private admission.

"It is okay. You are good and nice to me. Dagfinn don't know. It belong to another man." The giant sleeping bag wiggles like a fat misshapen caterpillar on the floor as Pharaoh's head nestles its way between her breasts. Her disclosure causes her heart to pound against his ear, and he realizes how traumatic the experience has been for her.

"You are not worried that some day he will find out?"

"Who will tell? I trust you." She pauses, as if she is actually uncertain whether to trust him with her secret. "It do not matter. He only work and sleep. Once while he sleep, I draw on his face in black marker. It don't come off in his shower, and he go to work and everybody laugh and tell him to call home."

He can tell that she has been eating oranges in her kitchen because her lips taste like marmalade. "You can trust me, Anna. I am not an evil person, but people seem to be afraid of me."

"You hate abortion?"

"Nope."

"Why? Americans hate abortions."

"I don't."

"You hate me?"

"No, Anna. I don't hate you."

"Good. I give you a surprise drawing next time. It make you come to me harder."

He laughs. "I can't wait."

"You hungry?" she asks, giggling.

"Why is that funny?"

"You know. You hungry?"

"Not really. You have something that I can eat?"

"You not eat meat?" She tickles him and seems surprised when he jumps. "You tell me secret, too?"

"I have no secrets."

"All have secrets."

"Why are you so afraid of roller coasters and flies?"

"My aunt, her hair stick in roller coaster wheels when I was a child. She lose all her hair after roller coaster stop. Now she bald. Look like cancer."

"She lost all her hair?"

"Everything."

Pharaoh thinks it must have been a strange accident.

"You love my hair?"

"It's nice," he says, and rubs her soft belly.

"You love it more than me?"

"It's part of you," he says. He is tired of her love questions.

"What happen to Stig?" Her laughter resumes but now sounds disingenuous. Her question surprises him.

"I guess he ran away."

"I hear about Stig."

"Me, too. He ran away."

"They don't believe you. I hope so. I don't like them."

"Who doesn't believe me?"

"Everyone, but not me."

"Well, he ran away."

"You tell me secret, too. I never tell no one."

"Really, I have no secrets."

"All have secrets. You also. I tell you about my secret. You next," she says.

He feels compelled to share with her an admission of the same magnitude as that of her abortion. He confides to her about the fight in the city with the three Norwegians. Although the risk is great, he believes her need for his confidence. "There. I have no more secrets."

She does not seem content. "You kill Stig?" Her heart begins to pound again, but he does not understand her fear.

"Stig ran away. He's probably living in someone else's garage."

"You cook Stig?"

Also thou shalt take of the ram the fat and the rump, and the fat that covereth the inwards, and the caul above the liver, and the two kidneys, and the fat that is upon them, and the right shoulder; for it is a ram of consecration.

"He ran away, Anna," he says. His hand dances across her pubic hair and he buries two fingers deep inside her vagina.

Things between the two of them are deteriorating. She abhors his African clothing, storing it in a dank, outside room that smells of mold. His refusal to cut or comb his hair has led her to clip Amaryllis bald without his consent. Their conversations about meaningful topics are scarce, and they always seem on the brink of an argument about life in Norway or his distant family. He notices that she is spending more time with her brother, Knut, as evidenced by her increasing attempts to use historical facts about her country to discredit his new African awareness. He ridicules her ignorance, knowing that she will report whatever he says back to Knut.

"Norway was the first country to boycott South Africa!" she says.

"South Africa should be boycotting Norway!" he snaps.

"We're not as racist or dumb as your African friends want you to believe."

"Then why is it so many Norwegians are registered as mentally challenged compared to people from other EU countries? . . . Don't give me that look. It was in one of your Norwegian newspapers."

"That's stupid," Hannah says. "It was probably a tabloid newspaper!"

"See what I mean?" he groans.

"We're not an EU country."

"And they always make excuses. I know, I know, I know. Just a small country with four and a half million people."

"We're not the only ones who make excuses. Your friends sure made a lot of excuses when I was in LA. They blamed everyone for their problems but themselves. That's not gonna work here. I don't care what your new African friends say, or your sister. You think I haven't heard you and Gwen on the phone? You think I've forgotten how to speak English?"

"What the hell do you know about what my friends have had to deal with in LA?"

"I know they bitch a lot. Your sister makes way too much money for anyone to even take her seriously when she starts her preaching about every black person being oppressed. She's not suffering."

"Hey! Just because we're married doesn't mean you get to be a minority. Leave Gwen out of this! You have no idea what she's been through in LA."

"Like hell! So what's she gonna do now, knit a quilt?" Hannah marches past him on her way to the storage room.

"Well, I'd rather she knit a quilt than blow her brains out, if that's what you mean. That's just not in our genes. She's not that weak. And I might be a lot of things, but at least I don't beat on women like Knut does. And I'm no convict. Maybe your gene pool needs a filter."

"It's too late for that now!" Her anger at him results in slammed doors, rugged churns of knobs on the washing machine, and a long silence, before she marches back in. "At least my brother can hold a job," she says, flinging a pair of his dirty underwear at him.

"What's this?" he asks.

"That's new."

"What is new?"

"That!" she points at his underwear as he examines it. "What is *that?*"

"Fruit of the Loom," he says. "Made in the US of A."

"They stick gum in them, too?"

"Of course not!"

"Then how did that get in there?"

"Beats me. Is that really gum?" He does his best to seem incredulous.

"Well, were you chewing it and dropped it in your pants? Did you sit somewhere in just your underwear with it turned inside out? I don't get it." Her eyes are fixed and unblinking. She clearly does not believe him.

"I don't get it either, Hannah. Maybe Amaryllis stuck it in there."

"Nice try."

"Well, I don't know how it got there." Her protracted questioning irritates him.

"Maybe it belongs to one of your African friends."

"And what's that supposed to mean?"

"You tell me. They're your underwear."

"You're not making sense, Hannah."

"Like hell I'm not! Anyway, they're ruined now and you can't put them in the machine."

It worries him that she ends the conversation so abruptly. He must be cautious about further contact with Anna. He wonders what Hannah is thinking and planning.

Anna parades past her kitchen window dressed in clothes he does not recognize. She waves to him, then motions for him to come over in five minutes, pressing her fingers against the window. Pharaoh is unable to wait, however, and darts over to her front door as soon as she disappears from the window. She opens the door with the doorbell still ringing, and displays her new look to him.

"You like what I wear?" She is in a blue beret with a bow on one side. Glitter spots the lid of the beret and the bow. A fat ponytail hangs out from behind the beret. Its bulbous end swings from the braid like an errant piñata. Anna has also sprinkled glitter in her hair. She is wearing a loose denim blouse and a skirt with beads around the waist that makes her legs look short and emphasizes the familiar bulge in her belly and hips. She is also wearing unlaced black army boots. She turns around and lifts the skirt to reveal a bikini panty whose seat has disappeared deep within her buttocks.

The flimsy waistband rides high and taut atop her hips. Pharaoh frowns at the sight of her.

"You are angry today? You hate me today, no?"

"Very nice," he tries to reassure her, examining her makeup.

"You have a favorite?"

"The bikini panty, of course."

She laughs, placing a hand to her mouth. A ring with a diamond attached to the end of a short chain dangles from her plump pinkie finger. "I will give them to you after you are nice. Today, I like you to give me bruise."

He swings the door shut behind him with a nudge of his arm and stands on a rubber mat at the entrance to the wide living room, hustling to get free of his coat and Caterpillars. The room resembles a rotunda, with family pictures and black-and-white photographs of jazz instruments along the walls. Anna points to a framed drawing of Dagfinn in dark glasses with a saxophone's tip hanging from the corner of his mouth. He is wearing a long leather jacket that looks heavy on his droopy shoulders. An old tenor saxophone, its once shiny gold having long since lost its luster, hangs overhead from a withered strap nailed to the middle of the ceiling. According to Anna, Dagfinn purchased the saxophone at a flea market a few years ago after he had decided to embrace jazz, but he has never learned to play the instrument. It is difficult for her to reach to keep clean, but she has allowed it to stay where it is as long as her old Volvo remains parked outside. Pharaoh does not have time for a tour of her house.

"Where is everyone?"

"No one is here in the house." She backs away from him playfully, unbuttons her blouse, and tosses it at him. He springs at her half-naked body as she tugs frantically at his belt.

"It is hiding from me, no?" Her confidence is growing along with her vocabulary.

"You have been drinking," Pharaoh mumbles between their wet mouths, after smelling the sour odor of wine on her breath.

"A glass of wine only. I have no favorite pills today."

"Perhaps I can have some wine also."

She pulls her mouth away to look at him, as her hands attempt to loosen his belt buckle. "You not miss me?"

"Well, I have been very busy lately."

"You forget about me?"

"Not really, Anna."

"Why not? You not get pussy from Hannah. She fight you too much. Have my pussy."

"About that word," Pharaoh says.

"What word?"

"Pussy," he says.

"You want? It is right here, always."

"It is not the right word to use."

"Don't be teacher right now. Have my pussy!" she says, opening his shirt and her legs and pulling the skirt up above the bikini panty until it settles around the bulge on her waist. Her comment about Hannah has surprised and angered him.

"I must go home."

"Now?"

"Now," he replies.

"You are angry? You do not love me?"

"That's not it, Anna."

"You will not come back later?" she asks pleadingly.

"No." Pharaoh shakes his head. But Anna will not give up her coaxing. Finally he submits himself to her with the assurance that this will be their last time. She turns on music in a panic, aiming the remote wildly, while wriggling out of her skirt and tossing her boots on the floor. He climbs reluctantly onto her sprawled, plump body. Their lovemaking is not the same. They strain until they both reach orgasms. But it's clear to Pharaoh that his involvement in the organization and Hannah's anger at his new identity have eroded his personal attachment to Anna.

"Bad music," Anna says as an apology. "Very bad music." She scrambles to find a CD, but settles for Paul Young's "I'm Gonna Tear Your Playhouse Down" on a Norwegian radio station.

"It is not the music, Anna."

"So, you do not speak truth. You never love me." She begins to cry like a teenager, burying her face in the ball of clothes that they now use as a pillow on the living room floor.

"It is not that either." He feels the room become warmer as they wriggle from the front door during more foreplay. The heat makes his ear itch.

"Ah, I see it. It does not lie," she says, as she discovers his penis becoming erect once more against her thigh. Anna lowers the remote control and makes her way toward his groin.

"You don't have to do that, Anna." But she insists, almost ritually, bobbing her head up and down on him in a continuous rhythm.

"Okay. Okay." He pushes her away gently. Anna interprets this as a sign that he wants another type of gratification. She dangles her bottom at him expectantly as he creeps toward her. He enters her from behind on his knees as he gazes up at the twirling saxophone. As Paul Young fades in the distance, he examines the curves of her naked back, now stiffened to receive his thrusts. She still has an artificial tan, but around her bottom and waist where the color has faded are scarlet patches that resemble blotches of ringworm. He wishes he could drape her bottom with a piece of clothing; perhaps the scarlet patches are contagious.

"You have smooth, very soft skin. Very dark." She reaches back blindly to caress his thigh. He feels a loathing for her and for everyone else in this country who treats him as a racial, sexual stereotype.

"You are the same, but not quite as dark."

"What happen? You do not like me today? It is okay. I stop say bad words."

He does not hear the front door open though he does feel a cold draft of air sting the sweat on his back. Anna feels it, too, and is resourceful enough to begin screaming immediately. Her sudden cries leave him frozen in shock on his knees as she scrambles away. He feels flakes of dry wax fall in his outer ear as he attempts to move. He rises weakly and turns toward the door, expecting to see Dagfinn. Instead, Sara and Lena stand at the entrance to the living room, their eyes transfixed in horror at the sight of their naked mother scrambling away from Pharaoh's naked body. It makes no sense to try to cover up or explain. He simply continues to stand there with his legs bent weakly at the knees, spent and exhausted, his arms dangling loosely at his sides like an oversexed orangutan. Finally, he collects his clothes, his movements slow and sloppy, as if he is uncertain of their use. He looks like an old man as he fumbles to find the correct hole to fasten his belt. He walks past Sara and Lena with his head bowed and his back bent forward slightly at the waist. He can hear Anna's caterwauling follow him out the door.

Pharaoh is sitting with Amaryllis on his lap as they watch an old Disney cartoon about a rambunctious cat whose mischievous antics frustrate a black mammy. The cat pretends to be asleep until the mammy, her legs thick and dangling in red and white–striped stockings, leans her chair backward against a wall. She falls asleep immediately, producing snores that vibrate like a pneumatic drill and make the cartoon picture tremble. The cat opens an eye and leaps to her lap, sending the startled mammy crashing to the floor as Amaryllis giggles and points at the screen.

Hannah's disappearance as soon as he sits down with them is not uncommon when her parents are upstairs, and her behavior no longer alarms him. Today he attributes it to her admitted disdain for his change in appearance. Bariti has offered him African clothes to wear at home, and Pharaoh has accepted the bright colors out of politeness. Black and red are now his favorite colors, but Hannah hates both.

"They are evil colors," she had said upon seeing his new wardrobe.

"Why? Because they are the colors of my skin and blood?"

Pharaoh sings to Amaryllis more often now, so that despite his colorful clothing and burgeoning dreadlocks she will recognize his voice instantly. His and Hannah's relationship has become filled with cartoons when Amaryllis is awake and sitcoms when she is asleep, with Hannah silently nodding and blinking at dialogue that she believes describes some element of their relationship.

He is glad that she has left him in peace so that he can be with his daughter, but he begins to think more and more of Anna. He has not seen her since their last meeting. Her kitchen curtains remain motionless in the window, as if her house has been completely shut out to the world. He hears the heavy crunch of footsteps in the snow and answers a knock at the door with Amaryllis in his arms, playfully tugging at his amulet.

They are not the ordinary police.

"*God dag.* You are Pharaoh Chisholm?"

"That's me."

"You live here?"

"Uh huh. Is there a problem?"

"May we come in?"

"Perhaps you would like to speak to my wife. She is Norwegian."

"No. It is you we are here to see."

Amaryllis ceases her play as Pharaoh's embrace tightens around her.

"How can I help you?" He has overheard people say that temperatures are expected to warm up as they enter April. The cold wind, however, surprises him each time he steps ouside. It still freezes the SHO on some mornings, but most people here act as if summer is approaching, even as embankments of snow hide pedestrians from motorists on the streets and ice remains on parked cars until noon. Outdoor workers go without coats, as they drink coffee and stare up at the sky.

"The child can be with her mother," a policeman says, and

Hannah appears as if on cue, with Trine holding her hand, escorting her toward Amaryllis. Pharaoh grabs his winter coat from a nearby hook and bundles Amaryllis in it before passing her reluctantly to Hannah. A policeman enters and immediately begins to question him about his involvement in the assault on the three Norwegians. Pharaoh cannot believe that it has taken them three months to get around to him.

"I do not understand," he says.

"You have committed crimes against Norway and violence against the Norwegian people for which you must take punishment," the policeman reads from a sheet of paper he has unfolded. There are three of them, as if two may not be enough to apprehend him. The rote policeman is in a shortsleeved blue shirt despite the cold and appears rebellious in his summer uniform, while the others wear leather jackets with the word *Politi* and the Monarchy symbol emblazoned above the front pockets. The leader holds the paper at arm's length, reading from behind glasses with large frames which make his eyes seem glassy as they shift from side to side. He folds one arm across his belly, and the other he places perpendicular to it, while he taps the side of his temple as if he is sending coded signals. The two policemen behind him are massive men, their jackets and uniforms stretching around flesh as snow melts from their boots.

"What crimes?" He laughs awkwardly to hide his discomfort. "Have you spoken to Peter? They attacked him first," he says. It was time to tell it all to someone, and he was prepared to sing like a bird. But then he was made aware of the real reason for their visit.

"We have had a complaint from your family. It is a very serious matter. You must come with us now. We must take you into custody."

Pharaoh has barely enough time to put on his Caterpillars before they escort him out in handcuffs to an idling van with tinted windows that reminds him of limousines in LA. His gait resembles someone old and infirm who is afflicted with gout. He stumbles along, off balance in the snow, stepping down on the back of his boots as if they are slippers. He attempts to act as if his arrest is no big deal. He assumes that his neighbors, whom he knows must be watching, are more capable than he is of assessing the seriousness of the scene before them. It does not occur to him to request a moment alone with Hannah to say something, anything, that can alleviate her pain and humiliation. All he knows is that he must avoid Amaryllis and any acknowledgment of his humiliation in her eyes. He hurries to the idling van, glancing at Trine and Hannah in an upstairs window as he ducks inside. Amaryllis is not with them at the window, and he finds himself nodding appreciatively. They only stare at him. For a moment, a wry smile appears on Hannah's face as Trine rubs her daughter's cheek with the back of her hand. He slips into the vehicle and discovers the jacket he had moments ago used to bundle Amaryllis in. It has been carelessly tossed onto the van floor.

During the ride to the police station, Pharaoh hears bells ringing as the van approaches the city. The bells are not an official declaration of his capture but an official greeting for a member of the Monarchy who is visiting the city in preparation for independence celebrations in May. He needs to pee but the procession delays the police vehicle so that Pharaoh sits folded uncomfortably in his seat wishfully contemplating the Monarchy's demise.

"I have to pee," he finally says, after the van begins to move again.

"Do not pee in here," one of them warns, removing his hat and tossing it on the seat next to Pharaoh. The policeman leaves his head bare, even after the queen's motorcade passes. "And do not pee in my hat!" They assume he does not speak their language, and the driver mutters, "Se på han. Herregud! Han har likedan klar som Yoruba Konge." They all laugh.

"So, you have been to Africa," Pharaoh says. They do not answer him but instead continue to talk about nothing special. He crouches in the seat, holding his bladder and reviewing in his mind the convoluted series of events that have led to his arrest here in Norway. He feels as if each event is an element in a Rorschach test that will determine his integration into their society. One of the policemen witnesses Pharaoh's shrinking in his own humiliation and discomfort and attempts to ease his anxiety about what will happen next.

"So, what do you think of Norway?" he asks.

"You've got to be fucking kidding me!" Pharaoh mumbles.

"Forget it! It is not a good question at this time. Maybe when your troubles are over," the policeman says. His troubles, apparently, have only just begun. He places his head on the cold window to avoid peeing himself like a coward. He remembers Oobamcee telling him that in some villages in Uganda the tongues of dead black men are removed and burned before burial. People fear that tongues carry spirits that seep into the earth. A tongue hanging from the roof of a black man's mouth has always been an intimidating sight to his countrymen. Pharaoh thinks about his own tongue and inexplicably begins to lick the cold glass of the vehicle. He decides to say as little as possible to avoid incriminating himself or the organization, advice he believes that Clint would give if he were representing him as his attorney. He removes his head from the cold window as the van leaves the city and enters a road surrounded by ploughed fields. Birds trail loud tractors with thick smoke rising and hovering in the crisp air like billowing gossamers. He wonders what farmers are sowing in fields that are still covered with snow. Pharaoh shuts his eyes and fantasizes that the American embassy has authorized US troops to rescue him en route and take him to a waiting official who will simply shake his hand, apologize, and welcome him home with the words, "*Mi casa, su casa!*"

He opens his eyes instead to an isolated compound, surrounded by a large fence and barbed-wire fraise. As they approach, he sees observation cameras mounted above a gate with a giant turnstyle. He feels cold and numb. When the van stops to unload him, he refuses to leave his corner. Bariti's prediction about his good soul has not prepared him for the loss of his daughter or his freedom. Perhaps she might have served him better if he had purchased a lottery ticket and had asked her about his chances of winning.

"Welcome to your new home. Our prisons are nice. We take care of our criminals here. They have rights here. We have not harmed you, not like in the US where you will get beaten and raped," the concerned policeman says, stepping into the van and tugging on Pharaoh's sleeve. It takes two of them to slide him along the wet seat toward them and out of the van.

On his first night in custody, Pharaoh tries to proclaim his innocence to the policemen while he remains in handcuffs. A doctor dressed in sandals and white scrubs that look like wrinkled pajamas examines him and prescribes medication that Pharaoh refuses to take.

"It is all a misunderstanding, *en misforståelse.* It was not rape. *Ikke voldtekt!*"

They ignore his explanations and strip him of his clothing, inspecting his amulet and bracelet as if they are ancient artifacts. Then they escort him to a small room with a metal door.

"You will see a magistrate." It is all the information they give him before locking the door.

He sits on the bed, the thin mattress and wood barely giving under his weight, and he feels his stomach churn into knots. His face is hot. Beginning to sweat, he holds his head at the temples to prevent his loud thoughts from escaping.

"Fuck! Fuck! Fuck!" he shouts.

"That is the reason you are behind this door." It is the voice of someone he has not met before who is about to enter his room, and Pharaoh stands and moves toward the door as if whatever stance he takes can return the principles he has abandoned upon entry into this little land.

"I have done nothing wrong!"

"That is for the magistrate to decide," the voice says. "When I open the door you must move back and give me your hands. I will lock them, and you will sit down. Understand?"

The door opens and a large policeman and a stoic policewoman stand shoulder to shoulder as if they are attempting to block his exit. The policeman is rotund but not muscular, and has a small, pink bald head, layered with loose, fat flesh and indentations that resemble ping-pong fractures. The policewoman grips a pad to her bosom with folded arms, as if it will protect her from being raped. She looks at her watch, then at Pharaoh, with an odd combination of indifference and urgency. Pharaoh's eyes follow the rotund policeman as he enters the room and snaps the handcuffs onto his wrists. The man's weary eyes are hollow, sunk deep within their sockets, and give him a starved, coiled appearance. Pharaoh thinks for the first time about the prospect of meeting a relative of the slain Norwegian who has made recent headlines.

"Do you speak Norwegian?"

Pharaoh shakes his head.

"You will be here for questioning until the magistrate decides if you are guilty or not guilty. You will have no visitors and no telephone calls while you are here. You will not write letters or get letters here. You will work every day here, and it is not easy work. Understand?"

Pharaoh nods nervously.

"Now we are here because you will not take your medication."

"I am not sick. There is nothing wrong with me."

"That does not matter. Our doctor has decided that it is necessary. For your safety."

"I cannot take medications just because I am ordered to. I am not sick. I would like to see someone from the American embassy."

"Who would you like to see?"

"A representative, anyone. This is all a mistake. I have done nothing wrong."

"Very well." The policewoman glances at her watch and then steps out of the way to allow a male nurse to enter. "He has refused." The nurse's thick hands unwrap a pair of latex gloves with little attention to sterility and slip them onto broad fingers. The gloved hands grasp Pharaoh by the shoulders and force him to a kneeling position. He flails wildly at the nurse, who seems unperturbed as he lowers Pharaoh's sweatpants to below his buttocks. Pharaoh ignores the request to lie still and, as a result, feels a heavy knee on his back as the rotund policeman flattens him to the floor.

"Son of a bitch! Motherfuckers! Hey, cut that out!" Pharaoh is prepared to fight an injection, but a suppository is inserted instead. A fat latex finger with no lubricant forces its way into him and remains ensconced inside his rectum to prevent him from expelling it while he continues to wriggle and kick. "I am an American! I am a warrior, motherfuckers! Tell that to your stupid magistrate!"

"You will get a chance to tell the magistrate what you want."

"Tell it to your king asshole the next time you give him *his* medication. Up the ass, King! Up the hole! Does he squeal? He is no warrior then."

The finger is yanked free, without ceremony, and Pharaoh feels a new pain on the side of his neck that ricochets throughout his limbs, leaving them heavy and numb. His brain also becomes heavy and lethargic, and he cannot tell if it is as a result of the stun gun or the medication's sudden effect.

He is left cursing them in a lethargic drawl after they remove his handcuffs. The pain in his neck from the stun gun has returned, and there are blisters under his fingers that he cannot explain. His vision has begun to play tricks on him, and he staggers over to the bed and collapses on it face down, unable to summon the energy to pull up his sweatpants or prevent his legs from dangling over the side. He tries to think of what Gawne and Perry and Meg and the African students will say or believe once they find out, but his thoughts are too scrambled. Their images remain, helping him to keep from thinking about Amaryllis or Gwen. Feelings of trauma and shame have shifted to a disbelief about his plight, and the need for someone to blame. Who is responsible for his treacherous slide? Is it Anna? Is it Hannah? Whom could he have avoided? He refuses to accept any responsibility for his own fate. He casts a wider and wider net for someone to blame, and his thoughts tug ferociously at the memory of his dead mother.

He falls asleep cursing her religious beliefs and her preoccupation with an old Bible she kept under her pillow. She would not have approved of Hannah. Like Pharaoh's father, she had held onto antiquated beliefs that would have ostracized Hannah and Amaryllis, even as she maintained her devotional vigil to proselytize Pharaoh. Her piety had not been restricted to the privacy of her home. The yard behind their one-bedroom house had a deep well where a single fish had lived for years. Pharaoh remembers pelting it with rocks while his mother was at work and he and Gwen were at home after school. They had continued to drink the water with the fish living in the well, and on late evenings, his mother would sometimes kneel at the well as if it were an altar, peering into the dark water at the fish. He could not tell if she had been praying, but he knew she was uttering words.

She comes to him now in a sleep filled with strange images. He dreams that Thor and Trine invite him for coffee one afternoon in the interest of creating peace. But Pharaoh leaves the table somewhat rudely to watch a movie in progress on the national channel. His sudden departure is not in the interest of peace. They sit through a poorly translated version of *Mississippi Burning,* with Thor chuckling insensitively during the exploitation scenes. Pharaoh decides to go to the city, boards the trolley, and sprawls himself on two seats in the back row as houses and streets rush past. He sees a row of toilet bowls surrounded by snow on display as part of the landscape in someone's backyard and is impressed by the pretty flowers sprouting out of the bowls. But he does not believe they are real. The trolley stops suddenly. The driver opens the doors and all the passengers leave, guided by dim lights along the floor. The driver is the last to disembark, folding the doors shut. Pharaoh sinks back into his seat to enjoy the darkness and his solitude, but he is not alone. A figure emerges at the very front of the train and stands at attention without uttering a word. The body seems familiar to him, but it remains frozen, hidden by the dark, completely still. Suddenly the train sways forward, and he sees the figure of a black man lean in toward the curtain that surrounds the driver's seat. Pharaoh recognizes that it is Sail. He wonders why it took Sail so long to move. He rises and walks forward along the aisle to tell Sail that he recognizes him, but the Nigerian disappears. The trolley arrives at its next stop, sounding an alarm to disperse a crowd of passengers who gather onto the tracks. The people scatter and leave behind a little girl's body bound with a rope. The trolley increases its speed, gliding along the tracks, and severs the trapped body. Pharaoh runs to the back to see the victim but glimpses only Sail among the crowd making obscene gestures at the trolley. He awakes, disoriented and doused in sweat, to the sound of loud knocks and a request to get dressed.

"I will be back in ten minutes to unlock. You will have your hands out so we can lock them. You will take your medicine by your mouth or it will be given to you as before. And you will begin to work today."

Pharaoh does as he is told.

CHAPTER 18

PHARAOH HAS VIVID DREAMS now, side effects from his medication for anxiety and aggression. He is sensitive to light and does not want to admit that he may need glasses. Because of Anna's drawings, he sees parts of his anatomy and those of others as pieces of a jigsaw puzzle. He is in a small cell with a wooden bed and three shelves above his headboard on the wall, a black-and-white television set, and a small cupboard. A toilet and sink are against the wall at the foot of his bed. There are no mirrors. Three normal strides in any direction bring him face to face with yellow-painted concrete. His dreams are entangled with the contents of his small cell. This morning has been a dry one. He does not have to tell guards that it is sweat today and hear them threaten to put him in diapers. They can tell the pampered from the laborer and have assigned him toilets and snow removal from outside drains and sewers. At 16:00, when sewage trucks return from collecting sewage from underground tanks on farms and residences in remote areas around the countryside, Pharaoh dons his plastic suit and climbs inside to scrape the bilge free and mix what has begun to harden into a soft constituent that will be used as compost in flower gardens around the city. It is a challenging job, even if it is only temporary, and he returns to the washroom where he must carefully dispose of the suit, which is heavily caked in sewage.

Last night, he dreamt that he visited Oobamcee's village. While walking through streets filled with dirt and pebbles, he kept stopping to stamp his Caterpillars free of the dust. Villagers on rusty bicycles with noisy bells swerved into his path and then out again to avoid denting their bicycles. Women balancing baskets with goods on their heads cupped naked, malnourished breasts and offered them to him, squeezing and wringing them dry as if they were the last local supply of drinking water before a seasonal drought. Occasionally, clouds of dust appeared in the distance, followed by the sounds of horns from big green trucks with rusty gears that noisily zigzagged through the streets as if the drivers were drunk. People parted the streets to allow them to pass, but Oobamcee and Pharaoh would not stop. They continued as if daring the trucks to run them over. At the last minute, the trucks swerved wide of them and kept on their way. Pharaoh turned around to see their packed cargo of military men dressed in green uniforms, gripping their rifles and gear with stoic faces as they bounced up and down on the uneven roads. "They're on their way to a safari," Oobamcee said, never turning around, and they kept walking and walking until Pharaoh opened his eyes.

He has made only three requests since his stay here began. Surprisingly, his captors have honored two. His African clothes have been replaced by plain, yellow sweatpants with drawstrings at the waist and matching shortsleeved shirts. But Pharaoh keeps Anna's drawings and a Bible tucked under his mattress. As evidence of his tribulations during solitary confinement, he underlines scriptures when he reads the Bible. He looks at his clock on the middle shelf. His medication will be arriving soon. Pharaoh strips and reaches under the mattress for one of his drawings. It is a drawing of Anna's feet. He sits at the edge of the bed and opens his legs, holding the drawing at eye level in his left hand and his already erect penis in his right hand. His rubbing begins slowly, as he studies her ugly feet. They are narrow but thick, and her big toe protrudes too far out of proportion from the rest of her toes. She has included the hair above the knuckles on her toes and has blackened her jagged toenails to indicate that they were polished at the time she drew them. It is an honest rendition, with no embellishments or absence of flaws, and his excitement at the prospect of seeing her again, in spite of what has occurred, causes him to rub his penis harder and faster until he collapses backward on his mattress. Still gripping himself, he feels the warmth seep through his fingers, and he prepares himself to beat back the same paranoid thoughts that disturb him after each climax. It cannot be. Anna's strong lusts and oft-proclaimed love for him had quickly turned into an accusation of rape the moment she swung around and saw what she had to lose. He tells himself that there has been no conspiracy between Hannah and Anna to accelerate his downfall, yet his paranoia has taken on demented proportions. Once during their lovemaking, he had withdrawn his penis from Anna's mouth before ejaculation because he had been afraid that his sperm might have ended up between Hannah's legs. He is careful not to soil the drawing and returns it under the mattress after wiping himself with a towel. While he gets dressed, his medication arrives promptly at 06:15. The guard bangs on the door before entry.

"I will unlock. Step to the bed, lad, and put out your hands."

Pharaoh does as he is told. The solid metal door opens with a buzz and the twist of a handle. Two policemen enter like bodyguards, wearing disheveled uniforms, followed by a gloved male nurse with bottled water. Pharaoh is handcuffed before being given his pill.

"You are healthy, lad. Our prisons agree with you here? They make you a better person."

"I am only in custody," he says. "Prisons are for the guilty."

"It is the same. You'll see when you get there."

"Your whole country is a prison!" he shouts. The male nurse looks sternly at the policeman who has broken the rules. Their visit is not a social one.

"Open," the male nurse says.

"Swallow."

"Drink."

"Open."

"Close now." He runs a gloved hand along the bed. "Still sweating?"

"Only when I jog." Pharaoh frowns at them.

"Open again." This time he uses his index and a penlight to look for the pill. "Close now." He whispers in Norwegian to the guard and they leave. It is how his day begins every morning in this cell that has begun to feel like his home. Pharaoh has thirty minutes to read his Bible before his interrogation begins.

"Our English, is it difficult for you to understand?"

"No, sir."

"It is good practice for us also."

"Yesterday you told us you did not know your father-in-law had a weapon. He has one. Did you not find it?"

"No, sir."

"Did you not find any weapon in his house?"

"No, sir."

"Did you not look into his garage?"

"No, sir."

"But it is gone!"

"I never saw it, sir."

"You did not believe he had a weapon?"

"Well, he had threatened to shoot me with a pistol."

"Did you ring the police?"

"No, ma'am, but neither did he." He focuses on gold letters on a patch on blue sleeves.

"Why should he ring the police?"

"To report it missing, if it was missing, ma'am."

"So you knew he had a weapon."

"I-I guess so."

"Tell us about your immigrant friends."

Pharaoh moves his hands from above the table to his lap. The handcuffs jingle like heavy bracelets while the policeman waits for him to respond. The policewoman continues to write as Pharaoh looks at a cell phone's digital display.

"We are not really friends."

"You do not know them, then?"

"Well, who do you mean? We were all immigrants in that class."

"The men from Africa." A longsleeved arm with a large hand and fingers reaches into a blue shirt pocket and withdraws a plastic pouch with tobacco and wrapping paper. Pharaoh watches carefully as another large hand joins the tobacco, unwrapping the plastic roughly, noisily. He is distracted and must be asked again.

"How long were you friends with the men from Africa?" The policewoman stops writing and whispers in her partner's ear. His hands continue to roll a cigarette but he moves his chair backward, smoothly on its wheels, and guides it to a television set at the end of the room. He turns on the television. On the left side of a split screen, there is applause and jubilation from a room filled with people dressed in suits and Norwegian *bunads*. Glasses are raised with shouts of *"Hoorah for Norge!"* On the right of the split screen Pharaoh learns that Norway has been granted United Nations membership for two years from a contentious panel of local female politicians. The women are debating the likelihood of the Nobel Committee bestowing the Peace Prize on the UN as an expression of gratitude. After more eruptions of cheers, an index finger turns off the television in the middle of an official address to the Norwegian people. Pharaoh listens to the wheels roll toward him on the other side of the table. The policewoman pinches the cartilage between her nose, rubs the residue between her fingers, and wipes it on a blue sleeve.

"The men from Africa. They are not your friends?"

"No, sir. They argued too much."

"Why did they argue?"

"I don't know." Smoke curls before them, and Pharaoh begins to shake his leg nervously.

"You know what they argued about?"

"No, sir. I could not understand their language."

"So how you know they argued?"

"I could tell."

"How could you tell?"

"They swore and used their fingers."

"Which language they curse in?'

"Why?"

"Which one?"

"Norwegian."

A knock interrupts the policeman's grin. A lady in civilian clothes places a plastic bag in his hand and closes the door. The cigarette is held between protruding lips while both hands open the plastic bag. One hand withdraws photographs from the bag.

"They are here." The hand places three photographs on the table in front of Pharaoh, who leans forward to view them. They are enlarged passport pictures of Oobamcee, Sail, and Peter. Oobamcee's face is grim, and his eyes are swollen. Sail's eyes are closed and swollen. Peter's eyes are wide open, and he is smiling. The police-woman stops writing to look at the pictures and lick her yellow teeth.

"Which ones do you know?"

Pharaoh continues to examine the photographs. "This one, this one, and this one. Uganda, Nigeria, and Ghana." He returns his handcuffed hands to his lap.

"Here are these." A hand gently lays down six more photographs. He recognizes the rest of Oobamcee's family, but the pictures are not passport photographs. Everyone is asleep for the camera.

"I don't know who they are. They weren't in my class." He uses the handcuffs as a weight to prevent his legs from shaking.

"Is somebody missing?"

"Oobamcee? I don't know. How should I know?"

"Look again!"

"When can I see my daughter?"

"You must answer our questions."

"I need to see my daughter."

"You will see her when you are released."

"When is that?"

"She is with her mother."

"Fuck you! That is not what I asked. Fuck all of you! You know that is not what I asked!

"Here! Is somebody missing in these pictures?" The hand extinguishes the lighted cigarette by squeezing its tip between thick fingertips, then spreads itself motionless before the pictures.

"I'd like to see my fucking daughter first! I am an American! I demand to see someone from the American embassy and my goddamn daughter! Fuck you people! I'm not answering any more fucking questions!"

One hand is on the table. Another appears next to it holding a stun gun, the painful bolts of which he has become familiar with. The switch is in the armed position.

"Who is missing here?" A chair rolls back on its wheels and stops abruptly. The chair relaxes and continues to roll slowly, freely, without its cumbersome weight.

"I am!" A longsleeved arm swings along the edge of the table, hugging corners playfully on its way toward Pharaoh. The policewoman stops writing. Pharaoh backs away and begins to rant. "Fuck you! This is nothing! Fuck everybody! All your motherfucking Highnesses! Fuck your king! Fuck your queen, too! Great bells, you fuckers! Great fucking bells!" He stiffens his body to receive the jolt.

"Have you killed dogs in the US before?"

"No, sir."

The policewoman has already begun her frantic scribbling.

"Only in Norway?"

"Nowhere, sir."

"Do you like dogs?"

"Yes, sir."

"For pets or to eat."

"Pets, sir." Pharaoh smiles stiffly. "Can I ask her a question?"

The hand relaxes on the table.

"We will ask the questions now. You are not in a position to ask questions." A hand covers the face of the Nokia phone. One finger, too fat for the keypad, punches up and down. "What is your question?"

"Why is she writing?"

A hand reaches into a pocket and withdraws a plastic pouch. Another hand helps balance the pouch's descent onto the table. Tobacco has escaped from the plastic into the pocket through a creased opening. A large fleshy index finger presses on tobacco scattered on a spot on the table, and two fingers grind the deposit back into the pouch. Pharaoh does not get an answer.

"Do you belong to a cult?"

"What?"

The hand stops rolling a tobacco cigarette. The policewoman continues to write.

"Your friends and you. Are you members of a cult?"

"No, sir."

And he said unto Aaron, Take thee a young calf for a sin offering, and a ram for a burnt offering, without blemish, and offer them before the Lord.

"Then where is the dog?"

And ye shall know the truth, and the truth shall make you free.

"I suppose he is still in Norway."

A hand surrounded by smoke halts in midair as if contemplating whether to lift the cigarette to its owner's lips or put it out in an ashtray.

"She will only stop writing if you do not answer questions for the magistrate."

The lips receive the cigarette with a pout. Billy smokes his joint the same way, Pharaoh muses, but his fingers and lips are black. It is a sin to smoke, and the magistrate can kiss his black ass.

"Will the magistrate let me see my daughter?"

"And your wife, if you answer all questions correct."

"Perhaps I can talk to the magistrate alone, about something."

Ye shall not respect persons in judgment; but ye shall hear the small as well as the great; ye shall not be afraid of the face of man; for the judgment is God's; and the cause that is too hard for you, bring it unto me, and I will bear it.

His handcuffs are heavy, if nothing supports his hands.

"The magistrate only speaks Norwegian. It is not his job to speak to you. It is ours."

Two fingers on one hand extinguish the cigarette. The same hand picks up the phone and returns it immediately. The wheels on a chair roll toward the television, the same finger used to punch key-pads presses the *On* button, and a woman in a black-and-white jumpsuit stands next to a weather map of Norway. Her protruding breasts prevent viewers from seeing the southern tip of the country.

"You must have more than one magistrate."

"Only one and he is out skiing."

"I don't believe you."

"You are not in Los Angeles or Hollywood. Norwegian police-men do not lie to get the truth. More snow." A fat finger presses the *On* button off.

"What time is it?"

"Your breakfast is coming."

"Cereal and coffee only. Nothing else."

"Why not?"

"That is all I will eat."

"You do not want waffles or pancakes or eggs with ham? Maybe we must bring your car around also?" The policewoman stops writing.

"More snow tomorrow? Maybe sunshine on the weekend."

The large hand collects different items. Pictures are placed back in a plastic bag. A hand reaches in again and flashes a photograph to the policewoman, who licks her teeth again. His breakfast tray arrives with three nectarines, an apple, a thin, long cracker with a slice of cucumber and tomato on top, and a small, soaked paper cup of orange juice sliding in a ringlet of liquid. A fat hand picks up the cracker whole and returns it again with a chunk missing. Pharaoh can hear a mouth chewing above his head.

"Fifteen minutes! Tomorrow you shall have a menu." The fat hand disappears outside the door. Pharaoh hurls a nectarine at the door and hurries toward the television.

Breaking news on CNN. Denmark says no to a Euro currency. Pharaoh is angry and feels cheated. He waits for subtitles while eating his sweet nectarine. There are no subtitles. Digging up fresh graves and robbing and sodomizing the occupants are on the rise in Murmansk. Pharaoh presses an arrow pointing up. Ricki Lake has gained weight again. Rap artists have problems with their spelling and vocabulary. *Bootylicious* does not exist in any English dictionary. *Two tripple O* is 2000. *Ricki, why can't we be creative? We don't gots to always talk like the man, baby.* Applause. *Ricki, this is a societal problem. It must say something to you if these kids, who are flunking out of middle school, already know the meaning of words like "incarceration" and "methadone."* Weak applause. *Go ahead, caller. Ricki, I remember when "bonehead" was a bad word. I don't understand why these beautiful, young black darlings have to make up so many mean words.* Boos. *Hip-hop is not a mean word, caller.*

The channel changes without him fingering the knob. Suddenly he is watching Disney's *101 Dalmations.* They are up to their old tricks again. He looks around the room as if to reassure himself that he is not under surveillance and sees nothing but a door, a desk, two empty chairs, and four walls. They have allowed him a single channel again, but today he does not watch. He stares at the black screen, and a painful image of Amaryllis appears before him. She is running on her little legs, but it is not a playful run. She is being chased by angry old men and women who are tossing at her whatever they can lift along their paths. They are screaming obscenities and vituperations. One lady throws a hardcover book by Henrik Ibsen that misses. Another member of the mob retrieves the book, aims, and hits Amaryllis squarely in the back of her head. She is bleeding but continues to run, picking up speed. Someone tosses a thick wallet filled with Norwegian coins that knocks her down, but she is up again running on her little legs toward a field. Finally, an accurate arm levels another hardcover book, and it topples Amaryllis as they surround her. A late arrival with a heavy backpack parts the mob, removes a curling stone from his backpack, and smashes Amaryllis's skull. Others join in with their own items, amid a chanting chorus from some Norwegian canticle. She shall not contribute to the preservation of Norwegian language, culture, and identity, the chorus insists, until her body is nothing more than a purulent pulp. Pharaoh begins to cry. He is filled with so much anger that he bites down on the nectarine seed, cracks it open, and spits the bits at the television screen. He swallows his orange juice, dismissing the thought that Oobamcee would not approve of his behavior. A warrior's arsenal does not include tears and spit. He must see Amaryllis soon. If answering questions that have nothing to do with why he is in custody will accelerate his release, Pharaoh is prepared to answer. But first they must hurry back to escort him to pee.

At times, he can still hear Hannah's toenails scrape the sheets, even though he is confined to his room. It is all he allows himself to summon of her. He sits in the dark in his room, flicking the light on and off for hours, cringing pathetically at the memory of the sharp sounds she made as she kicked at the length of their cover to spread it above them. He does not hate her now. Instead he feels relief. He knows she will never understand what he has done or why he had to do it. She has suffered great humiliation at his expense in her little land, but these are her dues. Pharaoh's humiliation has been greater. It is the price she and her country must pay for importing culture and exporting xenophobia.

He presses the *On* button on the television. Multiple channels have returned. But the screen immediately turns black. They have frustrated him again. He feels angry and helpless, and with no outlet for his anger and hopelessness, he pulls out his dick and douses the television with urine.

"You have eaten all? Let me see. No, you do not like our *knekkebrød?*" Fat fingers, swollen and sweating inside of thin latex gloves, pick up the sliced cucumber and tomato and turn them over on the cracker. "They are fresh."

"I prefer meat."

"You prefer what we give you to eat. Do not forget you are a prisoner."

"I am also an American citizen. I demand to speak with someone from my embassy."

"After you have answered our questions, they will also like to speak to you." A gloved index points to Pharaoh's hands in his lap under the table. He displays the handcuffs, tugging at the links to demonstrate its hold. The policewoman begins to write, then stops, wrinkles her nose, and continues writing, frowning as she prints on the pad.

"Useless bitch!" Pharaoh mutters.

The scratching of pen on paper resumes. The female civilian enters without knocking and places an envelope and a white plastic bag on the table next to the gloved hands. Pharaoh rattles his handcuffs. A small waist and flat bottom revolve at the door and retreat, pulling the door toward a drooping, buxom chest.

"Here you are in a queue. A very good picture. You are looking into the security camera direct." Pharaoh fidgets in his seat and wonders how long he had been under surveillance. He remembers the store and the items he purchased. A thick index finger slides the picture toward him. "Is it you? Correct?"

"Yes, sir. That's me."

"Here is a copy of your receipt."

"Okay."

"You buy these items here? Am I correct?" A gloved hand delves into the bag noisily and withdraws six bottles of seasoning.

"Yes, sir. If that is the receipt."

"Why so many of these?"

"I prefer spicy foods."

"But six?" Fingers cover the bottles, then twist caps off to smell the contents with a pale nose. The policewoman inhales, smiling.

"There were no complaints. Everyone enjoyed the meal."

"Even your daughter?"

He steadies his knees. "She ate fish."

"What did you eat?"

"Fish."

"Did you tell them what they were eating?"

"They knew." Two fingers reach into a blue pocket and pull out a tobacco pouch. A half-smoked butt is difficult to grasp.

"Who else ate fish?"

"No one."

"Did anyone ask about the meat?"

"Trine asked."

"Did you let her know what she was eating?" A gloved hand pushes the bottles to one side.

"It's possible. I can't really remember," Pharaoh says.

"You are losing your memory?" A hand disappears beneath the table.

"I may have said, *woof, woof,* but I told them that I was kidding. It was only meant to be a joke."

And his mouth was opened immediately, and his tongue loosed and he spake and praised God.

"Did they laugh?"

"Yes, sir. But not at my joke."

"Why not?"

"I was dancing for them."

Fat fingers light the cigarette, then squeeze the tip between pursed lips.

"You were dancing?"

"Yes, dancing. It was an African dinner dance performed to give thanks. You have probably heard of it, or maybe she has?"

"Did they enjoy your dancing?" Fat fingers drum the table.

"I didn't care if they enjoyed it. It was not meant to entertain them."

"But why did you do it?"

"I have told you. It was an African dinner dance."

"But you are not an African."

Pharaoh drops his chin to his chest and stares at the wooden table. It is happening again.

"I know who I am," he shrugs.

"Yes. We have written it down many times. You are an American warrior and an American citizen at the same time, with a history of some problems." The policewoman stops writing and pushes the pad toward a fat gloved thumb that is moistened on a tongue, then flips pages backward to find a particular item.

"No, you are not from Africa." The policewoman taps at a spot on the page repeatedly and wrinkles her forehead. She scratches through the words and returns to her original place on the pad.

"I support their cause," he mutters. "You will never understand."

A gloved hand warns him to be silent. They listen to the scratching of the policewoman's pen while she sticks the index finger on her idle hand deep into an ear, rolls the wax lengthwise with the help of her thumb, then continues to twirl it around between her fingers. He realizes that her role as a stenographer annoys him because she is unclean. Pharaoh starts to disobey the policeman's order to be silent but remembers the television at the end of the room. The scratching stops abruptly, and he hears whispers, a startled laugh, and the rattling of jars.

"This is the truth? You do not like the company name on these bottles? What do they say? Oh, Black Boy. They are not named after you. It is a Norwegian company." Fat fingers hang limp atop the jars. More astonished laughter. The policewoman only smiles, proud of her instrumental role in what she believes is a breakthrough.

"The name was of no use to me at the dinner, only the spices," Pharaoh says. "I did not buy them because of the brand."

And the Lord said unto Pharaoh, I did not create you in the likeness of a king to suck the white man's dick.

"Do you think our company will change its name because you don't like it?"

Pharaoh does not answer. They are idiots. He does not expect them to understand.

"I am thirsty!"

"Water will be arriving soon."

"I would like a cigarette in the meantime, then."

"No cigarettes!"

"Why not?"

"You are not allowed cigarettes." Fat fingers coddle the jars, then push them away again. The chair rolls back sluggishly and moves forward again.

"Tell her not to do that. It is unclean. And tell her to stop writing!"

A gloved hand silences him. Two fingers reach into a blue pocket. The contents of the tobacco pouch do not look all that different from the contents of a jar. Fat fingers wrap a cigarette and offer it to his lips from across the table. It is lighted, and the handcuffs feel like lead as Pharaoh raises his hand to his lips. He exhales smoke toward the ceiling, coughing, and tells them what they want to know.

CHAPTER 19

DESPITE HIS CONSTANT PLEA to speak to an embassy representative, Pharaoh is surprised one morning when his request is finally granted. His decision to tell his interrogators what they expected to hear about his relationship with Anna has cost him dearly. He learns that Hannah has surrendered his passport to the American embassy. He is offered a cigarette, which he accepts with the grace of someone trying to convince his persecutors that, unlike them, he faces a new and more intimidating enemy.

"You've gotten yourself into quite a pickle." A short, prematurely balding man offers his outstretched hand as the fat-fingered policeman escorts Pharaoh into the room. Pharaoh shakes it, rattling his handcuffs noisily. He would have preferred that the embassy had sent someone taller, and perhaps older and more muscular. He releases the plump hand. The man's voice discloses a youthfulness that makes Pharaoh uneasy.

"Finally! An American," Pharaoh says.

"Lou Thistle, Mr. Chisholm. Born and bred. They treating you all right? You need anything, Mr. Chisholm?"

"Pharaoh, please. We're both Americans here. No need for all that."

"You guys wanna loosen him up? I got him."

Pharaoh is cautious. He believes the character before him might be a Norwegian masquerading as an American, a clever attempt by the Norwegians to get him to behave. He does not believe Thistle is a real name.

"It took you long enough to get here. This is all a mistake. I've been trying to tell them that, but they won't listen. They've been giving me pills, trying to sedate me against my will, and stunning me when I don't answer their stupid questions. And they won't let me see my daughter. She's my daughter, for chrissakes!"

"Now hold on a minute there, son. One thing at a time. I've already put a stop to the pills. Did that as soon as I found out. No more of that," he says. "But I'm afraid you still have to work. Can't do much about that. No strings there." Lou Thistle, seated beside Pharaoh, places a thin leather briefcase upright on the table and allows it to fall toward him with a sharp noise that sends up dust and reveals his inexperience more than his resolve. It startles Pharaoh. "We'll straighten this out," he says winking at Pharaoh. "Unity does not always mean homogeneity, son."

"And that stun gun? Put a fucking stop to that, too!"

Lou Thistle and the policeman exchange glances as if to confirm that Pharaoh's outburst proves that his occasional shocks are warranted.

"Trust me, son. We'll straighten this out."

"It is not that easy for someone in his position. It is a very serious charge against him. Understand?" Fat fingers are clasped on the table as the thumbs form a tapping pyramid. The policewoman has ironed her uniform and sits erect, poised to begin her dictation.

"Serious charge, my ass! From what I could tell she was fucking him, and when her kids walked in she yelled rape to holy hell. Ain't that right, son?"

"Exactly. The bitch betrayed me!" Pharaoh says in a brash tone as he stares at the policewoman, daring her to write down Lou Thistle's account.

"Seems cut-and-dried to me!"

"We must investigate such a serious charge, anyhow."

"Sure you must, but y'all seem to be doing things ass backwards here. Y'all always arrest first, then investigate?"

Fat fingers remain calm, clasped, then unravel. The policeman's agitated tapping is replaced by the sound of locks snapping open on Lou Thistle's briefcase.

"Did you know the children were standing there watching? Were y'all putting on a show?" Pharaoh feels Lou Thistle's elbow nudge his arm.

"Absolutely not!" Pharaoh says, embarrassed and offended, but careful not to alienate his only counsel by reacting ungratefully. Perhaps it is too late. Lou Thistle, with thumbs halted on the upper flap of his briefcase, leans toward Pharaoh.

"Were y'all smitten?"

"What?"

"How serious was this? Were y'all planning on doing something about it, leaving your partners, running away like in the movies?"

"Are you for real? Don't be ridiculous. And what does that have to do with these guys jerking me around?"

Lou Thistle opens his briefcase carefully, as if to prevent its contents from spilling over, then pulls out a photo and slides it toward Pharaoh. "It is the best I can do on short notice," he says.

Pharaoh picks up the photo delicately between two fingers. His attempt to prevent himself from squeezing the corners together causes a trembling of his hand that subsides only when the photo drops from his grip.

"Why don't y'all step outside and give us a moment," Lou Thistle says, placing a comforting arm on Pharaoh's shoulder.

"We cannot allow that," the policeman says.

"Hell, y'all can't allow much now, can ya?"

"Do not forget, sir, that he is in custody." Fat fingers tediously, noisily, unwrap a tobacco pouch.

"Fine. Why don't we give him some time to collect himself. We'll be back in a few minutes, son. I'll clean this mess up."

Pharaoh does not welcome the unfamiliar clap between his shoulder blades. They abruptly leave the room and Pharaoh realizes that it is the first time he has been left alone in the room without being handcuffed.

Pharaoh remains seated. He cannot control the bouncing of his knees under the table. An opportunity to turn on the television passes him by. It no longer interests him. From her picture, Amaryllis stares back at him with a big smile that seems to weigh her head down so that her features resemble old women who smile with the corners of their eyes. It is a recent picture. She is sitting in her chair during the Christmas dinner, but the flash has turned her elf outfit into a darker green than Pharaoh remembers. He is concerned now more than ever that he will never see Amaryllis again, and his desire to protect her from harm from others now shifts to protection from himself.

Pharaoh continues to study the photo, blinking and bowing toward the table to make certain that what has come to him is not just a weak intuition that, because of his unfortunate predicament, he forces into a wild suspicion. He is becoming more and more aware that he may need to check his vision. He has begun to see faint objects flashing out of the corners of his eyes, but he has kept this to himself. Sometimes the objects appear jumbled, a knot in a piece of wood, a spectral light, a fly, a mosquito, or stars from an oncoming headache, but they are manifested as extensions of objects that are real. Perhaps it is the medication. He has no time for those tricks now. Someone conveniently found Trine's missing camera and developed the roll of film. He wonders if it had really been missing. Hannah's accusation that one of the African students may have stolen the camera now seems like a plot between mother and daughter that has gone off with surprising simplicity and flawlessness. Pharaoh can think of many reasons why the African students may have taken Trine's camera, but they all involve the students' aversion to technology and not the camera's value. Still, they are warriors. It is why their faces were swollen in their photographs. Oobamcee's son is not in any of the pictures. He can picture the lanky boy staring at the police like a beleaguered praying mantis with headphone wires dangling from his ears while he, too, betrays Oobamcee and tells all that he knows. He covers Amaryllis's smile with a palm and can hear Hannah's voice as she calls his daughter Amy. He cringes and uncovers the photo, which seems to blur before him, and with an index finger traces around Amaryllis again and again, as if bounding her in concentric circles will protect her from harm. His conversations with Oobamcee about warriors have come to nothing. He cannot protect what is most important to him without feeling also that he must first protect himself. Pharaoh can feel his enemy's omnipresence. He is vulnerable like Thor's stupid fish, lost in shallow water and swimming close to the surface, aware that there are vultures circling above, ready to swoop down and snatch them with spread talons. But they cannot go deeper. Pharaoh cannot escape the mess into which he has gotten himself. It is hopeless to even entertain the idea of a gift if he is away from her. "Bullshit on the sly," he hears himself mutter, and he flips the photograph on its face before sinking into his chair to wipe his eyes.

To lift himself out of his moroseness, Pharaoh rolls his chair toward the television, pushing himself along the side of the table with both hands. The use of his hands without handcuffs is awkward. He turns on the television in the middle of *World News Now* on CNN. It is great that the news is not breaking, Pharaoh muses, but the world is still falling apart. For Pharaoh, more calamitous news is not a good omen. He turns off the television and stares at his reflection on the black screen. His demeanor has changed of late. He has become more serious, more pensive, and despite his quiet jubilation at being freed from the handcuffs, he notices his slouched shoulders.

They remind him of Anna's depiction of Dagfinn as a jazzman. It has been four weeks since his arrest in front of Amaryllis, and the fear that he has seen her for the last time has intensified with Lou Thistle's grandstanding as Pharaoh's counsel. He has a wild suspicion now that everyone he has met since his stay here began has been part of a conspiracy that he does not fully understand but that he recognizes as the culmination of Anna's betrayal.

There is a rattling at the door, and Pharaoh quickly crumples the picture of Amaryllis and tosses it along the length of the table. He folds his arms on his chest and sits rigid, as if preparing for defiance of handcuffs, questions, tears, the unexpected.

"You all right, son?"

"Never better," Pharaoh answers.

Lou Thistle's assuredness becomes a groan when he sees the crumpled picture. He slides his thin leather briefcase softly before him. Pharaoh notices that it is not as thin as he first thought, although it is still dusty. Its surface is worn and undulating, giving it a bituminous glow when Lou Thistle raises it slightly to unlock the latches. The policeman and his stenographer return and make their way around the table in what has become a stiff routine, but Pharaoh continues to monitor Lou Thistle's movements.

"It's good," he says, "that you're all right, because I'm afraid you've got some bad news. Your wife filed for divorce and sold the car, son. Told me to tell you."

"You didn't know that before you left the room?" Pharaoh feels his muscles go taut on his chest. He does not care if the car has been scrapped and the tires used as swings in playgrounds, but he cannot forsake his daughter.

"It just came in, son. Brand new info."

"That is not our concern here, Thistle. We must go on with our questions so that he is not late for his work." Fat finger points to a wristwatch.

"You go ahead, then." Pharaoh feels a nudge under the table.

"We'll answer your questions," Lou Thistle continues with a collaborative tone.

"Did she say anything about my daughter?"

"Your daughter's all right, son. They're all at a cabin, according to my information."

"What did she say?" He suspects that Trine and Thor may have influenced Hannah's decision to go to their cabin, and it angers him to think they are on the run with his daughter.

"We'll let them get to their questions, then you and I'll talk."

Pharaoh nods and places two fingers to his lips.

Fat fingers without hesitation offer Pharaoh a cigarette.

"You were paid by the Africans to belong to this?"

Pharaoh exhales quickly but cannot avoid the bitter taste in his mouth. He ignores a copy of the organization's manifesto before him. "No. I was not paid by anyone."

"You are lying to us?"

"I was not paid by anyone!"

"You belong to the group for free?"

"Hold on now, there. You have his answer," Lou Thistle says, resting his hand on Pharaoh's shoulder. It is a heavy hand with a short, thick forearm, like an elephant's trunk, and from its weight on his shoulders, Pharaoh believes it can uproot a small tree just as easily as it can pick up a spoon.

"How did they earn money?"

"Don't know," Pharaoh mutters.

"Do you know this book?" Fat fingers push the booklet closer toward Pharaoh.

"No, sir."

"Are you certain about this?"

"Yes, sir."

"Give it here," Lou Thistle says, drawing it in with one hand and examining pages with an index and thumb. A scowl envelops his face. "Son, you a part of this?"

"Of course not."

"This what you impersonated a military man for? Hell, this is a crock of shit, if you ask me! You ought to know better than that, son. Anti-capitalism, my ass! Your warrior friends were probably running a little scam already and ran one all over you."

Pharaoh remains silent.

"Looky here! What's this all about, son?"

"You wouldn't understand."

And the Lord hardened the heart of Pharaoh, King of Egypt, and he pursued after the children of Israel. And the children of Israel went out with a high hand.

"Try me," Lou Thistle says, grinning.

"Looky here, son! You've been duped all the way around."

They are alone. By placing a call to the embassy, Lou Thistle has managed to convince his superiors to pull more strings. Pharaoh shows his appreciation by reluctantly disclosing the nature of his relationship with Anna to Lou, whose grins and astonished expression reveal the absurdity of it all. Pharaoh asks to call his sister, certain that the request will not be granted, but still he crosses his fingers. He knows that Gwen will never be sympathetic about his relationship to Anna. Gwen would quickly make Anna seem as significant as a strand of hair. Then she would chastise Pharaoh.

"I have learned a very difficult lesson," Pharaoh admits.

"Not quite, son!" Lou's grin has disappeared. "Uncle Sam isn't too happy with this crock you're mixed up in. Hell, impersonating US military personnel in a foreign country? You could end up in a brig, son, if Uncle Sam stays pissed off long enough!"

"Where will I go then? I cannot stay here in this country any longer," Pharaoh says, ignoring the threat but acknowledging Lou's tacit admission that his release is imminent.

"Don't know, son, but we'll get this mess straightened out," Lou says, tapping his briefcase.

"I have done nothing wrong," he mutters.

"Son, you let that woman almost send you to prison for a piece of ass? Hell, if you ask me, it's a little too late for you to be worrying about your daughter," Lou says.

Pharaoh's heart begins to race, and his chest feels like it is exposed to the sun. He thinks about the telephone call that he must soon place to Gwen.

"I have nowhere to go," he says. "Where will I go?"

Lou shakes his head and places an arm on Pharaoh's shoulders. It is an insincere gesture, but Pharaoh is unable to shrug it off.

"Your belongings are in the garage, according to your wife. You will be released today," Lou announces, and claps Pharaoh on the back.

Pharaoh reluctantly dials Gwen's number from a public phone, while two uniformed policemen with watchful eyes prepare to transport him back to his belongings. He is in the same clothes he wore when they took him into custody, but his Caterpillars are now laced properly. He checks his pockets for Anna's bundled drawings and his amulet, allowing Gwen to vent her frustrations about her father as he shivers from the cold air that gushes in when the sliding doors are activated at the entrance.

"Well, he's gone. You missed your chance to make good," Gwen says.

"He knows where I am," Pharaoh replies. "Why is it I who always have to make the first move?"

"That a rhetorical question, or you want a real answer?"

"Well, he's not busy. He can call."

"He tried, child!"

"Oh," Pharaoh says in a dejected tone. "Did he talk to Hannah?"

"Why don't you ask him?"

"He didn't have to leave without saying goodbye," Pharaoh says.

"He's retired, Pharaoh. It's not about goodbyes! Maybe the man just wants to drink rum out of coconuts and hang around cricket fields all day with his grandchild. Who knows?"

"Perhaps you ought to give him one, then." There is a vexed silence from Gwen's breathing. Pharaoh remains silent.

"What does the devil look like over there?"

"Me," he answers.

"What's wrong?" Gwen asks.

"Everything."

"Well, child, stuff is happening over here, too." Pharaoh is surprised that she isn't more curious about what he has to say. "Billy is in prison," she continues.

"No surprise there," he answers. "What'd he do? Shoot Tia?"

"Something about drugs," she says. "Don't know what it is with black people and drugs."

"I got into a little trouble here, too. But I'm out now. False arrest."

Gwen does not allow him much room to soften the impact of the news. "You don't hear me laughing!"

"It is not a joke," he says.

"Arrested?"

"Yes, Gwen."

"In a foreign country?"

"False arrest," he repeats. "It's no big deal, sis."

"Don't *sis* me! Child, you pack and get back where you belong! I am not kidding, Pharaoh. There are four of you. I always knew two of you would end up in jail but I never thought it would be my own brother. You black men can't fight the statistics, even all the way over there, it seems, child, and you shouldn't even try. What was it?"

"False arrest. Nothing the embassy couldn't handle."

"The embassy? Have mercy! The *embassy* was involved? What was the charge?"

"Oh, I'll tell you about it when I get home," he says, but stops short of telling her when he will be returning home.

"What about my baby?"

He remains silent.

"You're not answering, Pharaoh. I don't like that sound you're not making. Child, you're not leaving my baby over there. Come on, Pharaoh! What have you done?"

"Nothing I can't fix," he says.

"You need money? If you want, I can open up that war chest I've been putting money into. You hear me? And you need anything more, you call and let me know." There is fear in her voice.

"I am not sure when I can come home. Hannah and her parents are on the run with Amaryllis, and I don't have a passport."

"Sounds like you're caught between the devil and the deep blue sea, Pharaoh." She does not say it, but he knows that for the first time she is considering praying for him. He turns to see an official-looking man approaching with a bouquet of flowers.

"Did you send me flowers, Gwen?"

"For what, child? You don't get flowers for being in jail!"

The flowers are wrapped in thin plastic and presented to him casually with a handshake and regret at his strange incarceration. Pharaoh accepts them with one hand. He has no idea what type of flowers they are and twists the transparent plastic to try and trace the stems to the blossom. When he describes the colors and petals to Gwen she sucks her teeth in ridicule over the phone.

"That's snapdragons! You're talking about daisies! You sure that's not leek? Smell it. What does it smell like?"

Pharaoh does not care for the bouquet nor the gesture behind it. He tells Gwen that the African students were not what they had claimed to be. He has come to accept that he was used and manipulated.

"Come on home, Pharaoh." Her appeal is soft now and sincere.

"I have to find Amaryllis," he says, and promises to call Gwen later. Pharaoh hangs up the receiver and surrenders himself to the waiting policemen. They walk through sliding doors to the idling police wagon. A German shepherd pacing in its kennel greets Pharaoh with violent barks. He freezes at the opened door until a policeman shouts out commands in Norwegian that silence the dog. He wonders if it is all a clever joke by his fat interrogator. The German shepherd remains alert, and Pharaoh enters the car uncertain of where he will stay. He has lost track of the days. He is surprised to learn that he has been released on a Sunday and ironically chose to leave his Bible behind. With any luck, he will see Amaryllis tomorrow, while everyone is at work. His wife and her parents follow routines. They will be back with his daughter, he thinks, and he is prepared to wait.

Chapter 20

PHARAOH RETRIEVES his belongings from Thor's garage while his police escort watches as if on patrol. He pulls the wooden door shut and walks toward the trolley with his bouquet of flowers and two heavy suitcases. The driver places the car in reverse and drives off slowly as Pharaoh turns the corner. Nothing much has changed in the community. He can see swift shadows in windows as he makes his way to the trolley stop. It is late in the afternoon and already it feels like midnight. Pharaoh loses his footing occasionally on icy patches in his path, having to accustom himself to walking on ice and snow in his Caterpillars again. He does not care to know what Hannah has packed in his suitcases. She is predictable, and he expects there will be pictures of Amaryllis, his rumpled clothes, his books, and perhaps a picture of his car and one of Anna for spite. Pharaoh smiles. There will be no pictures of Hannah for him to keep and stare at. He continues his walk toward the tracks but does not rest in the booth. He drags his suitcases over the tracks and trudges through fresh snow, leaving a thick trail of footprints that lead into the forest.

Getting into Thor's house is not a difficult feat for Pharaoh. He evades the watchful eyes of neighbors who are more alert and curious now because of the unwelcome publicity Pharaoh has brought into the little community. He simply walks further into the forest, covers his bouquet and suitcases in a pile of snow, crosses the tracks toward the back of Dagfinn's house, and hides beneath an awning under the balcony. No one is at home, and they have not been there for days, if the cold chimney is any indication. They will not be at the same cabin. Anna's Volvo is gone. It has been moved recently, and the thin film of bush and snow that now occupy its place causes Pharaoh to grimace with the memory of Anna's exploits in the Volvo. He enters the unlocked garage, retrieves from a hanging nail the key to the front door, and then enters Thor's home upstairs as if he is an expected guest who has finally arrived at his destination from a long journey. Pharaoh locks the door behind him and hurries downstairs.

There is no evidence that Pharaoh has ever been here. It as if he has committed suicide; Hannah has removed any connection he has had to the apartment. He sits in the dark living room, a defeated warrior whose only concern now is becoming a survivor. He considers calling Oobamcee but remembers the photos of the African students. He wishes to hear no more warrior speeches. He dials Gawne's number, and a woman answers the telephone. He asks to speak to Gawne, but she does not understand. She does not speak English. Her chant of *"feil nummer"* annoys him, and he hangs up the receiver hurriedly. He makes himself at home in the dark, ducking into the kitchen shower room and closing the door to conceal the light he needs to identify things that are unfamiliar to him. He remains fully dressed in shoes and coat, ready to leave on short notice. While drinking orange juice from a carton, he notices Amaryllis's birthday invitations scribbled in Hannah's linear penmanship. He frowns. He finds a pen, scratches through *"Amy,"* writes his daughter's full name on all the invitations, and places them in his jacket pocket.

Pharaoh sits down to wait. Overcome by sadness and grief at

what he is prepared to do, he begins to weep, a guttural explosion that causes his temples to hurt. He reaches into his pocket and pulls out the foolish remnants of his pain: Anna's multiple drawings, his amulet, and his bracelet. He imagines Anna stripped naked and without makeup deposited on a busy boulevard in Compton while niggers drive by and tug at her prehensile ponytail, spinning her around like a piñata. But he realizes that this might not cause Anna the least bit of humiliation or pain. He examines the amulet and bracelet and decides that they are worthless, both in real and symbolic value, with no actual connection to Africa. His stomach contracts. How could he have been so stupid? He remembers the kid selling Afro combs in Oobamcee's apartment complex, and he wishes now that he had taken them all and destroyed them, eliminating the kid's appanage to the Monarchy. Pharaoh's burden, although self-inflicted, is too heavy to carry alone. He makes a second attempt to contact Gawne, and after a series of calls to an operator, he finally dials the right number.

"What's up, G-man?"

"Hold on. Let me turn this volume down on homeboy . . . Shit! Where you at? In the pen?"

Pharaoh feels his pain subside. "Nah. I'm out, man—false arrest. You believe that nonsense?"

"Damn. Too bad, holmes." There is an uncomfortable tone in Gawne's voice, as if he is ashamed to be talking to Pharaoh. The volume is still high on the TV.

"How's it going?"

"Man, that class is different now. Everybody's serious, studying like crazy. All the clowns left." Gawne chuckles.

"Even the Africans?"

"Man, them brothers raised up! Nobody's seen 'em since you left, holmes. Thought they were with you. Heard they were into some scary shit."

"I haven't seen them," Pharaoh says. "How's Perry?"

"Guess you haven't heard, holmes. We hardly talk. Think he and the instructor got something going on ever since his Portuguese girl-friend left him."

Pharaoh laughs uneasily. "Anybody ask about me?"

"Hell, we been readin' 'bout your ass in the papers, holmes. This place loves you. You helpin' us with our Norwegian!" Gawne yawns as if he is bored or about to fall asleep.

"Oh," Pharaoh mutters.

"You going back home, holmes?"

"Soon."

"Damn!" There is a long pause, and Pharaoh wonders if Gawne is watching a mystery.

"Well, I'll let you go, man. Just thought I'd give everyone the right scoop on what happened."

"Yeah, yeah. Sure you right. Talk to you later, holmes," and the connection is gone.

It is almost midnight when Pharaoh hears footsteps upstairs. They are the nomadic steps of Trine moving from the kitchen, up the steps to the bedroom, then down to the kitchen again. Not long afterwards, Pharaoh hears heavier steps hurrying along the side of the house. It is Thor carrying Amaryllis in his arms. Pharaoh hides in the shower room and locks the door. He hears Thor enter the apartment and place Amaryllis in her crib before locking the front door and walking through the living room on his way to his place upstairs. Pharaoh's heart pounces at the thought of being able to see Amaryllis, even if she is asleep. It is how he prefers to see her any-how, and he recalls when he used to hover around her crib observ-ing her peaceful sleep. Perhaps he will read a bedtime story to her while she sleeps before Hannah enters the apartment, catches him, and raises hell.

Pharaoh unlocks the door and hustles across the living room to the bedroom. Amaryllis is lying in her crib, still bundled in blankets. He begins to caress her cheek and stroke her soft hair. She has changed. She seems more comfortable sleeping on her side and not crouched on all fours, and her hair has grown out from Hannah's spiteful clipping. Her forehead is darker and seems to protrude more than he remembers, but he cannot tell if it is the result of her receding hair. He hears footsteps meet in the living room above his head and realizes that his problems with Hannah are still there. Pharaoh picks up his daughter, wrapping her in more blankets, and paces around the bedroom with Amaryllis tucked to his chest. Her breathing remains undisturbed. He kisses her warm face and listens to the soft sounds she makes in her sleep. He is overcome by tears again. He squeezes Amaryllis to his chest while he unlocks the door. She does not stir in the cold air as Pharaoh begins running over snow and ice toward the forest and his buried suitcases.

With any luck, Pharaoh believes, he will get deep into the forest and far away before Hannah and her family can alert the police. He does not care if they follow his trail. He places Amaryllis on the snow and frantically uncovers the largest suitcase. He opens it quickly and, with no concern for its contents, makes room in the middle for Amaryllis by littering the snow around him with clothes and books. He keeps her well bundled, further insulating the suitcase by rearranging its contents around her, and then closes it shut with Amaryllis tucked inside. He wonders now about the mythical Trolls as he seeks refuge deeper in the forest. They are ferocious trees shaped in the form of humans, according to stories he has read to Amaryllis. Perhaps one hundred years from now, his retreat into the forest will also be the stuff of bedtime stories. He remembers Oobamcee's insistence that a warrior must have a purpose and not only think of himself. Pharaoh smiles as he kicks away snow-covered branches in his path. It is a moonlit night, but the dense trees allow only enough light on the scattered patches of snow for him to avoid falling on the slippery rocks. It is not the jungles of Africa, but it will have to do. He continues his flight into the forest, dragging his two suitcases along the snow. He begins to think about calling his father. Amaryllis is safe. No one will call her Amy, he reassures himself, not as long as she is with him. He stops and listens, but hears only faint cries in the distance. Amaryllis is awake. Her muffled sobs present a new challenge for this brave warrior, who must now find something for his daughter to eat.

Also from AKASHIC BOOKS

SOUTHLAND by Nina Revoyr
*Nominated for an *L.A. Times* Book Prize*
348 pages, a trade paperback original, $15.95, ISBN: 1-888451-41-6
"*Southland* merges elements of literature and social history with the propulsive drive of a mystery, while evoking Southern California as a character, a key player in the tale. Such aesthetics have motivated other Southland writers, most notably Walter Mosely."
—*Los Angeles Times*

"If Oprah still had her book club, this novel likely would be at the top of her list." —*Booklist*

SEED by Mustafa Mutabaruka
*Selected for the *Washington Post's* Best Novels of 2002 list*
178 pages, a trade paperback original; $14.95, ISBN: 1-888451-31-9
"Mutabaruka's deft maneuvering between past and present, Morocco and the United States, blurs distinctions and creates a mystical and frightening story . . . [P]lain prose and interesting characters keep this novel on its feet and make it dance."
—*Library Journal*

SOME OF THE PARTS by T Cooper
A Barnes & Noble Discover Great New Writers selection (fall 2002)
A Quality Paperback Book Club selection (February 2003)
264 pages, a trade paperback original, $14.95, ISBN: 1-888451-36-X
"Sweet and sad and funny, with more mirrors of recognition than a carnival funhouse, *Some of the Parts* is a wholly original love story for our wholly original age."
—Justin Cronin, author of *Mary and O'Neil*,
2002 PEN/Hemingway Award–Winner

BEULAH HILL by William Heffernan
288 pages, trade paperback, $13.95, ISBN: 1-888451-40-8

"The whispered revelations that come spilling out of *Beulah Hill* are like ghostly voices you sometimes hear in the attic—soft, sad and disturbingly urgent."—*New York Times Book Review*

"William Heffernan is one of the rare mystery writers who cares about soul."—Martin Cruz Smith

ADIOS MUCHACHOS by Daniel Chavarría
Winner of a 2001 Edgar Award
245 pages, a trade paperback original; $13.95, ISBN: 1-888451-16-5

"Daniel Chavarría has long been recognized as one of Latin America's finest writers. Now he again proves why with *Adios Muchachos*, a comic mystery peopled by a delightfully mad band of miscreants, all of them led by a woman you will not soon forget—Alicia, the loveliest bicycle whore in all Havana."
—Edgar Award-winning author William Heffernan

SPEAK NOW by Kaylie Jones
A new novel by the daughter of James Jones
249 pages, hardcover; $22.95, ISBN: 1-888451-53-X

Clara Sverdlow has been stalked by Niko Kamenski, her high-school lover, for almost twenty years. A recently sober alcoholic in her mid thirties, she has found happiness in a tenuous new marriage to Mark, another recovering alcoholic. Yet the past lurks over them like a great shadow, always encroaching on their happiness.

"A rich and splendid book." —*Roger Rosenblatt*

**These books are available at local bookstores.
They can also be purchased with a credit card online through
www.akashicbooks.com. To order by mail send a check or money order to:**

**AKASHIC BOOKS
PO Box 1456, New York, NY 10009
www.akashicbooks.com   Akashic7©aol.com**

**PRICES INCLUDE SHIPPING. OUTSIDE THE US,
ADD $8 TO EACH BOOK ORDERED.**